A
THOUSAND
LETTERS

INSPIRED BY JANE AUSTEN'S PERSUASION

STACI HART

Cover design by **Quirky Bird**

Photography by **Perrywinkle Photography**

Editing by **Love N Books and Rebecca Slemons**

Book design by **Inkstain Interior Book Designing**

BOOKS BY
STACI HART

HEARTS AND ARROWS
Rereleasing in 2017

CONTEMPORARY ROMANCE
Hardcore
With a Twist
Chaser
Last Call
Wasted Words
Tonic
A Thousand Letters

SHORT STORIES
Once
Desperate Measures

*To those of you who have known
the mercy of a second chance.*

*When pain is over, the remembrance of
it often becomes a pleasure.*

—**ANNE ELLIOT, Jane Austen's** *Persuasion*

ALWAYS

I've never understood why the heart always reacts.

A shot of adrenaline is all it takes, triggered by a thought. A word. A memory. And every time the reaction is singular, a fingerprint of a moment.

Sometimes it's a flutter, a flicker of wings in your chest. Others, it's a relentless vise that stops the beat, if only for a second. It might be a hot burn, spreading like wildfire in your ribs, or an icy cold space, empty and void.

But the heart always reacts. Even after seven years, just hearing his name inspired any of those reactions or a dozen more. And there was one every single time.

TIME

The ticking of the clock
Marring the deafening silence,
Time's footsteps toward an end
Or a beginning.

—M. WHITE

ELLIOT

I *didn't hear the knocking until* I closed the door to my nephew's bedroom, and my first thought was that I hoped it wouldn't wake him from his nap. The second was wonder over who it could be as I hurried to the door of my sister's brownstone. But nothing could have prepared me for the turn my life would take when I opened it.

My best friend stood on the steps, her dark hair hanging over her bent shoulders, tears falling from sparkling gray eyes, her mouth gaping in pain as she reached for me, falling into my arms.

"Sophie," I breathed as I held her trembling frame as best I could.

Sobs racked through her, and her hands fisted my sweater. She couldn't speak, so I held her with my mind racing, heart aching with dread, and her father's name echoing in my head. She'd come from the hospital, and she'd brought news. News I didn't know that any of us were prepared for.

"Come inside," I said gently, guiding her into the house, down the stairs, and into my room.

We sat on the edge of my bed, and Sophie hid her face in her hands as her shoulders shook. I turned to her, laying my hand on her back, waiting.

She wiped her cheeks with the flats of her fingers, though tears kept falling as she looked at me with crisp eyes and a trembling chin and said words that would echo in my heart forever.

"The stroke … it was because he's …" she struggled. "He has cancer, Elliot, and … and …" Her thin composure had nearly shattered, her face bending under the weight of the words, and my fingers went numb as my heart split open. "He's dying."

She broke, folding over, and I pulled her into me, wrapping my arms around her, pressing my cheek to her crown as my tears fell, blinding me.

He was more my father than my own. And now … now …

"Wade …" she started, but couldn't finish; the words held too much power.

Even the one she uttered had power over me, the same power it always had. His name. That name I'd heard a thousand times, a thousand ways, and still — even under the shock of the moment — his name crushed my heart, splintering it like broken glass.

"Wade's on the plane," Sophie said, her words uneven. (Again, his name, my heart murmuring fresh pain.) "I can't … he doesn't know. There's no way to tell him what happened, not until his flight lands. He's on the plane, and he doesn't know … doesn't know that Dad only has weeks …" she said as she clutched my sweater. "Weeks. That's all we have left. I don't … I can't …" The words dissolved into sobs.

"Shhh," I soothed, rocking her until she found her voice again.

"I need Wade," she whispered. "I don't know what to do. But he'll know. He always knows."

My heart thumped hard, bumping the broken glass, nicked by sharp edges. "He'll be here soon."

She nodded against my breast. "And Sadie. What will I do about Sadie? She's still at school … I came straight here." She moaned gently. "I don't even know what I'm doing. I didn't even tell my own sister. I should … I should call the school. But how will I tell her? How can

I? I can't do this without Wade." The words split and cracked, sending her over the edge again.

There was nothing to say, no words of comfort to offer; it wouldn't be okay, time wouldn't heal her wounds, it wouldn't work itself out. Her father was dying with no warning. A seizure at work the day before sent him to the hospital, and the diagnosis gave him a life sentence. An expiration date.

I had no way of comprehending what was happening to the man who had been like a father to me. My best friend's father. Wade's father.

Wade ...

My heart folded in on itself for a beat. He was coming home. Seven years without a word. Seven years without seeing his face.

It was all too much.

I squeezed my eyes closed and rested my cheek on top of her head.

Her sobbing ebbed, and she pulled away, though her eyes were trained on the ground, barely open.

"I don't know what to do."

My fingers wound together in my lap, squeezing and twisting. "For now, wait for your brother." I couldn't say his name, such a simple thing, still beyond me. "How long will your dad be in the hospital?"

"Two days. He's stable now, speaking, but he can't walk, can't feed himself. He fell asleep and I couldn't ... I couldn't be the only one who knew. I needed you. God, what are we going to do, Elliot?"

Her eyes were bright and sparkling behind thick, dark, tear-soaked lashes, her brows stitched together with fear and sadness and grief.

"Have you spoken to hospice yet?"

She shook her head and buried her face in her hands. "We're meeting tonight with a social worker. Dad wants to come home, so we've got to make a plan, figure everything out, but I ... I just ..."

"What can I do?" I laid a hand on her back.

"I don't even know. Wade lands at five-thirty at La Guardia —

we're meeting at the hospital. He doesn't know, I don't want to text him, don't want him to find out that way. I've got to tell him when he's here. But I … I don't want to be alone until then. Please, will you come with me to the hospital?" Her eyes were big, shining, begging me. "I wouldn't ask if things were different."

I swallowed my emotions, swallowed my fears. She needed me, and I'd be there. "Of course I'll go with you."

She looked sorry she'd asked. "Are you sure? It's been so long."

I shook my head, just a small motion. "Don't think about that. I'll take care of everything, okay? I need to make some calls, though. Will you be okay here in my room? I'll be just outside if you need anything, just call for me."

She nodded again, looking grateful and relieved, and I guided her to lie down, tucking her into my bed. I closed the curtains and left her there in my room.

Fresh tears fell as I walked through my sister's quiet home, up the stairs and to the window seat overlooking the Manhattan street. My sister and her husband were at work, and the kids would be asleep for a little while yet. I had time to help, and I'd do whatever I could.

First, I texted my sister Mary and told her what happened. My phone dinged within minutes with a reply, rare because she was a resident at Mt. Sinai and was always busy. Also uncommon because she was one of the least affable people on the planet, rarely showing concern for anyone other than herself, outside of her job. Her cold detachment helped her disconnect from her patients, and her bedside manner left something to be desired. But today she was obliging, offering promises to have Charlie come home early to take care of the kids so I could go to the hospital with Sophie.

After that, I texted Sophie's younger sister and asked her to text me when she was home from school in the hopes I could keep the lid on it all until her brother was home.

Wade.

His name again, the sting of it ever unexpected.

As I sat in the window seat, bathed by the cool winter sun, I thought of him, worrying as I so often did. I imagined him on the plane over the Atlantic, not knowing what was going on. Not knowing what he was walking into.

I knew what his father meant to him. He'd already lost his mother, and now … now everything would rest on his shoulders.

More tears fell, and I pulled my legs into my chest, head pressed to my knees, shoulders sagging, heart aching as I mustered the strength to calm myself so I could check on the kids.

I climbed the stairs to the third floor, peeking in on the sleeping children. They were peaceful, faces slack and lips puckered, lashes against their cheeks and chests rising and falling. I wished for a long moment that I could find relief that complete.

Down I went again to the second floor and took my seat once more, my head resting against the glass as I sifted my way through all that had come to pass.

In an hour, my world had been brought to a stop. In five hours, it would begin to turn backward, back to my past, back to the boy I loved. The boy I ruined.

The first time I saw him, I was fifteen and he was sixteen, the boy with the dark shock of hair and broad shoulders, with eyes gray and cool as December and a smile as bright and warm as June. I remember walking into their house with Sophie just a few days after we met and finding him there in the living room, tall and beautiful, the light shining in through the window as he worked on his homework. He saw me, and I stopped, and he stopped, and time stopped.

The last time I saw him, I was seventeen, and he stood before me with tears in his eyes as he begged me to say yes. Begged me to go with him. Begged me to be his forever. Begged me to change my mind. But I couldn't. Didn't matter how much I wanted to, because I did. I would have given him the world. But in the end, it hadn't been up to me.

He left the next day for the Army. That was seven years ago.

It felt like yesterday. It felt like another lifetime. It felt like I relived the moment every single day.

I'd written him almost every day, pleading at first for forgiveness, telling him I'd changed my mind, begging him to come back to me. After a year, my letters grew angry, accusing, my hurt and rejection pouring out of me and onto the paper, though the transference never relieved me. And then I found resignation, and I'd stopped sending my letters completely.

He never answered me. Not once. Not a single word, not from any avenue.

But I was still connected to him through Sophie and her dad, though they rarely mentioned his name around me. I knew when Wade came home, though he never stayed for more than a night or two before moving on, back to wherever he was based, back to Iraq. Afghanistan. Now Germany. I knew very little, but I took comfort in that he was alive — fear had weighed on me every moment he was deployed throughout the course of the war.

That was the sum total of my knowledge, but I was never able to let him go. Didn't matter that I knew nothing. The boy who I walked away from lived on in the wreckage of my heart, and I never stopped wishing things had been different.

Maybe he hadn't gotten my letters. Maybe he'd never know how I felt. Or maybe he'd read every one. Maybe he'd burned them all without breaking the seal of the envelopes.

Maybe I'd never know.

My niece Maven woke from her nap — her little voice carried over the monitor as she played in her crib. And with that, I wiped my tears and made my way to her room, grateful for her love, which she gave freely and without condition. She hugged me around the neck, reminding me just what it was like to feel tenderness after so long without.

WADE

I took a deep breath as the cab pulled to a stop outside of Mt. Sinai, eyeing the entrance to the hospital with my throat in a clamp. My father was in that building, lying in a hospital bed.

I had no idea what I would find inside those walls.

The second Sophie had called me, time began to move differently, fast and slow. The words had turned around and around in my mind as I spoke with my supervisor, who granted me leave. I'd packed my bag and rushed to the airport, getting on the first commercial flight I could. And I spent eight hours on the plane, staring out the window with every fear whispering to me.

A stroke. I didn't know what it meant other than he needed me, so here I was.

My mind was everywhere but where I was as I paid the cab driver and unloaded my duffle bag. I didn't feel the fatigue of the flight or the hunger from not having eaten, only icy dread as I walked to the nurse's station, then down the cold hallway to my father's room.

The door swung open, and I stood in the threshold, still and silent as my eyes found my father. He looked smaller than I remembered him, lying in that hospital bed with tubes and wires twisting away, connecting him to machines that blinked and beeped. They didn't seem to disturb his sleep. Even at rest, I could see the slackness of the left half of his face from the stroke, his mouth downturned and drooping open.

He'd always been strong, larger than life. But lying there, he was vulnerable, shrinking under the weight of his body.

My bag fell to the ground with a thump next to my boots, my chest rising and falling painfully with every breath.

Sophie drew a breath from the corner of the room; her face bent and tears streamed as she flew across the room and into my arms. That was all it took for my composure to crack and crumble, emotion climbing up my throat, stinging my eyes, burning my nose. I closed my eyes to stop the tears, but it was no use. They seeped from the corners, defying the physics of my pinched lids, and my sister sobbed in my arms, clinging to my shirtfront.

I held her tight, wishing I could change everything, rearrange time and space and make it all right again.

She stilled after a moment, pulling away. Something in her eyes stopped me dead.

"I need to talk to you," she whispered, casting a furtive glance over her shoulder at our sleeping father.

I nodded, moving my bag out of the way as she took my arm and guided us into the hallway.

When the door was closed, she stood before me for a long minute, wringing her hands, lip between her teeth. She couldn't look at me.

"Soph," I said softly, gently, "what's going on?"

She opened her mouth to speak but took a shaky breath instead. Then she met my eyes. "It's not just the stroke, Wade."

I couldn't swallow my fear. I tried, but it stayed lodged where it was. "What do you mean?"

"They did scans and … and …" Her eyes darted, her bottom lip trembling.

I reached for her hands, willing her to look at me as my pulse raced, hands tingling from adrenaline and foreboding. "Sophie, just tell me."

A fat tear slipped down her cheek as she looked into my eyes and hit the detonator on my heart. "He has brain cancer, Wade. They've given us a few weeks before he's gone …"

If she said more, I didn't hear her. My knees buckled, and I reached for the wall to brace myself, turning to press my forehead against the cool veneer. It couldn't be possible, couldn't be real. It was a dream. A nightmare.

Gone.

I fought the truth. He was too young, too healthy. He was a superhero: immune. I wasn't old enough to lose him — I was supposed to have years. Years and years. I'd already lost one parent, a loss I'd never recovered from, a loss that changed the course of my life. And now, I'd be alone.

He taught me how to be a man. He gave me everything.

I was supposed to have more time.

Time, time, time.

I'd been gone too long. I'd avoided coming home, and because of that, I wasn't here for him, for my family. I'd abandoned him, and now … now … now I'd lose him forever.

I sank to my knees there in the hallway with my sister sobbing at my side, wrapping her arms around me as best she could, and we cried together. If only our tears could change what had come to pass.

Now I just had to make up for my absence as best I could in the time I had left. Now I would be present, consequences be damned. I'd handled so much, seen so much, witnessed war and death and suffering firsthand. I knew what to do and how to do it.

I also knew it would be the hardest thing I'd ever do.

We stood and held each other a little longer, hanging on to one another. Because we were all we had left.

I pulled away when I could finally speak. "Where's Sadie?"

Sophie drew in a breath and let it out, trying to calm herself. "She's at home. I couldn't tell her without you. I'm sorry … I wish … I wish …." She shook her head.

I swallowed again and pulled her into a hug. "It's all right. I'm here. We'll do it together, okay?"

She nodded.

I looked toward the door to his room, seeing nothing. "What do we do now?"

"We have an appointment with hospice in an hour to talk about our options."

Options. The remainder of my father's life had been whittled down to options for his death. "Is he … can he speak? How is he?"

Sophie rubbed her nose and let me go. "They say he was lucky. The clot was in the right hemisphere, so he can speak and comprehend, but he can't read. His speech is affected because of his paralysis, but he's already more clear today than he was yesterday. The doctor says that will get even better, but he probably won't be able to use his left hand or walk again before …" She looked toward his door. "He knows this is it, and he wants to go home."

"Then that's what we'll fight for."

We stood in silence. Sophie finally broke it, touching my arm. "Are you ready?"

I took a breath and squared my shoulders as best as I could under the weight. I didn't answer her question. There was no way to be ready for any of it, but I opened the door anyway and stepped into that room to face fears I hadn't even known were real until a few minutes ago.

When the door closed behind us, he opened his eyes, turning his head to the sound. And half of his face came alive with joy and pain and fear when he saw me.

"My boy," he said, the words thick.

"Hey, Dad." My voice was rough, and I cleared my throat as I walked over to him, reaching for his hand. He squeezed it hard and let it go with tears in his eyes, and when I bent, he cupped the back of my neck and pressed his forehead to mine.

"Long time," he muttered, the words shaky.

"I'm here now," I answered, begging his forgiveness.

"Glad," he whispered, and I pulled away. Sophie stood back, her fingers pressed to her lips, tear-stained cheeks shining as she watched us.

The door opened behind me, and I turned, unprepared for who I found.

Her cheeks were flushed, eyes big and shining, wet with tears, chest heaving from running or from proximity to me, I didn't know.

Elliot.

Her name in my mind was a curse I couldn't escape, a ghost that haunted me day after day, year after year since I'd seen her last so long ago.

Time stretched out in the moment, the two of us caught in it like a web, but we didn't struggle, didn't fight. Instead, we witnessed the past standing in front of us, alive and intact. She was the past I'd been running from for seven long, lonely years.

Dad cut the tie, saying her name with reverence, and I stepped back as she stepped forward, keeping my pain in front of me, as if it could shield me from her.

She tried to smile, forehead furrowed and brows pinched with her sadness as she turned all of her attention to him.

"Rick," she whispered, bending to kiss his forehead, and he looked at her just like he did my sisters. She'd been a part of our family from the second she crossed the threshold of our home.

"Sadie?" he asked, wondering after our youngest sister.

Elliot glanced at me, just a flick of her eyes to me and back to my father, but I felt the burn of her even in that small moment.

"She's at home. Sophie and Wade haven't told her yet."

He closed his eyes and nodded, his Adam's apple bobbing. "I'm sorry," he tried to say, but the words were muffled and slurred.

"No," Elliot said, her voice shaking, her lips smiling sadly. "There are no sorrys, not for anyone. Especially not for you. Everything in its time. *Now let the night be dark for all of me / Let the night be too dark for me to see / Into the future. Let what will be, be.*"

He smiled. "Robert Frost."

She smiled back, though her chin flexed, trembling as she held his hand. "Don't be afraid. You exist. You'll never cease."

He nodded again, a tear slipping down his temple on his left side, and she wiped it, knowing he couldn't. And I broke, not able to show it.

AS AIR

For every breath
And every beat of my heart
Carries me farther away
From you.

—M. WHITE

ELLIOT

squeezed Rick's hand and backed away, slipping into the background as Sophie and Wade took my place by their father's side. Sophie sat on the edge of the bed, caging Rick's hand in both of hers as if she could hang on to him forever, if she were strong enough. Wade pulled up a chair, his profile cut out against the shadows behind him, jaw firm, throat working, brow low. He'd changed so much, aged into a man, hardened into stone and muscle. I didn't recognize him, and yet the familiarity of him sang to me, called to me.

But he wasn't mine. He hadn't been for a long time.

And he didn't want to be.

So I sat in the back of the room in the shadows, shouldering my pain and all of theirs, wishing I could take it from them. I could be strong for them. I wanted to be strong for them — I had a feeling they'd need that in the days to come. It was a small offering, but an offering I had to give nonetheless.

The proximity to Wade was stifling, the shock of seeing him stripping me bare every few minutes, over and over again. I thought I'd find my footing and lose it, my feet slipping out from underneath as the undertow dragged me beneath the surface.

I'd loved him since the second I first saw him, and though time had passed, though I thought I'd buried that love, it sprang fresh the second I saw him again. The moments I kept locked away broke their chains and pressed themselves into my mind.

Long nights with his lips against mine, my body entwined in his, our hearts wrapped in each other. Simple, happy moments of his smile, his laughter, his love. It had always been him, from the first. There had never been anyone else.

The pain of our last words slipped in like a fog, banishing the warmth of the good. He'd asked the impossible of me, but that it was impossible didn't stop my regretting everything.

But it wasn't supposed to happen like that. We had a plan, a plan that he redrew without me.

Enlisting in the Army had always been part of that, a part that had never been contested. I was to stay in New York and graduate from high school, and then we would get married, start our lives together. Where he would go, I would go.

The night before he left, he came to me with his grandmother's ring and changed the rules. He couldn't leave without me, he'd said. He needed me to promise him, to come with him. And I wanted to.

But I was seventeen, too young, too afraid, and I didn't have my father's blessing. Why couldn't he wait? I asked him the question, begging him as he begged me. He wanted me to choose him.

I didn't know how to walk away from my life. And my biggest regret, my biggest shame, was that I wasn't brave enough to do it anyway.

The proposal devolved into an argument as his pain twisted him until he was angry. But he wanted me to leave everything. He wanted to burn the plan and fly off instinct. And I wanted time, that was all. But it was more than he could give.

He said if I loved him, I'd go.

Time, I begged.

Now, he pleaded.

And in the end, it was over, his anger sending the shrapnel of his pain into my heart, shredding it to ribbons.

The wounds never healed. I was acutely aware of every rip, every tear, as I watched him from the shadows of the room.

Sophie and Wade both stood after a while, and so did I. Wade turned for the door, his eyes passing over me like I was invisible. Sophie reached for my hand.

"Will you stay with Dad while we meet with the social worker?" she asked quietly.

I squeezed her fingers. "Of course I will. Go."

She closed her eyes, bowing her head slightly in thanks, and then she turned to leave, following Wade out the door.

He took my heart with him when he left. It had been his, always — he'd possessed it since the beginning — and being near that atrophied piece of me after so long had the broken muscle thumping in my chest, erratic, beating again for the first time.

I took Wade's place by his father's side, resting my hand on his.

"Glad," he mumbled, pausing, "you're here."

"I'm always here for you, Rick."

He blinked back tears, eyes moving to the door. "Wade …" He didn't finish.

I didn't speak.

His eyes found mine again. "You okay?"

I smiled. "Only you would be worried about me right now."

Half his face lifted just enough to soften it. "You okay?" he pressed.

"I'm okay. You think he's okay?"

"No."

I pulled in a slow breath and let it out. "It's been a long time."

"Too long."

"He was surprised to see me. He didn't know … I should have waited to come."

"No," he said, squeezing my hand. "Needed you."

I wondered for a fleeting moment whether he meant himself or Wade.

I reached into my bag for my book, eliciting half a smile from him when he saw the cover. He couldn't read, but he recognized the book.

"Whitman," he said.

I nodded, pleased that he was pleased. "I thought you might like me to read to you."

"Please," he said and closed his eyes, and I turned to "Song of Myself," one of his favorites, and I began to read.

Rick was part of the reason I studied literature at NYU — he'd cultivated my hobby of writing poetry, turning it into an adoration of literature, putting books of poetry in my hand, prompting discussions after school that rolled into dinner with me and his children. They were used to it, consequences of having a father who was a Lit professor at Columbia, but I wasn't — those moments fed my soul.

I kept my voice steady and smooth, though I could feel the heat in my cheeks from the emotion, knowing he knew every word by heart, though he couldn't speak them, could never read them again, and a tear slipped from the corner of his eye as I read on.

The last scud of day holds back for me,
It flings my likeness after the rest and true as any on the shadow'd wilds,
It coaxes me to the vapor and the dusk.

I depart as air, I shake my white locks at the runaway sun,
I effuse my flesh in eddies, and drift it in lacy jags.

I bequeath myself to the dirt to grow from the grass I love,
If you want me again look for me under your boot-soles.

You will hardly know who I am or what I mean,
But I shall be good health to you nevertheless,
And filter and fibre your blood.

Failing to fetch me at first keep encouraged,
Missing me one place search another,
I stop somewhere waiting for you.

I took a breath, overcome for a moment, unable to continue as my tears fell fresh. And he opened his eyes, the man who had been one of the constants in my life, the man who believed in me when no one else did, the man who would depart as air in just a matter of days, slipping away from me forever.

"Don't cry." He reached for my face, and I leaned forward for him to cup my cheek.

"I can't help it. What will we do without you?"

And to that, he only had one answer, and he gave it to me with strength his body no longer possessed, but his soul always would.

"Live."

WADE

The meeting was one of the hardest of my life.

I sat next to my sister, back rigid, listening to the options, the choices we had. Care plans and insurance and needing nurses every day. Transporting him home, readying the room for his hospital bed, the equipment, the space he would need as his body betrayed him.

There were plans to be made, a million things to do when all I wanted was to sit with him in that room and beg him to stay with us as long as he could.

Sophie cried silently through the conversation, and I took the lead gladly, finding comfort at least in that. In being a doer. In being a fixer. But frustration twisted through me at the futility of it all. There was plenty to do. There was nothing to fix.

So I put on the mask I wore, the mask I'd perfected over seven years, the one that buffered me against war, against Elliot, and now against this.

But as the meeting wore on, I considered the fact that Elliot was sitting in the hospital room just down the hall. She was older — it seemed impossible. The vision of her when I'd last seen her was a part of me, a part of my mind and soul. I could still hear her say goodbye, still feel her slipping away from me.

Although she was older, she was otherwise unchanged. Smaller, maybe. Quieter. But she was still so beautiful, her eyes so dark. Bottomless. Infinite.

It wasn't any easier to see her than I imagined it would be. Given the circumstance, it was exponentially harder, wider, taller than I could have believed. I didn't want her here, couldn't deal with her in that moment when I needed all my strength for my father. And with that realization, I found the deep burn of resentment that sometimes accompanied my thoughts of her. But it wasn't resentment for her; I resented myself.

We walked out of the office and toward the elevator, my feelings a nebulous cloud, ever shifting, charged and crackling.

Sophie sniffled, and I pressed the button to call the elevator, thinking about what waited for me downstairs. My father. Elliot.

My chest ached as we stepped onto the elevator. "Sophie, why …" I stopped myself, drawing a heavy breath. It wasn't the time. I could handle this, handle Elliot.

"Why what?"

I clenched my teeth, flexing my jaw. "Never mind."

Her brow furrowed. "No, Wade. Please, tell me."

"Don't worry about it, okay?" My voice was more gruff than I meant for it to be, and I cleared my throat.

She squared off, turning her body to mine. "Tell me what you were going to say," she insisted.

I faced her, trying not to accuse, but I knew my eyes were hard, and I could feel the stiffness of my body, my heart. "Why did you bring her? You know …" I paused, unable to find the right words. "Just … why *now*? Why *right now*?"

"Because I asked her to be here." She frowned, her face tight. "It's been seven years."

I ran a hand through my hair. "You know damn well we haven't spoken since then. And to see her now …" I swallowed hard. "I just don't want her here, not yet. I need time."

Sophie fumed. "She's a part of our family, and she's been here all the years you haven't."

I angled away from her, the sting burning deeper than she could have known. "Not fair, Soph. Not fucking fair."

The doors opened, and we stepped off, legs moving fast with our hurt.

"What's not fair is you denying me the right to have her here. What's not fair is you denying her the right to see Dad." She grabbed my arm, pulling me to a stop. "Wade, I know it hurts, and I'm sorry. But I need her. Please tell me you can find a way to be okay with it, because I don't know if I can get through this without her." Her voice cracked, and tears filled her eyes.

I stood there in front of my sister, who asked me to do the impossible, and I couldn't say no, and not just because I didn't want to hurt Elliot, but because Dad wouldn't have wanted me to either. He loved her, and having her there was the right thing, even though

I hated the position I found myself in. I hated her, and for a reason I could never utter: I still loved her. I would love her forever. But there was no way back to what we were.

"Fine," I said curtly. "But please don't ask me for anything more than tolerance."

She nodded, and we turned, heading for his hospital room.

Elliot sat next to his bed, reading him Whitman, her voice strong and sure, words leaving her lips with the intimacy of them being her own. A flash from a thousand nights before overcame me — Elliot in my arms, reading me Byron with all the passion and love in her heart.

I pushed the thought away, holding it back with the truth of our circumstance.

She turned to us, closing the book and slipping it back into her bag. Dad opened his eyes and tried to smile as Elliot moved out of the way again.

She was so quiet, disappearing like smoke, just as she had before.

I moved to the edge of the bed. "Hey, Dad."

"Go okay?" he said through the side of his mouth.

"Yeah, it went okay. The social worker is going to meet with all of us tomorrow with the plans so we can make a decision."

"Just want …" he paused, struggling, "go home."

I swallowed. "I know. It's just details, like how many nurses they'll need, what days they'll come. That sort of thing."

He nodded.

I watched him for a moment, not wanting to leave. "Dad, Sadie's at home waiting for us. She … she doesn't know."

His eyes closed, chin trembling. Another nod.

"We've got to go, but we'll be back." I turned to Elliot, voice hard, addressing her for the first time in seven years. "Will you stay with him?"

She blinked and nodded — I didn't think she was breathing.

"Thank you."

"Y-you're welcome." As hard as my voice had been, hers was soft and quiet, all the strength she'd given to my father gone. And I knew it was because of me and for me. It would seem neither of us had escaped the other unscathed. I was just so much better at hiding it than Elliot could ever be.

SMALL
COMFORT

To make the best
Of what you have:
A small comfort
In a big world.

—M. WHITE

ELLIOT

An hour passed quickly as I read to Rick, thankful for something to do that felt productive, as if every turn of the page brought me closer to something. To what, I didn't know. Everything had shifted, gravity tilting, leaving us all sideways and scrambling for purchase, throwing us into each other, leaving us bruised. And it had only just begun.

My phone buzzed in my bag, and I grabbed it, surprised to see a string of texts from my sister.

Hope everything's okay.

Just checking in, do you know when you'll be home?

Just got here and you're not home yet. Let me know when you'll be back.

The kids are asking for you, are you leaving soon?

I bit my lip and messaged her back. *Sorry, phone was in my bag. Is everything okay?*

Within a second, she texted me back. *I could really use your help. I don't mean to interrupt, but if you could come home soon, it would be great.*

I sighed, sadness anchoring my heart as it did so often.

There were days when I looked back at my life and wondered how I found myself where I was. At the fulcrum was Wade and the decision which had sent my life down this road.

I was the caregiver for my niece and nephew, and my payment was that I had a place to stay. But I received my other, more substantial income in the form of macaroni art and messy kisses.

When I looked up from my phone, Rick was watching me.

"You okay?" he asked.

"Yes, I'm sorry. It's my sister — she needs help with the kids."

He tried to smile. "Go."

I reached for his hand. "I don't want to."

"Don't worry. Tired."

"I promised I'd stay."

"S'okay." The words slurred together. "Go."

I looked down into my lap, torn.

"Elliot," he said, and when I met his cool, gray eyes again, they were full of understanding. "Go. M'okay."

I let out a heavy breath. "All right. I'll come see you tomorrow, okay? I promise."

He squeezed my hand, and I let him go, firing off messages to my sister and Sophie before packing my things, except the book, which I slipped under his hand. He flexed his fingers, trailing the canvas cover with his fingertips.

I smiled and cupped his jaw, which was strong, just like Wade's. "I'll bring more tomorrow. How about Emerson?"

"Yes, please."

And then I kissed him on the forehead, smoothing his dark hair before I turned to leave, hating that I had to choose. But my family, those children, were my world, and I worried over what was going on at home that was so important that she'd interrupt this. Interrupt my time with Rick.

So I hurried home, anxious about them, and when I blew through the door, I found a disaster zone.

Toys were strewn all over the entryway, and Mary looked frantic, her dark hair in disarray and brown eyes wide. A crying Maven sat propped on her hip, and Sammy was in tow, his face smeared with jelly.

"Thank God you're here," she said, passing Maven to me.

She stopped crying the minute Mary let go of her.

"What happened?" I asked as Sammy twisted away from her and ran down the hall.

"Get back here!" she called, chasing him down, marching back over to me with him under her arm. "It's just been a mess ever since I walked in the door."

I glanced at the clock on the wall. She'd been home an hour. "Where's Charlie? Did the kids have their snack?"

She huffed, shifting to keep the wiggling boy in check. "He's in the office, working, just dumped them on me the second I walked through the door. Can you believe that?"

"Shocking." I smiled at Maven, wiping the tears from her cheeks. "And the snack?"

"Who knows, Charlie was on duty." She readjusted her grip on Sammy, but he thrashed, making monster noises.

"I left him a list."

She rolled her eyes. "I'm sure you did. Doubt he read it. Here," she said, passing Sammy over. "It's bath time."

I frowned at her as Sammy chanted *Elliooooot, Elliooooot*, over and over again, dragging the word out. "They ate, right?" He wrapped his arms around my neck and planted a sticky kiss on my cheek.

Mary waved a hand, already turning to leave. "I didn't feel like cooking, so they had sandwiches."

I nodded and moved to the stairs. "Sounds yummy," I said to Sammy, setting him down so I didn't topple over trying to carry them both up. I bent down to get eye level with him, smiling as I dipped a finger in the purple massacre on his cheeks, pretending to lick it. "Mmm. Grape?"

He nodded, smiling wide. "With goldfishes!"

I opened my mouth in mock surprise. "Goldfishes *and* grape jelly? What a feast."

"It was good, good, good," he said, hopping up the stairs with each word.

"Ready for a bath?" I asked Maven, whose nose was still red, her little finger hanging in her pouty, red lips. She nodded, and I kissed her on her cool cheek. "Then let's get cleaned up, shall we?"

I followed the bounding four-year-old up the stairs and into the bathroom.

The routine was automatic, easy, bringing me a little bit of joy with every action: making sure the water was just right, adding the bubbles, singing them silly Beatles songs — "Octopus' Garden" was their favorite, followed by "Maxwell's Silver Hammer." I stripped the sweet babies down and took care of them, washing them tenderly, and as they began to play on their own, my mind wandered.

One whole hour, and she'd blown up my phone to get me home. Not even an hour — she'd barely been home at all when she texted me, put out I supposed because Charlie passed the kids off on her. Heaven forbid she cook or bathe them. I was hurt that she'd given up so easily, knowing I needed some time. And I'd already been late leaving because Charlie hadn't gotten home in time for me to leave with Sophie … I'd barely had any time with Rick tonight at all.

I sighed as I straightened up the bathroom, putting the kids' dirty clothes in the hamper and getting fresh towels out from the linen closet.

She had her reasons for being so unwilling to help. In part, it was bred in her by my father who indulged her at every opportunity — she'd always been this way. Past that, she was so busy at the hospital, and when she came home, she was tired and overwhelmed. Charlie too. He was an attorney and brought his work home with him nearly every night.

I also made a quiet concession that they hadn't planned for this, even for each other. They'd only been dating a few months when she found out she was pregnant, and their solution was to get married. I thought they'd been in love, but the strain of the kids and their jobs was so much, and things had deteriorated over the years. It was another reason I was happy to help, hoping I could take some of the pressure off of them so they could get back to each other.

I'd lived with them for nearly four years, since just after Sammy was born. My father moved to Miami with our younger sister, and Mary asked me to move in to help out. It was a perfect situation — I was in college at the time and needed a place to stay, and they'd just bought their brownstone, which had plenty of room. She offered me the guest room downstairs at the back of the house where I could look out on the patio and write.

I jumped at the chance.

Of course, as the years wore on, they came to depend on me more and more. And when I'd graduated with my literature degree, I didn't know what to do with it. Didn't know what to do with myself.

The boldest thing I'd done since Wade left for the Army was to go to school. But even in doing that, I was still only going through the motions without an end game.

He'd been my end game, and when things ended, the path of my life had been erased, left smudged and blurry. I hadn't found my way since.

So it was easy, convenient, to be a live-in nanny, working my schedule around theirs. The kids were in private preschool three days a week, and I took care of them from the time I picked them up at three until they went to bed, and all day the rest of the time. Charlie and Mary always had places to be, benefit dinners and the opera and other sorts of social things — frankly, I lost track. And I enjoyed the solitude when they were gone.

But before I knew it I was … stuck. I didn't think about it overly much, mostly because I didn't have a plan for the rest of my life and it was easier to just put it off. I felt no urgency — I had my degree but no idea what to do with it. And helping Mary gave me a sense of purpose, gave me a solution to a question I didn't want to answer myself.

I pulled the plug on the old clawfoot tub and helped the kids out, drying off Maven before handing Sammy his hooded towel, knowing he'd want to put it on himself. Then Sammy ran off to his room to get dressed, and I carried Maven to her room.

It was all pink and purple with butterflies and flowers hanging from the ceiling, with a white sleigh bed topped with pillows and her favorite stuffed animals. Her room always reminded me of *Peter Pan* and what I imagined Wendy Darling's room to look like, classic and Victorian, sweet and pretty, just like Maven.

The toddler hummed tunelessly as I dressed her, and then we climbed in bed with a book while Sammy brushed his teeth. And when we were all finished with *Olivia*, I tucked her in and turned down the lights, clicking on her nightlight that threw stars all over the ceiling. I sang her a soft song, and she gave me a hug, and when she told me she loved me, my heart ached.

Guilt sprang in my chest — I'd forgotten for a moment what the day had held, the sadness crushing me in a wave. But I caught my breath as I walked into Sammy's room to find him bouncing on his bed with a *Pete the Cat* book. His room was like Maven's, but all shades of blue and dark wood, with a captain's bed and a nautical theme that had skewed in the pirate direction over the course of the last year. He leaned against me as we read, though he knew all the words and recited them with me. And when all was done, I said goodnight with a wave and a kiss on the cheek before making my way wearily down the stairs.

Mary sat in the living room on her phone, long legs crossed, wine glass in hand. People always said we looked alike, but I didn't see it.

Mary was all sharp edges; even her dark eyes, the one part of her I did see myself in, held a hardness to them that I'd never understood.

"Everything go okay?" she asked, not looking up from the screen.

"Just fine. They're all off to dreamland."

She sighed. "Good. I hope they don't come out a thousand times."

I tried to smile, but I found it hard to pretend. "Well, I'm heading downstairs for the night."

Mary looked up to meet my eyes. "Oh, I didn't even ask you how Rick is."

This was her way of asking. "He's …" I swallowed. "He's okay. I read to him while Sophie and W-wade had a meeting with the social worker." His name hitched in my throat, catching, snagged by my heart.

"Wade's here?" she asked, one dark brow climbing.

I nodded. "He flew in from Germany tonight."

"Huh. Great place to be stationed. Have you even seen him since he left?"

"No," I answered quietly.

Compassion passed across her face and was gone. "I'm sorry. Was it hard?"

I took a breath. "It was."

"Is he just as handsome as he was?"

"More. He's … he's a man now. I barely recognized him."

She shook her head. "Well, he's really done well for himself in the military. I hate that he's back under such awful circumstances. Poor Rick. Those poor girls."

I found it so strange that she approved now when seven years ago she was so quick to judge, so quick to steer me away from him. Another attempt at a smile had me wanting to leave. "Okay, well … if that's all, I'd really like to lie down."

"Of course," she said with a wave of her hand.

I started to walk away but stopped, turning back to her when I remembered something. "Oh, I'm sorry, one more thing."

She was already back on her phone. "Mmhmm?"

I clasped my hands behind my back, pulse speeding up at the prospect of her saying no. "The next few weeks are going to be … well, they're going to be a lot for the Winters family. Sophie's asked me to help out, and I'd like to do what I can. Do you … do you think it would be possible to put the kids in full-time school for a while?"

Mary looked up at me, frowning. "That will cost a fortune, Elliot. I don't even know if the school has space."

My cheeks flushed. "I know, I just thought—"

"I mean, I can ask them, if you want to pay for it with your money. And if they have room, I guess that would be fine. But I still need you to pick them up every day."

I blinked, simultaneously surprised at her solution and not surprised at all. "O-of course," I said, not thinking twice about doing it. I only had a few weeks left with Rick, and I wanted to be there as much as I could, whatever the cost, regardless of the slight.

She looked back at her screen, thumb scrolling. "Unless Charlie will help out, but I doubt it. You know how busy he is."

I pursed my lips and nodded. "All right."

"'Night, Elliot. Get some rest."

"'Night," I echoed and descended the stairs to the bottom floor, then into my room where I closed the door behind me with a snick.

I loved the room, loved the creaky floorboards and the dark wood wainscot, loved the old brick fireplace and elaborate mantle. The house had been built in 1910 and remodeled, but they'd left so many of the original fixtures that it still held the charm it had always had.

Mary's words and the stress of the day didn't ebb as I made my way through my room putting my things away, changing into more comfortable clothes, finding myself on my bed, notebook in my lap, pencil flying as I poured my heart onto the page, thinking of everything and nothing, possessed by my emotions.

My family and my responsibilities at home, my sister … today I felt stifled and trapped, but it was less about them, I knew.

It was Rick lying in a hospital bed. It was Sophie crying in my arms. It was Wade standing before me, a man I didn't recognize, though I knew him all the same.

Wade.

He was home, appearing at the edge of my universe after what felt like a thousand years without him. *Changed* was the word that circled my thoughts. Hardened, colder. The boy I knew was gone.

No, not gone — he was there, somewhere. But I couldn't see him; I could only see what he'd become. I wondered how much of what he was now was due to me.

I set my pen down in the crease of my notebook and leaned back, my eyes on the fireplace as I thought back to the night he asked me to marry him, the last time I was truly happy, even though it was only for a moment.

It had been summertime, just after his graduation, a bittersweet affair. It was a celebration of all he'd accomplished and a moment that marked the beginning of the end. Because once he had graduated, he'd enlisted in the Army.

The lights were off that night so long ago, and I lay in bed, waiting for him with the moonlight bathing my room, casting long shadows in the corners as I listened for him.

In two days, he would be leaving for boot camp, and we'd made a pact, a vow to stay together until I finished high school. Then I'd graduate, and he'd come back from his first deployment, and we'd marry. It was going to be the longest year of our lives and then … well, after that I didn't really know what would happen. I could get an online degree, find a place for myself wherever we were. Maybe I could go to a local college, transfer when we were re-stationed. Make it work. And for Wade, I'd make it work.

That didn't mean I wasn't scared. Because anything could happen in that year. He could meet someone else. He could change his mind. Or the unthinkable could happen: he might not make it home from the war.

I remembered breathing through the pain in my chest, wishing I could say that love would conquer all, that our love was too strong to break. But life didn't work that way, and believing in that particular fairy tale wasn't something I could ever be so innocent as to pin my hopes and dreams on.

When a quiet thump sounded from outside my window, I sat up in bed, smiling, my worry forgotten.

Wade.

My heart filled up at even the thought of his name, blooming, spreading warmth through my ribs. And he opened the window, perched on the fire escape platform. His face was in shadows, but I could see he was smiling — the high curve of his cheeks gave him away.

I whispered his name, and he whispered mine as he climbed into bed with me, wrapping me in his arms, and I closed my eyes, breathing him in, wishing I could make the moment last. But the clocked ticked on, and instead I made a tally of everything I could. The feeling of being surrounded by him. The smell of his soap. The hardness of his chest under my palms. His soft lips against mine.

He laid us down and looked down at me.

"Hey," he said in a whisper.

"Hey," I said, smiling.

And then he kissed me again. He kissed me with a thousand promises on his lips, his fingers tracing my jaw, tilting my chin, telegraphing his love through his skin against mine.

When he pulled away, he watched me for a long while, and I memorized him some more. His dark hair, a little mussed. The line of his jaw. The curves of his lips.

"I love you, Elliot," he said softly, as he'd done a thousand times. "I've loved you from the second I first saw you. I might have loved you before I'd ever met you. I think … I think I'd been waiting on you, and I think if I hadn't met you, I'd have just gone on waiting."

My chin trembled, his departure too soon, too close. There wasn't a way to make time stop, so all I could do was love him as much as I could in the time I had. My hand cupped his jaw, and emotion climbed through my chest as I tried to speak.

"I love you, too. More than anything."

He turned his head to press a kiss into my palm before pulling me up to sit face to face with him. I'd never forget that moment — half of his face in moonlight, the other in dark, save his eyes that shone, looking into mine with depth I'd never be able to put into words, as much as I'd tried.

His eyes turned down as he reached into his pocket, and when he opened his hand, what sat in his palm stopped my heart.

He opened the black velvet box, and inside sat a ring, a beautiful ring with a large square diamond in the center and smaller diamonds framing it, the band simple and delicate and absolutely the most brilliant thing I'd seen in my life.

I couldn't breathe as he watched me hopefully.

"I know we said we'd wait. I know we're young, and I know things won't be easy. But I can't leave without you. I can't *be* without you. The thought of leaving you here … the thought of spending the next year without you is too much. I don't want to live without you, not for a second longer than I have to. Marry me, Elliot."

"Wade," I breathed. "Of course I'll marry you. But—"

His lips were on mine, his arms around my waist as mine circled his neck blissfully, all the 'buts' flying away on flickering wings.

I laughed softly as he pulled away, and he laughed into my neck, peppering it with kisses.

"I'm only seventeen, Wade."

"Just until September, and then you're legal." I could feel him smirking against my skin.

"What about high school? I can't exactly leave right this minute."

He leaned back so he could look down at me with a smile on his face. "I'll go to boot camp, get stationed, and I'll come back just after your birthday. That's when we'll do it."

My hands rested on his shoulders as I watched him. "What about our families?"

He shrugged, and my arms rose and fell. "What about them? We can take care of ourselves. I'll have a job with a salary, hopefully base housing, insurance, the works. And I know Dad will help however he can. As for your family — who cares? Because they'll never be there for you, not like we want them to be. Not like I can be there for you. And as for high school, you can finish your classes online. Easy."

I laughed and kissed him. "Easy to *say*."

He tightened his hold on me. "We can run away. Elope. Have a huge party. Get married in a church. Get married by an Elvis impersonator. I don't care how. I just want you to be mine, forever. I want you where I am. It's that simple."

I took a breath and let it out. "And when you're deployed?"

"Come back and stay with Dad and Sophie. Stay wherever I'm stationed. Whatever you want."

"You make it sound so simple."

He pulled me even closer, bringing my body flush with his. "I love you. You love me. Everything else is details." He angled for my lips, kissing me between hushed sentences. "Wherever I go, you go. Forever. Because I'll love you forever, Elliot."

My heart burned, lit up like a beacon for him, and he lay me down, held me, whispered his promises through the night, that one perfect night where everything in the world was right.

It was the last night we ever got.

The next morning, the sky had lightened only by a shade when he left me with a kiss and a promise, and I lay in bed for hours, smiling, dreaming of everything to come.

It was what I wanted. He was what I wanted, and even though I was afraid of what we would face, it was right. I would be with him, so everything would be just fine.

So naive.

I climbed out of bed when the sun had broken over the horizon, the glint of my engagement ring catching my eye with every motion of my left hand. My family was asleep, so I sat in the kitchen with my notebook, sipping coffee in the quiet morning, putting all of my emotion into words of love and hope, phrasing verses in an attempt to explain the inexplicable.

After a while, I turned my face to the sun, looking out the window, considering what would come next as I anxiously awaited my family's awakening, fashioning the speech in my mind. We'd agreed to meet at his house afterward to spend time with his family, maybe even trying to get both families together for dinner later. I smiled, imagining it all, elated to celebrate.

My father woke first, shuffling into the kitchen to pour himself coffee — I'd made enough for everyone, as I always did. I didn't look much like him, more like my mother, her dark features and big eyes present in all three of her daughters' faces. He was lighter in coloring, shrewd in the eyes, his lips set in judgment, even when he slept, which was unnatural. Happiness was not a trait that most of my family knew, ever since my mother died while bringing my younger sister Beth into the world.

My mother was the last happiness I'd known, until Wade.

Dad sat across from me with the newspaper, taking every

opportunity to give me his opinion on what he read. We rarely agreed, and I never said so because there was no discussion, only his opinion and everyone else's, and everyone else was wrong. But that morning I just smiled and listened, wondering if he would notice the sparkling diamond on my finger or the fact that I was floating above all of us.

He didn't. But I didn't mind.

Mary was next up, also unseeing. Then Beth, my younger sister and father's shadow and favorite pet. As we sat, none of them saw me. I was virtually invisible in my own home, the odd duck. Where my sisters were like my father, a little vapid and a lot opinionated, I was more like my mom: quiet, reserved, content. And it wasn't as if I didn't see them for who they were, it was just that I accepted them for who they were unconditionally. I knew there was no changing them, and they were happy with who they were. And I required no watering, no tender care. I found ways to feed my soul from a very young age, knowing I couldn't depend on them for that.

The practice made me feel whole, self-sufficient.

I closed my notebook, laying my hands in my lap, with a whisper of a smile on my face.

"I have something to tell you all."

Dad didn't look up, just shook his paper to straighten it. "Oh?"

My sisters didn't look up either — Beth took a bite of her bagel, and Mary got up to pour more coffee.

"Wade asked me to marry him."

Everything stopped.

Dad's paper dropped by an inch as he glared at me over the top. Mary turned, coffee pot in hand, looking shocked. Beth slowed her jaw, a wad of bread in her cheek like a dairy cow.

"What?" Dad asked, the word hard.

My smile slipped. "He … he asked me to marry him, and I said yes."

"You've got to be kidding me," Mary said, annoyed. "You're

seventeen, Elliot. You can't get married."

I watched as my hope for their support slipped away. "We would wait until after my birthday. This … this was always the plan, though we'd always planned on waiting until after I graduated. But he asked me to come with him sooner, and I said yes."

Dad's face was red as he huffed and blustered at me from across the table. "You said yes, as if you have any right to agree to such a preposterous thing. You can't do anything, not while you're still living under my roof."

"Dad—"

He slapped the table, making the coffee cups jump and us along with them. "This is ridiculous, Elliot. You're still in school."

"I'll finish school wherever we end up," I answered, undeterred.

He paused for a split second. "You can't marry your high school crush."

I drew a long breath through my nose. "You did."

He gave me a look. "I sure did, and instead of marrying *John* like I really wanted, I married your mother and was miserable until the day she died."

I jerked away from the shock of his words, not that it was the first time he'd said something so horrible. It's just that it never ceased to hurt me. "Marrying her was *your* choice, a choice you made for what, for money? She's the reason you have all of this." I motioned to the home around us, the food on the table. "But I suppose I should say I'm happy to hear that her dying released you from your prison. Is that what you'd like to hear?"

He rolled his eyes, his face still red and eyes still hard. "Don't be dramatic, Elliot. Of course it's not her fault that I'm gay, or that I asked her to marry me. I loved her in my way," he said, conveniently ignoring the rest of what I'd said. "I'm just saying that you and Wade staying together is unrealistic. You're too young to know what's real and what isn't. He's leaving tomorrow, and what — you're just supposed to wait for him? Move far away, be all alone when he's deployed? When they throw him on the front lines in Iraq? Why would you want to be a widow at twenty?"

I breathed again. "It's my decision to make, and I choose him."

His brow dropped, eyes leveling me. "It's *not* your decision to make, Elliot Marie Kelly. I won't allow it."

My cheeks burned with anger, but my voice was even, containing a calm I didn't feel. "And how will you stop me when I turn eighteen?"

Everything about him challenged me, his posture, his tone, all of him, and the air between us crackled with tension. "I refuse to support this. If this is what you choose, what you want? Well, then you can find yourself somewhere else to live. You can find someone else to feed and clothe you. Can he do that? Will he take you in? And is that what you want? To abandon us?" He touched his chest. "To sacrifice us for him? Because that's the choice you'll have to make. I just hope he doesn't turn you out, because we won't be here for you when it all falls apart."

Anger and sadness and confusion rolled through me, disappointment over how everything had gone hanging over me, pressing into my chest, suffocating me. Abandon them? They would abandon me. But how could I survive without them? They were everything I'd ever known, my last tie to my mother.

My sisters watched me through my mother's eyes, nodding their support like mob lackeys, and my father was the Godfather.

"Why are you doing this?" I breathed.

"Because you're not smart enough to make the decision yourself. I'm your father, and I know more about the world than you do. It's my job to protect you from that," he said piously.

I didn't even know what to say through the shock of the moment; his words stopped me dead. It's not that I believed what he said or subscribed to what he proposed — I didn't. But what he said hit me deep, not only because some of it struck a chord — being alone, lonely while he was deployed, praying he came home to me — but because I was afraid. I felt my age, like a silly little girl with dreams too big and feelings too grown up. If I left, I'd have no one other than Wade and his family. And if he died … would Rick and Sophie keep me?

The thought of choosing between my past and my future overwhelmed me. I didn't know how to make that decision.

But Wade … Wade would understand. He loved me — he'd never force me to choose. I believed with all my heart that he would wait, that we could go back to the old plan. The alternative was too much to even fathom. I just had to talk to him, and we could sort it all out.

But I was wrong. So, so wrong. And that mistake had haunted me ever since.

RAZED

Burned down
And singed,
Razed to ash
And blown to the wind.

—M. WHITE

WADE

The living room walls closed in on me as I sat with my sisters in my arms, wishing I were strong enough to save them. They clung to each other and cried as I held them together as best I could. Sadie's face was in my mind, the words echoing as I spoke them … it was a moment I'd never forget, as much as I wanted to.

As their emotions poured out of them, I found that I was numb, razed from all that had happened. A few hours, a few words, and everything had changed. I could hear the clock ticking, the sound taking on a new meaning as I imagined what would come, as I realized how little time I had left.

Time, time, time.

The word pulsed around me, a chant that ticked up my heartbeat with every second that passed. I didn't know how we would survive this, didn't know how we'd ever get through the next few weeks with him or the rest of our lives without him.

It was a long time before the shuddering stopped and their breaths evened, tears ceasing for the moment.

Sadie looked up at me, her gray eyes shining like I had all the answers. She had no idea that I didn't have a single one.

I cupped her cheek and wiped a tear away with my thumb. "Do

you want to see him tonight?" I asked gently.

She nodded, chin quivering.

"Visiting hours end soon, so we should go."

"O-okay," she said, and I stood, helping my sisters up.

"I just … I need a minute, okay?" Sadie blinked, eyes darting between us. She was so young in that moment, and I saw her as a little girl again instead of seventeen, needing my comfort after a skinned knee. If only this were so simple. If only.

Sophie smoothed Sadie's dark hair. "Whatever you need. Just let us know when you're ready."

Sadie nodded and left the room, and Sophie turned to me, shaking her head.

"How did this happen, Wade? How did we get here?" The words were agony.

"I don't know, but I feel like I've stepped into hell." I took a deep breath and let it out slow, but the pressure remained in my chest, heavy and aching. "I'm gonna go put my stuff in my room before we leave."

"Okay. Maybe I'll make some coffee."

"Good idea." I grabbed my duffle bag and headed upstairs. At the mention of coffee, exhaustion washed over me — I'd been awake close to twenty-four hours at that point, and adrenaline had carried me through it. But now, nearing the end of what had been the longest day of my life — and I had endured some very, very long days — I didn't know how much more I could take.

My boots might have weighed a hundred pounds each as I climbed the stairs, turning down the hall and into my room.

Nothing had changed except me.

I dropped my green canvas bag into the closet, leaving it there to deal with later, parking it under my old letter jacket and other clothes that had been mostly forgotten. And I sat on the edge of the bed, looking around the room.

Everything reminded me of her.

There were so many reasons why I'd avoided coming home over the years, and this room was one of them. When I left, I left part of me here, part of me I'd never quite found again. War changes you that way.

I left here without Elliot, and that alone hardened my heart. But nothing could prepare me for war. The things I'd seen, the things I'd done … when you're over there, you can't think about life back home. You can't think that everything is going on as it always did, that your friends are out working desk jobs or going to school, hitting happy hour at bars, living a normal life.

Life inside of war is no life at all. It shrinks your world down to a thirty-mile radius, and everyone in that radius is living the same hell. There's a comfort in that. But there's also fear, fear that you'll never live that normal life again.

My family was my only connection to that normal life, and even that at times had been thin.

I'd poured myself into the Army, volunteering for tour after tour because it was easier than facing the life I'd left behind. I knew my Army life. I knew how to exist there. I didn't know how to be a civilian anymore.

So, I didn't come home much. But my family and I were close despite the fact. We spoke daily in the form of text, calls, emails, video chats. They'd visited me too, everywhere but Iraq and Afghanistan, and I think they understood why, though no one mentioned it. Especially not me.

But here, in this room, I was eighteen again. I was in love with a girl, with *the* girl, the one who I'd have moved heaven and earth for. And as I looked around, that past seemed so far away, like a story of a person I used to know.

Her pictures were on my cork board over my desk. Her poems were in my nightstand. That was the window she used to climb in when she was supposed to be in her bed at home. A sweater she'd gotten me for Christmas years ago was in the drawer still, I knew, and the box in the top of the closet held boutonnieres and notes we'd left in each other's lockers.

She was everywhere.

But then I considered my life for the last seven years. Considered what I'd seen. Flashes of memories flickered through my mind — an IED hitting the truck in front of us, my men, my friends wounded. My friends dead. Gunfire and the smell of mortars. The stars at midnight outside of Kardashar. The heat of the desert. The sickness of war, which hadn't changed since the beginning of man.

I twisted the black bracelet on my wrist, the reminder of those I'd lost. As if I could ever forget.

I'd convinced myself it had been easier without her. She'd been spared the pain, the fear she would have endured as I endured war. It was a mercy she'd ended it. I'd had no idea when I left here what the truth of my situation would be, but still, selfishly, I wanted her. I wished she'd chosen me. I wished that when the war and the world broke me, that she was there to hold me, to remind me there was still good in the universe.

Truth was, I didn't know if there *was* good in the universe. And losing Elliot was just another point of proof.

The memory of the last time I saw her crashed into me, and I closed my eyes against the force.

As much of a snap decision it had been to propose, I knew with every atom in my body that it was right, that it was time. Our plan had been on paper since weeks after I'd met her, but as I packed my duffle bag for boot camp, that two-dimensional plan rose off the page, every detail in high relief.

I was leaving, and I didn't know if I'd come back.

My sisters had been crying almost every day over my departure, and Dad, though I knew he supported me, couldn't hide his anxiety.

He tried, but I felt it in every word, behind every hug, in every moment. Sadie was the same age I'd been when I lost Mom, and I felt her pain, her fear, just as fresh as if it were my own.

I felt like it was a betrayal, an abandonment. And that left me utterly alone.

I was leaving everyone I loved.

But I didn't have to leave Elliot. I could take her with me in a small way. I would have her always, if she would marry me.

The plan had been to wait to marry until she'd graduated, when I came back from my first tour overseas, to Iraq, if I had to guess. I'd wondered, as my hands stilled over my bag, if I would make it back.

It wasn't the first time I'd considered it, but it was the first time I *felt* it. I imagined it, imagined them sending my body home, imagined Elliot standing over my grave, wondering what would have been, what could have been.

Something in me snapped.

If something happened to me, she would be the last to know. She would receive nothing, would have no means to take care of her. If something happened to me (I pictured it, saw the image of my broken body, the blood, the sand blowing over me), if it happened before I came back, I would never have had her at all, never called her my wife. Never placed the ring on her finger and told her I'd love her until my last breath. And that was the one thing, the only thing I wanted before I died.

I knew where Dad kept Gran's ring, and I swiped it in the dark, hurried to her house, climbed in her window, and I changed the rules. For us. For me.

And she said yes. She eased my mind, eased my fears. She said yes, and that made me the happiest man in the entire world.

The next day as I waited for her to come over so we could tell my family, the foyer seemed smaller than it usually was as I paced from end to end. My thoughts flew around my head — she was on her way. We were getting married. *Married.* She'd given me everything I wished for when she uttered that single word: *Yes.*

A knock sounded on the door, and I rushed to open it, knowing it was her, smiling the smile of a man whose dreams have come true. But the look on her face nearly brought me to my knees.

"What happened?" I asked, reaching for her.

Her chin quivered, face bending as she curled into my chest, crying. I held her against me with my hand cupping the back of her head, her silky dark hair between my fingers. We stood like that for a long moment, my heart sinking lower and lower until I was anchored to the spot.

When she pulled away, she swiped at her tears, avoiding my eyes. "I … I'm sorry."

"For what?" I asked, terrified, my voice quiet and still.

She shook her head. "I told my dad."

"What did he do?" I growled.

She blew out a breath and looked away, staving off more tears. "He said we're too young. That we don't know what we're doing. That he wants to protect me, so …" She met my eyes. "He told me I have to choose."

First was shock, zapping up my spine like I'd been electrocuted. Then anger, hot and slow in my chest, but not at her. For her.

"How could he do that? Why would he do that?" I asked, spitting the words, pulling her back into me, hanging on to her as if I could absorb the pain, or at the very least share it with her.

"Because he's my dad. He wants what's best for me."

I would have laughed if I hadn't been so angry. "No, Elliot. He doesn't."

"Of course he does."

I let it go, not wanting to argue with her, not now. "What did he threaten you with?"

"Everything," she said quietly. "He'll kick me out, disinherit me."

"As if he has something left to give you other than debt."

"That's not the point." She pulled away, eyes full of hurt. "They're my family. I'm just seventeen … where will I go? What will I do?"

"You'll be with me. I'll take care of you." I willed her to understand. "I'll always take care of you."

Her dark eyes searched mine. "What if we went back to the old plan? What if … what if we just have a long engagement? I'll finish high school, and then I'll be free."

Betrayal was all I felt, slipping over me like a storm. "I can't believe you're actually considering this. After last night, after everything …"

She touched my arm, her skin burning mine. "I love you, Wade. I want to marry you, but why can't we wait just for a year like we'd planned?"

I swallowed my fears, not able to speak the truth, not able to admit why I couldn't wait. I didn't want to scare her, didn't want her to know I was afraid too. "This isn't about them. This is about you and me. They don't care about you. They don't want your happiness, don't you see that?" I took her hands and looked into her eyes. "Don't let them dictate your life. Don't give them that power."

"Please," she said, her voice shaking. "Please don't make me choose, Wade."

My will hardened, digging in its heels. "I don't want to leave, go to war, *live,*" (*Die*) "without you. I can't. While I exist in this universe, I want you tied to me in a way that's unbreakable. Undeniable. And I know what you want — you told me last night. I know you want me, want *this*, just as much as I do. So just make the choice. It's easy."

"You keep saying that, but it's not." Her voice quivered, her eyes flashing with the hurt and betrayal I felt. "Nothing is easy. Nothing is simple. I'm seventeen, and you're asking me to commit to walking away from my family for my whole life without considering what it will mean for me."

"I'm asking for you to commit to *me*. I'm not asking for you to give anything other than *yourself* to *me*."

"There are consequences, consequences that will last my entire life. I'm just asking for time, that's all," she begged.

"I don't have time to give you." I fumed frantically, watching her, willing her to change her mind.

She shook her head, pulling her hands back, taking my heart with her. "I can't believe you're doing this. I expected it from them, but not from you. What I'm asking isn't unreasonable. I'm not saying no, Wade. I'm saying *yes*. I'm telling you I want you, but you're telling me that it's now or never. It's not fair. None of this is fair," she said, voice raising, trembling. In the moment, I couldn't see how right she was.

"You want to honor *them* over *us*." I watched her slip away, and there was nothing I could do to stop it. The finality of the situation dawned on me, our future, our dreams fading in the light. "They've done nothing for you but tear you down, and you're not willing to walk away from them. You're not willing to come with me. You're choosing them."

"And you'd rather lose me forever than give me more time?"

I took a breath and squared my shoulders. "I'm asking you to take a leap. To trust me."

"I do trust you, but you're asking too much. Too much," she whispered, eyes shining, heart broken.

"You would choose them over me when all they've done is hurt you. When all I've ever done is love you. And if you really loved me, you'd come with me." I watched her, resigned, defeated. "I don't know what else to say."

Her tears fell in sparkling trails down her cheeks, and I watched, my soul folding in on itself as she reached for her left hand, ring finger, and she twisted, twisting the knife in my heart along with it. The ring slipped off her long finger and she pressed it into my palm.

"Then I guess we say goodbye."

And I was so broken, so hurt, that all I could do was turn around and walk inside, closing the door to my heart behind me.

I'd never opened it again.

I left the next day with everyone sending me off but the one person I needed more than anything, and my anger, my hurt overwhelmed me. At the time, I felt like she'd abandoned me, that she'd broken the promise she'd made. That she'd left me the second she put that ring in my hand. I just didn't realize it was me who had forced her to take it off, not until much later. Not until it was too late.

Boot camp was a blur, and the second it was over, I was whisked away to my new station, my new life. And after a few weeks of training, I was on a plane headed for Iraq.

I had no idea what waited for me there.

In the back of my mind, I think I believed that when I finished my first tour, I'd go home and we'd find a way back to each other. A little bit of time was what we needed.

Stupid and young, that was what I was, so angry and betrayed at first that I couldn't see past the feeling. But when I did, I found regret.

I'd been wrong, so wrong, and I hated myself for giving her an ultimatum, for pushing her away. I'd lost her because of my fear. I could have had it all, if I'd only been more brave. If I'd only given her what she'd asked for.

A few weeks into my tour, I found myself in a convoy headed out for supplies with my buddy Perez sitting next to me, smiling and joking as he always did, making light — a useful skill where we found ourselves, when nothing was light or easy. We'd been together since day one of boot camp, not only stationed together but deployed together.

I thought we hit a hole at first — the truck bounced once, and time slowed as gravity shifted. Everything floated for a stretched-out second as the truck flipped, and when we crashed to the ground, there was only nothing, only the deep blackness of unconsciousness sweeping over me.

I came to a few minutes later with my ears ringing, the sound of my name far away, the scent of gasoline and smoke in my nose. And as I got my bearings, I found Perez lying across from me, staring at me. He looked strange, his eyes distant and glassy. Then I noticed the blood that seeped from his head in almost black threads as they wound through his hair and across his forehead.

It was only then that I realized he was dead.

I tried to call his name as they pulled me backward, into the blinding light. *Fire*, someone yelled — the truck was going to blow — and they dragged me away only a heartbeat before it exploded. Heat passed through us in an unbearable wave, knocking everyone down.

We'd survived. But as I lay in the dirt and sand, I had a singular realization.

I was right to be afraid.

I had nothing to offer Elliot. I had nothing to give her other than pain. If I died here, would she ever recover? Would she ever move on? I regretted so much. I'd hurt her so much. But this was one thing I could spare her.

It was then, in the heat of the desert, that I made the decision not to speak to her again.

At the end of every tour they would ask us who wanted to stay. I volunteered every time.

By the time the war was over, it was too late. It didn't matter that I wished I hadn't gone silent. Because by the time I realized my mistake, it was too big, the distance too far, the wrongs I'd done too deep and wide to breech.

My regret was infinite. And that regret had made me lonely. Angry. It had changed me, twisted me into the man I was now. And now … now it was impossible to see a way back.

I told her now or never, and that mistake would haunt me until the day I died.

THIN
SOUL

Thin soul,
Stretched and pulled
Left to bear the weight
Of the world
On its own.

—M. WHITE

ELLIOT

Sammy spun around in circles next to me, singing a song entirely composed from the word *truck,* as I slipped Maven's foot into her boot. The morning hadn't been any more hectic than usual, though I felt heavy, weighted. I hadn't slept well, spending so much of the night awake, thinking. There seemed to be so much to think about, and when I got up, I didn't find myself any closer to peace than I had when I lay down.

Instead, I took comfort in the routine of getting the kids ready for school. I'd spend most of my day at work, around books. For two years since I'd graduated, I'd been content not to decide what I wanted to do with my degree, to devote myself to the kids and writing, though I'd recently gotten a job at a book bar that opened near Columbia.

Wasted Words was its name, touting half romance, half comics, and a full bar. I'd convinced the owner, Rose, to add a small poetry section to the library, as well as adding some special edition Jane Austen hardbacks to the mix. Mostly, I kept to myself there, the big store full of big personalities. Being around the books all day, with no one to answer to, no one to be responsible for but myself — that was my happy place.

With everyone ready to go, I carted the kids downstairs and into the entryway where their backpacks hung. Charlie stepped into the foyer, looking a little sheepish.

He was tall and slender, with blond hair and an elegant nose that turned itself up to the world far less than Mary's.

He folded his arms across his chest and leaned on the banister. "Elliot, I wanted to talk to you before you leave."

Maven's hand blindly waved behind her for the backpack strap, and I chased the flailing limb with the loop. "Sure. What's up?"

"Mary told me about your talk last night. I'm really sorry she called you to come home. One hour alone, and she caved." He shook his head.

"Oh, it's all right." I smoothed Maven's hair and moved on to Sammy, who was turning around in a circle looking for his second strap. I touched his shoulders to stop him and slipped the other strap on.

"No, it's not. Listen, I know she told you to pay for the extra daycare, but it's not necessary. We'll take care of it."

I smiled gratefully. "Thank you."

He waved a hand and bent down to pick up Maven as she ran over to him. "Don't thank me. They're our kids, for God's sake. Also, I wanted you to know that we're here to help as much as possible, so if you need to be somewhere in the afternoon, just let me know. Mary or I will pick the kids up and hold down the fort."

I watched Maven squish his face around, and she giggled when he crossed his eyes and stuck out his tongue.

"Are you sure? Mary didn't seem—"

His face hardened. "Don't worry about Mary. If she gives you trouble, just let me know."

"Thank you, Charlie. Really."

"You're welcome, Elliot," he said as he set Maven down. "I'm working from home today, so I'll get the kids from school."

I nodded and took the kids by the hand. "All right. Just let me know if you need me back and I'll be here."

"We'll manage. Have a great day, you three."

The kids waved, and I offered another smile of thanks before we headed out into the chilly winter morning. The school was only a few blocks away, on the way to the bookstore, and we made our way, jumping over cracks and waving at dogs as they walked by. I felt a little lighter, largely in part to Charlie, who had given me a solution, an out. I'd felt very much alone for a moment, and to know at least someone was there to back me up made a difference. Usually it would be Sophie, but now she needed me far more than I needed her.

A little while later, I walked into the bookshop, surrounded by that magical combination of scents that made my heart flutter — books and coffee. I waved at Cam behind the bar, my tiny, spunky little boss who never failed to make me smile. She trotted around from the back of the bar, smiling as she approached.

"Hey, Elliot."

"Hey," I answered.

"I just wanted to check on you after the other day. Is your friend's dad okay? He had a stroke, right?"

The clamp around my heart squeezed until I couldn't breathe. "He … no. He's not okay. They found out it was cancer."

Cam's hands flew to her lips, and we slowed to a stop just outside the office. "Oh, my God. I'm so sorry."

"Thank you," was all I could say.

"Well, what do you want to do?"

My brow quirked. "Pardon?"

"About work. Are you okay to work? Do you need some time off?"

I blinked, surprised. "I don't know. I hadn't thought about it."

She eyed me. "You were just going to come in and work every shift without asking for any time off?"

"Well … yes. It's my responsibility to be here. And I love being here."

"I get that, I just know he's important to you. He's the poetry professor, right?"

I nodded, not trusting my voice.

"Elliot, I'm serious. If you need time, we can cover for you. Three days a week is nothing."

I swallowed and reached for her arm. "Thank you, Cam." I paused, considering her offer. "I need this place. It's my escape from all the rest of it."

She smiled sadly and placed her hand over mine. "It's mine too."

"But Sophie's going to need a lot of help, and we … we don't have very much time left with him. So maybe, if it's all right, it wouldn't be a bad idea to cut back to just a day or maybe two rather than three?"

Cam nodded once, standing up a little straighter, seeming relieved to have contributed. "That'll be just fine — let's do one day, and you can pick up if you need to get away. Any preference on days?"

"No, whenever you need me most is fine."

"Deal. And if you need to take off, just let me know."

I smiled. "Deal."

We parted ways, and I headed into the back to put my stuff in my locker, then clocked in, picked up a box of books at the register, and began walking around the store to put them away. It was a quiet morning, as mornings there usually were — afternoons and evenings were the busy times. I'd heard, at least, since I was always at home with the kids. Cam threw themed singles nights to try to mix up the comic book boys and romance girls, and they were a smash. She'd been trying to get me to come to them since she'd hired me, her requests bordering on relentless. It made me smile — I thought she might actually die of happiness if I found a boyfriend at one of her events.

Thing was, I didn't really want one. I should take that back — I wanted to eventually settle down, get married, have kids of my own. But for the time being, I was too busy and unsure of what I wanted out of life to commit to anyone, not that anyone had caught my eye.

I slipped *Jane Eyre* back in with her sisters and checked the next book, heading to its shelf, thinking about Wade.

It would be a lie to deny that he had something to do with my loneliness. With me. With everything.

But it wasn't that I hadn't been asked out by other guys— I had, even recently, perils of working in a bar, even if it was a bookstore too. But secretly I compared everyone to him, and no one could measure up. The way they made me feel, the things they'd say, it was just never right, never even close to what I'd had. Every date I'd been on ended up being all wrong. Or maybe I was all wrong.

I'd thought so much about why I couldn't move on, what it was about him that I couldn't forget. I didn't know that I believed in soulmates, but I believed in compatibility and chemistry. I believed in the feeling of being so tied to another person that you didn't want to be without them. I believed in love that doesn't die, mostly because I'd lived in that hell for seven years, regretting all the reasons we were apart, wishing for forgiveness, wishing I'd made different choices, used different words, just ... wishing I'd done it all differently.

But wishing and hoping had given me nothing, only prolonged my loss.

And now, he was back. He was home. And he didn't want to see me, didn't want me there. It was clear in every muscle in his body, every molecule in the air between us — it only telegraphed anger and betrayal, even after all this time.

I placed JoJo Moyes where she belonged and walked around the corner for the Diana Gabaldon book in my hand. Outwardly, I was sure I looked perfectly fine, but inside, I was on fire, consumed by my losses. It was my version of a magic trick: it was easier to keep the truth to myself, because what could anyone else do? I carried the weight of my choices around with me always, and no one knew. No one needed to suffer along with me.

As I put away the rest of the books, I thought ahead to the afternoon when I'd see Wade again.

Sophie had asked me to come over to prepare the house for Rick's homecoming, and I would be there despite my fears, despite the warning that rang in my heart. I was torn between the want to be there for her and the knowledge that I wasn't wanted by him, opting in the end for Sophie, for Rick, for myself. I only hoped we would find a way to look past ourselves. But it was all up to him. It had always been up to him.

WADE

It was too quiet.

My sisters and I sat in Dad's library, rearranging the room for the hospital bed and equipment hospice had dropped off a few hours before. The only sounds in the room were the shuffling of books, the smoothing of sheets, the crackle and pop of the fire, and the occasional sniffle to betray what we were all thinking but couldn't say aloud.

This was the room where my father would die.

We'd spent the morning at the hospital with Dad and had sorted out the final details with hospice, then had come home to get everything ready for him. I'd moved out his heavy, mahogany desk — a relic passed down through generations along with the house, which had been in my family since it had been built — and we'd managed to create a space for the bed next to the window, leaving two armchairs and a couch, in case one of us needed or wanted to sleep in there. That was phase one.

Phase two was to fill the room with his most precious worldly possessions.

First and foremost were his books, which lined three of the walls. Thousands of books, some of which had lived in that room for nearly a hundred years, some Dad had acquired through his years of teaching literature, some that we'd given him as gifts. But those books fed his mind and soul through his entire life, and he'd be with them in the very end, even if he couldn't read them anymore. We'd read them for him.

Everything else was secondary, and my sisters were already planning what they'd bring down for him. We moved through our actions like ghosts, our thoughts turned inward, and we guarded them like we would a wound. None of us knew how to share our grief.

The doorbell rang, and the girls looked to me. They'd be looking to me for everything now.

"I'll get it." I turned to leave, my footsteps echoing in the too-quiet entry.

I pulled open the door to find Elliot, and my world shrank even more, consisting only of the two of us for seconds or minutes, I couldn't be sure. Her hands were deep in the pockets of her navy peacoat, a yellow knit hat on her head, and eyes so big, so full of sadness that I pushed away the urge to reach for her, wrap my arms around her small frame, hold her until we both felt right again.

I cleared my throat and stepped out of the way to let her in, saying nothing with words, only with my straight back, dropped brow, narrowed eyes, using my body as a weapon against her.

I had to keep her away.

I had to keep my heart away from her, because when she was near, when it came to life, the sensation was too much, too painful.

But how I wished it wasn't so.

If only.

She lowered her gaze and stepped in, walked past me without addressing me either, but she seemed smaller than before, as if she wanted to disappear, fade away. I wished for the same; she spun me around too quickly, and I couldn't find my footing.

Elliot set her bag down just inside the door and Sophie hurried over to her. They embraced, my sister's face tight as she hooked it over Elliot's shoulder.

"I'm so glad you're here," Sophie said, voice trembling.

"Of course I'm here. I'll always be here for you."

Sophie pulled away and swiped at her cheek. Sadie was waiting just behind her, twisting her hands, lip between her teeth, and Elliot moved to her, pulling her into a hug, rocking her almost imperceptibly. But I saw it. I saw everything Elliot did for what it was — kindness. She never acted under pretense or expectation.

It was one of the many reasons why I'd loved her.

Elliot let her go, but slipped her hand down Sadie's arm to hold her hand. "The room is coming along. What can I help with?"

Sophie glanced over the room. "I was just going to go upstairs to gather up some of his things to bring down."

"Great, I'll come with you." She unbuttoned her coat, her eyes finding mine for a fraction of a second before she followed my sisters. That tiny sliver of time could have been a year for what it did to me.

"I need some air," I grumbled, my heart drumming in my ribs as I blew past the girls, down the stairs, and to the backyard.

Yard was a generous word to use — it was a twenty-by-twelve patch of concrete and brick with an outdoor couch and two chairs, lined with bushes and flowers. But in Manhattan, it might as well have been an acre.

I couldn't sit, not with a hundred thoughts of Elliot zinging through my head. So, I paced. Confusion, that was the primary emotion. Having her there, seeing her, remembering her … it stirred everything in me that I worked so hard to keep down. Regret. Love. Longing. And now of all times when I had no reserve energy? When

I needed everything I had in me to keep my mask in place so that I could bear the days to come?

I felt exposed, thin, too small to contain all of the things I felt, too weak to fix a single thing.

But I had to find a way. I had to, not only for Sophie, who I'd promised, but for my father. He needed her here as much as he needed the rest of us. She was one of us, part of us. Part of me.

That was the part I couldn't process. That after all this time, after all the lies I'd told myself, she was a part of me. It was as fresh now as it was the day we said goodbye, and I hated myself for my weakness.

Elliot was a shock to my nervous system, a bucket of ice water down my back, and the clarity it brought stung all the way to my bones.

I'd read an article once about a theory that when adults returned home, the family slipped back into their old dynamic. I'd found it to be true — Sophie would call me a know-it-all and I'd call her immature. Sadie would turn into a fawn, deferring to me for everything, telling me about her life with the same enthusiasm she had when she was five. And being around Elliot took me back to the years I loved her.

But I didn't want to love her anymore. I didn't want to hurt anymore.

My phone rang in my pocket, and I pulled it out, answering without looking.

"Hello?" I snapped.

"Hey, man."

"Ben," I said, relieved to hear his voice, sighing as I raked a hand through my hair. "Sorry, didn't know it was you." I paced the length of the yard.

"Well, I'd hate to be whoever you thought I was."

I chuckled at that, just a puff of a sound.

"How are you holding up?"

The truth was that there wasn't enough time and there weren't enough words in the English language. "As well as I can. What time is it there?"

"Eleven."

"Late."

"Nah, not too bad. Hadn't heard from you today. Figured I'd check up on you."

"Thoughtful," I said, almost smiling.

"Well, I'm nothing if not thoughtful. And kind. And well-mannered."

That elicited a snort out of me.

"What? I'm well-mannered."

He'd done it. I smiled. "You eat like a hog."

"Only when it's MREs. You can't take too long to eat them or you'll start thinking about what you're putting in your body and gag."

"Aw, come on. Cheese tortellini isn't so bad."

"It is when it's got sand in it. And everything in Afghanistan has sand in it."

I chuckled. "Well, at least we're in Germany now. Nothing but beer and brats as far as the eye can see."

"I'll take it." He paused for a moment. "How's he doing?"

A lump formed in my throat, and I swallowed it. "He's okay. We're getting the house ready for him … he'll be home in the morning."

"And your sisters?"

"They're …" I sighed, feeling tired. "We're a mess, Ben. All of us. And the only thing we can do is take every day from breath to breath."

He sighed too. "You know, I've got plenty of leave saved up, and I'm sure I can get Sanders to approve me, if you want me to come. I think I can be there in a couple of days. All you have to do is say the word."

I slowed my pace and sat down, dropping my head into my free palm. "There's no point in you suffering through all of this too. I can't give you any of my energy if you're here. I'm already on reserve as it is."

"Psh, I'm easy — all I need are three hots and a cot."

It might have been nice, having him there as a buffer, but I couldn't accept the offer no matter how much it could help. He didn't need this in his life. "I'll be all right. But thanks, Ben. I appreciate it."

"Anytime," he said, sounding a little disappointed. "If you change your mind, just let me know."

"I will."

"So how is it, being back in the States?"

I looked around at my childhood home, feeling nostalgic and out of place. "It's weird. It's always weird."

"Feels like another life." He paused for a second, and I wondered warily what he was about to say. "So, have you seen her?"

Even without hearing her name, she invaded my mind. And Ben knew. He knew all about her, knew about us, knew she was friends with Sophie and all about her relationship with my dad. He knew everything about me — we'd been together since my first tour in Afghanistan.

He was my best friend. My only friend.

"She's here right now," I answered.

He drew a breath and let it out. "How bad is it?"

I ran a hand over my face and stood to pace again. "Bad. I can't deal with her on top of …"

"Yeah."

"But she's going to be around. A lot. And I have no idea what to do about it."

"How's it gone so far?"

"I don't know, man," I said, frustrated. "I'm not prepared for this, not for any of it, and she's the last thing on my mind right now," I lied.

"Liar."

I rolled my eyes. "What do you want me to say, Ben? I don't want to see her, but she's here and she'll be here, and I've just got to deal with it however I can."

He sighed. "Fair enough."

The doorbell chimed, and I stood. "Goddammit," I mumbled. "I've gotta go. Somebody's at the door."

"All right. Just hit me up and let me know how things are going."

"I will," I said as I charged through the hallway, hanging up and shoving my phone back into my pocket. I pulled the door open with a whoosh that sent the blond ponytail of the woman on my stoop swaying.

Lou, my cousin by marriage, stood on the front porch holding a casserole. She was tall and blond with high cheekbones and wide, blue eyes, and I'd never been so unhappy to see someone smiling than I was right then.

"Wade!"

"Hey, Lou. Come on in," I said gruffly, and she obliged without protest.

"I'm so sorry," she said as I closed the door. "For everything."

I cleared my throat, not sure what to say. Luckily, she didn't wait on me.

"Jeannie wanted me to bring this casserole by so you had dinner tonight. She would have brought it by herself, but she's at work and didn't want you to make plans." She offered the covered dish to me, and I took it.

"She could have just called," I grumbled under my breath as I set it on the hall table. Sophie and Sadie appeared at the top of the stairs with Elliot behind them. There were too many people, too many things happening, too much chaos, and I felt strangled by it all.

"Lou!" Sophie called, hurrying down the stairs to hug her.

She wrapped her arms around my sister. "Sophie. I'm so sorry."

Sophie's breath hitched. "Thank you." She pulled away and glanced at the casserole. "Oh, this is so thoughtful. God, I hadn't even thought about what we'd do for dinner."

Lou's brow dropped. "Have you eaten?"

We all shook our heads.

"Well, let me get it started for you, then."

"You don't have to do that, Lou," I said, hating that she felt obligated, wishing she would go. Wishing everyone would just go.

She smiled over at me. "Oh, I don't mind. I love taking care of people."

Lou hadn't seen Elliot standing behind the girls — this wasn't uncommon, most people didn't see her unless they were looking right at her. I was unfortunately not one of those people.

"Oh, hello. We haven't met," Lou said, and I caught a hint of confusion, tinged with wariness.

"Elliot," I said, and her eyes darted to me at the sound of her name just as my heart stopped at the feel of it on my lips. "This is my cousin, Louisa."

Lou gave me a little look, smiling. "By marriage," she added, propping the dish on her hip to free her hand, which she extended. "Nice to meet you."

"Nice to meet you too," Elliot echoed meekly.

Lou smiled. "I'll just be a second. Wade, did you want to help me out?"

Elliot and I glanced at each other and away just as fast. "Sure," I answered, following her into the kitchen.

She headed straight for the oven and turned it on, setting the casserole dish on the counter as I wondered exactly what I could help with. So I leaned on the counter and watched her, feeling useless and uncomfortable.

"I really am so sorry, Wade."

I shifted and folded my arms. "Thanks."

Her eyes were full of pity. "I know I haven't always been part of the family, but Dad and I have always felt like it, thanks to Rick."

I nodded, not sure what I was supposed to say.

"Anyway," she continued, turning for the cabinets next to me. "We're here for you guys. Just let us know what we can do to help.

You've got my number, so call whenever. I mean it." She picked up a stack of plates and wobbled a little — I was at her side in a flash, steadying her. Her cheeks flushed as she looked up at me, smiling. "Gosh, thanks, Wade. I'm such a klutz."

"No problem."

I took the plates and turned, not wanting to give her the wrong idea. In part because she was looking at me like she'd wanted me to kiss her. The thought was another in a myriad of events and feelings that I couldn't find a way to process.

Aunt Jeannie had married her dad after I left, so I didn't know Lou all that well, but from the first time I'd met her, she'd had a thing for me. She was always flirting, and though she wasn't unpleasant at all — in fact, she was beautiful — I'd never even considered her. That didn't stop her from trying.

The oven beeped, and she practically bounced to the casserole, popped it into the oven, and set the timer for twenty minutes.

"This'll be ready in a jiffy," she said with a smile. "I can't leave until you're fed and taken care of. Come sit down, take a break. This can't be easy on you."

I took a breath and let it out, taking a seat, not comforted by her endeavor to 'take care' of me. But I didn't think she'd take no for an answer, and I found myself without the energy or means to argue. She was trying to help, and the alternative was trying to avoid Elliot. The kitchen suddenly seemed as good a place as any to do just that.

Lou smiled and popped open the fridge, returning with a beer that she expertly popped the top of before handing it over, looking pleased.

"So, tell me what's been up with you? My God, I feel like I haven't seen you in years, but it was just Christmas-before-last, right?"

I took a long pull of my beer and nodded. "I wasn't here very long."

"Right, just dinner on Christmas Eve and then Christmas morning?"

"Yeah. I had to get back, but at least I didn't miss Uncle Jerry's drunken Bing Crosby karaoke."

She laughed. "The best part was the dried eggnog on his crotch. He looked like he'd been partying at a strip club instead of a family holiday dinner."

I relaxed a little, laughing at the memory of old Jerry swaying, eyes glassy, with a microphone in his hand and a crusty white stain next to his zipper. She laughed too, leaning on the island on her forearms, which incidentally put a little slice of tasteful cleavage in my line of sight.

I kept my eyes on hers, hoping I didn't look encouraging.

"I wish you could have stayed longer," she continued. "My Granny Eugenia played the ukulele Christmas night, and we had a repeat Jerry performance, though less drunk and somehow more lewd."

I chuckled. "Had to get back."

"You don't get much time off, do you?"

I took another drink to give myself a second to cultivate my answer. I had plenty of time off, and I could have taken more, if I'd wanted. I just didn't. It was easier that way, to bury myself in work, in my other life, my easy life where I knew where to be, when to be there, and what to wear. I didn't have to decide. I could just *be*, and that life, that new life was what I'd devoted myself to for seven years. The old life seemed like a dream most days, a story about a man who didn't exist anymore.

I set the beer on the counter and twisted it in a circle. "Nah, you know how it is. Things are busy, and flying home, especially when I'm overseas, isn't always an option."

"That's too bad. We miss you when you're not here."

I took a drink, hoping she wouldn't wait for an answer. She didn't.

"So, how's Germany been?"

"Great. You know, lots of castles." I didn't want to talk to her, but she didn't seem to pick up on it, no matter how perfunctory I was. She just smiled and kept firing off questions like I was the most interesting man in the world. My stomach soured.

"Is it easy to get around Europe?" she asked.

"Most everything is just a train ride away."

"Where all have you been?"

I shrugged. "All over. Italy, Greece, Spain, Switzerland, Belgium, France." She lit up. "Paris?"

I smiled at her reaction. "It was one of the first places I went." The smile quickly faded. The trip had only reminded me of Elliot. It was one of the first places we'd wanted to go, hoping we could get stationed in Europe. The list of sights in the city she'd wanted to see had been recited night after night, lying in my arms.

I'd only visited Paris once and had run from the city like she was chasing me.

Lou sighed dreamily. "I've always wanted to go to Europe. Maybe I'll come visit you." The statement was heavy with intention, and I picked up my beer again.

"It's definitely worth seeing." I took a sip, hoping she'd leave it alone. And she did, in part because we both turned to the sound of the door closing hard.

ACQUIESCENCE

To bend,
Breath still,
Heart stretched,
Is strength
In weakness.

—M. WHITE

E L L I O T

hurried down the front steps, pulling on my coat, breath puffing visibly in the cold and fading light.

I was not brave.

There were so many reasons why, I thought as I rushed away with tears stinging my eyes.

It wasn't only because I didn't know how to behave around Wade. It wasn't because I couldn't speak or think or feel anything but his presence when he was near. It wasn't because Lou had shown up, beautiful and confident with a casserole and an agenda.

I was not brave because I ran away, and today wasn't the first time.

I'd been walking down the stairs with a box when I glanced into the kitchen to see Wade with his arms around Lou and a stack of dishes between them. She looked up at him like she was waiting for a kiss, and when I saw them, my heart stopped. I'd nearly dropped the box — my arms, my knees lost all strength. But I hung on and walked as quickly as I could into the office, noting when I passed the kitchen again that she was smiling at him, and that she'd made him smile. And when I heard him laugh, it was all I could take.

A week ago, I didn't believe I'd ever hear that sound again.

I don't know quite what came over me, but I had to get out of the house. If I'd stayed, they all would have known how I felt. They all would have seen my pain, pain I guarded so desperately. So I hurried up the stairs and into Rick's room to lie, telling Sophie and Sadie I'd gotten a text from Charlie and needed to go home, promising I'd be there the next morning when Rick came home. I heard the deep rumble of Wade's voice on my way out, the word *Paris* hanging in the air, speeding my feet as I rushed through the foyer and out the door.

I was silly and stupid, I told myself as I flew down the sidewalk toward home with burning cheeks and stinging eyes. I was selfish, I realized with anguish, boots pounding as I picked up the pace, even though I didn't want to go home. At home, I was watched, opinions were made. The only place I was free to feel whatever I felt was in my room at night, with the door to the world closed tight.

I was overreacting, I knew this. He wasn't mine and I wasn't his, and it had been this way for what felt like an eternity. But it didn't change the fact that I didn't want to be privy to his relationships, however innocent they may be. I thought again about how Lou had looked at him. I knew that look — I'd given him a version of it nearly every day for two years.

The air was thin and chilly, but I took a cleansing breath anyway, forcing myself to slow down. It was better to get back to the kids tonight, because when Rick came home, I'd need to be there for him, Sophie, and Sadie, whether I was uncomfortable or not.

You're ridiculous, Elliot.

Shame crept over me for behaving the way I did, without even saying goodbye to Wade and Lou. It was terribly rude, and as my emotions ebbed and reason took its place, I made plans to apologize to them both when I saw them again.

I checked my watch —I had plenty of time to visit Rick, and then it would be about time for dinner. I felt relief at the thought of keeping busy with the kids. And once I was alone, I'd write, try to sleep, and steel myself for the day tomorrow.

Those were all the places where I was safe. Where I knew my place and my job and my self. Where I could do what needed to be done and know without a shadow of a doubt that it was right.

At the hospital, Rick seemed lonely, afraid, but he hid it as best he could, smiling the drooping half-smile, his silvery stubble shining under the hospital lights as I unpacked more books for him, including the Emerson I'd promised. And then I read to him for a while, and he'd closed his eyes, lips smiling peacefully on that one side alone.

And then I was walking home that evening, on to my next task, leaving the notes of my day singing sadly behind me.

I'd become an expert at compartmentalizing my feelings. It was the only way I survived, by stacking up dusty boxes in my heart for every hurt, packing them away in the dark. But times like these blew the dust off the tops, opening them up to free the old pain so they could do more harm in new ways.

Some boxes weren't dusty — those were lined up neatly, opened and closed daily. There was one for Mary. One for my father. One for the kids. And the new ones — Rick, Sophie, and Sadie. Wade's had recently been unpacked and set in its place next to the others, and as I walked home, I stowed my feelings away in the dark where they belonged.

But all my careful planning proved useless when I walked in the door.

The house was louder than usual, the air charged with new energy. I paused just inside the door, listening, aware. And then I heard my father laugh from the living room.

I swallowed and closed the door, taking my time hanging up my coat and bag, trying to prepare myself. And then I took a deep breath and walked into the room to face them all.

Dad was in the middle of a story, hands gesticulating, his little Chihuahua Rodrigo trembling in his lap, his natural state. He looked the same as he always had, calculating and critical, a little bit older and a little more flamboyant. I hadn't seen him in several years; once he and Beth moved to Miami, they lived in their little bubble, because nothing could *possibly* exist outside of *Miami*. Out of sight, out of mind. It worked well for me too.

Beth sat next to him, just as much of his pet as Rodrigo was, listening like she'd never heard the story — though he'd clearly told it a thousand times — snacking on a bowl of cashews that she chewed without closing her lips. Charlie seemed more interested in his scotch than he did my dad, but Mary listened intently, laughing.

They all saw me, but no one stopped what they were doing, though Charlie nodded to me in greeting. No one wanted to interrupt Dad — we'd never hear the end of it. So, I sat on the floor where the kids were playing quietly, which was a miracle on its own.

"And then everyone turned to him and said *Watch where you put that banana!*"

Everyone laughed except for me and the kids, and Rodrigo barked at the burst of noise. Dad finally turned to me. "Ah, Elliot. Come here and give me a hug."

I stood and did as I was told. "Hi, Dad."

"You look well. You were too skinny last time I saw you. How are you?"

"Fine, thank you," I said, knowing full well he didn't want a real answer.

"Oh, Daddy," Mary said, touching his arm. "Rick Winters has brain cancer, can you believe it?"

He gasped, touching his chest. "You're kidding."

Mary shook her head and took a sip of wine. "Elliot's been over there for the last two days. He's coming home tomorrow, but they've only given him a couple of weeks to live."

I twined my hands behind me — they spoke about me like I wasn't there, and they spoke about Rick like he was gossip fodder, not out of sadness or respect. Tears threatened my composure, and I squeezed my fingers tighter as I moved to sit back down with the kids.

Charlie cleared his throat. "How did it go today, Elliot?"

"Oh," I breathed, turning to face him. He smiled kindly, and for that I was grateful. "They delivered his bed and some equipment, and I helped prepare the library for him."

Dad's brow was judging. "Why were you there? Surely you'd have been in the way during such a trying time for their family."

"Sophie asked me to be there." I didn't mention how important Rick was to me, a topic that Dad hated. Strangely, I think he was jealous, though he'd made no real attempts to be close to me. We didn't bond over gossiping like he did with my sisters — he thought I was boring.

"Well," Dad said, gesturing with his glass, "I hope it doesn't interfere with Mary and Charlie's schedules."

Mary opened her mouth to speak, but Charlie cut her off. "We'll be fine. The kids are in school a couple extra days a week, and we're taking care of them in the afternoon when Elliot's not here."

Dad made a face and took a sip of his drink.

"So," I started, needing to change the subject, "when did you get in?"

He lit up at that, always happy to talk about himself. "This afternoon. We had the most awful flight. Sat next to some horribly fat man who wouldn't stay in his seat. And the weather here — I don't know how you stand all this cold. Miami is beautiful this time of year … I haven't used a coat in years!"

I smiled amiably, a complacent expression I used as a curtain behind which I could hide my own feelings. "I'm so surprised to see you. Will you be staying long?"

He shrugged and took a drink. "We didn't want to put a time limit on it, so we bought one-way tickets."

Mary laid her hand on his leg and smiled. "You can stay as long as you want, Daddy."

He patted her hand. "Thank you, dear."

STACI HART

I didn't miss Charlie rolling his eyes as he tipped his drink back until it was gone. "I need another drink," he said as he stood. "Anyone else?"

They chimed their yays or nays, and he turned to me.

"Elliot?" His brows rose, tone implying that he figured I needed one.

"I'm fine, thanks, Charlie." He left, and I kept asking questions, wanting to keep the conversation off myself. "What brings you to New York?"

He frowned, feigning hurt. "What reason should I have other than to see my daughters and grandchildren?" He said daughters, but didn't look at me. His eyes were on Mary, filled with something akin to worship. Maven toddled around the room and up to Dad, speaking gibberish, and he took her hand, making a face when he touched her. "She's sticky."

Mary gave me a look. "Elliot, maybe you should give them a bath?"

"But they haven't eaten. They'll just get all sticky again."

"Well, then maybe you should feed them first."

I put on the smile again and stood, picking up Maven and calling Sammy, relieved to be leaving the room. "Sure. Come on, kids. How's grilled cheese sound?"

The kids cheered and Dad brought his drink to his lips. "Not very nutritious," he muttered.

I ignored him. "Be back in a bit."

They'd already turned back to each other, whispering and giggling about who even knew what. I didn't even want to know.

Charlie was in the blissfully quiet kitchen, drinks already poured and his glass to his lips, checking his phone. He smiled at me when I walked in, taking Maven from my arms.

"You run away too?" he asked me.

I chuckled. "The kids needed to eat. I'd rather be in here with them than out there."

"Me too. Clearly."

I situated the kids with crayons and paper and gathered supplies for dinner. Charlie leaned on the counter next to me.

"I'm sorry about them."

I shrugged and buttered the bread. "It's okay."

"It's not really. They're horrible."

"I can't argue that," I said with a soft laugh and a smile.

He paused for a beat, watching me. "Why do you put up with it?"

I thought about how to answer as I built the sandwiches. "Well, it's easier with Dad and Beth living in Miami. When we're all together, things are … harder."

"Right, I get that. Your father loves to criticize everyone who crosses his path, but show him a mirror and he'll gladly bash you over the head with it. But still, you know you don't *have* to just … acquiesce."

"I know that, Charlie. And I don't always, but when I do, it's a choice. It's conscious. Their badgering doesn't typically faze me."

He gave me a look. "Judging by what I saw a little bit ago, I'd say that's untrue."

"That's different." My voice had shrunk, just a little. "Today … today it's different." I placed one sandwich half on another. "Anyway, they're my family, so if it means I have to be present to endure some vapid conversation, I can make that sacrifice. And when it comes to Mary, well, you have both done so much for me."

"You do so much for us. It only seems fair."

"But I enjoy this, you know? The kids, I mean. And I'm not sure what I want to do with my life yet, so it's really the perfect place for me to be. Our relationship is symbiotic."

He chuffed and said into his glass, "Even with Mary breathing down your neck?"

I shrugged and set the first sandwich on the pan with a sizzle. "She doesn't mean it."

He gave me a look.

"Honestly, I don't think she even realizes she's doing it. You know Dad and Beth. Maybe it's genetic and I just got skipped."

"Luckily."

I smiled, feeling the same. "In any event, I don't usually take it personally."

His eyes squinted in thought. "So you excuse them because you believe they don't mean to be assholes?"

"Basically." I flipped the sandwich.

"And why not tell them how you feel? Argue?"

"Because fighting with them is futile. There's no convincing them of anything. Their worlds are so small, and that's all they know. I mean, when was the last time you were able to convince my dad of anything?"

Charlie snorted. "Point taken." He sighed, pushing off the counter. "Well, you're a better person than I could ever hope to be."

"Hey, I'm not the one married to one of them," I joked. "You, sir, have the patience of a saint."

"Or the IQ of a carrot," he said with a smile. "Jury's still out. I'd better get back in there with drinks or they might invade the kitchen, and I feel like you've paid your dues today. Let me know if you need any help with the kids, okay?"

"I've got the kids if you can keep my family away from me for the night."

"Deal."

Mary stormed in. "What the hell, Charlie? What's taking so long?" She narrowed her eyes at me, and I turned my attention to the sandwiches.

Charlie sighed, a defeated sound. "I was on my way. Just got an email that required my attention, that's all."

"Whatever." She swiped her wine from his hand and turned to leave.

He shrugged and followed her out.

What I hadn't mentioned to Charlie was that he was another

reason I didn't leave, besides the kids. He was my only ally in the house, and a thin one at that — he wasn't much more prepared to get his hands dirty than Mary was, though he at least offered.

They'd met years ago on an introduction by me. Charlie and I had a mutual friend who had not-so-stealthily nudged us together. I found him charming, tall and handsome, smart and funny, and the only surprise I felt when he'd asked me out was that I wasn't at all interested in entertaining the idea. He wasn't for me, the moment just another echo of Wade in my heart.

He was terribly gracious about the whole thing, and we remained friends. And when he'd met Mary, they'd started dating right away, then married not too long after.

It had never been strange between Charlie and me — we got along well, finding a little solace in each other given the family we now shared. And he'd always accepted and respected the boundaries between us. We were still friends, though it was mostly because we lived in the same house and were part of the same family.

Mary, on the other hand, had never been silent about her resentment. Charlie had never even held my hand, but she still seemed oddly jealous, though whatever feelings she harbored weren't enough for her to refuse my help. She found ways to dig at me all the same. I just chalked it up to her own feelings — it was less about me and more about her own insecurities. Talking to her about it had proved fruitless over the years. So we were where we were, and that was that.

"Wook, Ellie!"

I turned to see Sammy holding up his picture: oblong people with stick arms and giant, wide-set dots for eyes, and crazy hair that stuck up like they'd all been struck by lightning.

"Great job, buddy!"

"Can you put it on the fwidge?"

"Sure thing, you wanna do it?"

He lit up and slid off the chair, bounding to the fridge.

I plated their sandwiches and one for myself, sitting with them at the table while we ate and talked about colors and numbers, throwing in a song or two for good measure. Once we were finished, I cleaned up the kitchen and took the kids upstairs to bathe, taking my time, hoping it would be late enough that I could duck into my room. By the time I'd kissed the kids goodnight, I was exhausted. It had been a long day, and tomorrow would be even longer.

Everyone was still in the living room by the time I came back down, with the exception of Charlie, who had been able to sneak away, probably holing himself up in his office. My sisters and Dad sat on the couch together with rosy cheeks and smiles on their faces, laughing, probably at the expense of someone else.

Mary looked over. "Kids in bed?"

"They are. I just wanted to say goodnight. I've got to be up early."

She must have been feeling sentimental, because she smiled warmly. "Don't worry about the kids in the morning. I'll get them. You just go help with Rick."

Beth cooed. "You're so sweet to do that, Mary."

She waved her free hand, the motion sending the wine sloshing dangerously in its glass. "Oh, it's nothing. Get some rest."

"Come here, Elliot. Hug your old father." He wiggled his hand in the air impatiently, and I bent to hug him. The embrace was thin.

"'Night, Dad."

"See you in the morning," he said, dismissing me.

I left gladly, descending the stairs and slipping quietly into my sanctum.

I clicked on the light next to my bed and peeled off my clothes, walking naked to my bathroom to turn on the shower. As the steam rose and curled around me, I stood in front of the mirror for a long moment, glancing over my quiet features, my dark hair, small nose, lips like a rosy bow. The only thing loud about me were my eyes, dark and shining, heavy with all the things I didn't say, and I wondered if there would ever come a day where I'd let all those words free.

HERE & NOW

Here
(Not there, not far)
Now
(Not then, not ago)
You will find a way
To love.

—M. WHITE

WADE

had no idea how I was supposed to feel.

My room was cold, my hands rough against the pages as I sat in my bed reading Byron, for lack of anything more constructive to do.

I shouldn't have been reading it, but it was a torture I'd come to find comforting, pouring over the poems she used to read to me like a prayer, an homage. It was like the pain that came from running until my body ached and my heartbeat rushed in my ears, a welcomed pain. A reminder.

The waves were dead; the tides were in their grave,
The moon, their mistress, had expir'd before;
The winds were wither'd in the stagnant air,
And the clouds perish'd; Darkness had no need
Of aid from them--She was the Universe.

I closed the book and closed my heart along with it.

Dad would be home that afternoon, and every moment pressed on me in anticipation of that event, that marker that would set us on the path to the end. It was the quiet before the storm. I took comfort in the fact that once he was home, I'd have something to do, someone to tend to. An objective.

Without an objective, I was untethered.

I'd spent the morning working, filing for extended medical leave, talking to Dad's lawyer, setting up meetings, speaking to hospice to coordinate with the nurse who would help us get set up. The things that needed to be done flapped their wings in my mind like buzzards, waiting. Always waiting.

But I did them, thankful for busy hands and a busy mind. When I was idle, the fear set in, and I had no room in my heart for fear.

Deep down, I knew it was only a matter of time until the fear broke down the door and took over.

Elliot had come over early enough that coffee had just finished brewing. She'd breathed life into the room with quiet purpose, a distraction, a buffer. For my sisters, at least.

For me, she was a curse, a presence that invaded my heart and thoughts.

Sophie had answered the door, and I found that the second she was in the room, I had to get out. Something in the way she watched me, something about her body language told me she wanted to talk to me. The thought of that conversation only spurred me to leave the room.

I wasn't ready. I didn't know if I'd ever be ready.

She held my gaze for a long moment, and I wished I could give her what she wanted.

But she was in the back of my mind as I checked tasks off my list. After all these years, I was still so affected by her. I'd convinced myself I was fine, made a new life for myself, but the old dreams never died, the imprints I'd made in my mind of what our lives would be together never fading. Her refusal was the moment that split my life into two paths — what was, and what could have been.

And now I would endure what would be the most trying time of my life with the woman I'd tried to banish from my heart by my side.

It was an impossible situation with no solution.

I glanced at the clock, wondering when they'd get here, when he'd be home. Like I'd been holding up the levee, but the pressure was too great, too much, and the second he arrived, it would fall and sweep us all away.

The doorbell rang.

My heart stopped.

Dad.

I walked out of my room with my heart thumping, meeting my sisters and Elliot in the hallway, all of us wide-eyed as I opened the door to a paramedic. I showed him through the house and to the library where they'd bring Dad, and he headed back out to the ambulance at the curb.

Elliot stood in the entry with her arm around Sadie and Sophie at her side — fear colored their faces, fear that I felt whispering in my ear, knocking at that door to my heart, but when I caught a glance of my reflection, my face was calm, stoic. A mask. A lie.

We waited for a few long, silent minutes before they carried him in on a gurney. He turned his head to find us as soon as he was able, eyes searching, body relaxing with relief at the sight of us. And his eyes stayed on us as we followed them into the library. He already seemed so much thinner, so much smaller even than he'd been when I'd seen him last night, his skin pallid and slack. I wondered if I imagined it, but when he squeezed my hand and I could feel his bones, delicate and hollow, I knew it was real. He was already leaving us.

The nurse showed up in the middle of the shuffle, and when the doorbell rang, Elliot let her in, a gesture I was grateful for. Dad was home, and I didn't want to leave his side.

The nurse bustled around, chatting pleasantly as she worked on getting him hooked up, explaining what we could expect, how to administer his oral medication and what times, discussing what we could feed him, providing the list of numbers to call should anything happen. Most of it had already been covered, but it was nice all the same, something to listen to, to focus on. And my father watched me silently with his hand in mine, as if he were trying to memorize my face.

The nurse left a little while later — an aide would be by later that evening to check on him again. And with that, we were all finally alone.

Elliot turned on Dad's wireless speaker and played Chopin as he looked around the room at his things. I'd brought in a dresser for his clothes, lined with photos — my grandparents, he and my mother on their wedding day, all of us as a family, baby pictures — his life chronicled in moments.

Sophie pulled an extra throw over his legs. "I'm glad you're home, Dad."

He smiled. "Me too." His speech had improved over the last couple of days, a glimmer of hope in the darkness.

No one seemed to know what to say, all of us quiet for a few minutes, standing mutely as we soaked it all in.

Dad chuckled. "So quiet. Not contagious, you know."

The girls chuckled, and I smiled, just the slightest pull of my lips. I couldn't find any humor, though. I wondered for a moment if I'd ever feel joy again.

Sadie sat on the edge of his bed, smiling at him. "What would you like to do?"

"Talk. Nap. Ice cream."

"In that order?" Sophie asked as she took a seat on the couch, and Elliot followed.

"Yes, please."

Sadie stayed where she was at the edge of his bed holding his hand, and I sat in an armchair next to Sophie and Elliot, keeping my eyes on Dad.

He asked us questions, prompting us, guiding us even when

we should be caring for him, knowing we didn't know what to say, what to do. There was too much in the air, too much between us, too many things we weren't ready to talk about, and I felt the pressure, the need to make every second count, every question, every breath and heartbeat. I wanted to tell him all my fears. I wanted to take away his. I wanted to scream and cry and fight for him. I wanted to laugh with him. But I found myself unable to say much of anything as we talked about the mundane, the meaningless, the nothings of our lives. All that in a moment we should have spent in the truth, not hiding behind cordiality.

The falsity of it all sank into my heart and twisted.

Elliot stayed mostly quiet during the light conversation, listening attentively without interrupting. And when he touched upon my life, I felt Elliot's presence as if she were tethered to me, so aware of her that I struggled to form the words to answer his questions. Because the words all held hidden meaning, underscored by the loss of her.

"Germany's beautiful."

I wish I could have taken you there.

"Ben and I went to Neuschwanstein Castle last month — it was like something out of a fairy tale."

I imagined you standing in the throne room with me, reverently reciting Byron.

"Skiing the Alps was a religious experience."

Would you have loved it as much as I did? Would it have stolen your breath like it stole mine?

And then he moved on to Elliot, prompting a discussion that led her to mention that her father had come to town. She kept her eyes trained on Dad, but I knew she was as aware of me as I was of her.

The urge to get up and leave the room climbed on top of me and squeezed until it was almost unbearable — the last thing in the world I wanted to even hear whisper of was her father, or her sisters, for that matter.

Seven years gone, and that wound still hadn't fully healed.

I took a breath, trying to be still and quiet while I dismantled an M4 carbine rifle in my head and reassembled it. It was a trick I'd acquired a long time before, after long nights in Afghanistan when sleep escaped me. The repetition, the imagined motion hypnotized me, quieted my mind. Like counting to a hundred, except it made me feel safer.

The doorbell rang, interrupting the conversation that felt like a lie, a charade, and frustration twisted through me. I jumped at the chance to escape, standing to excuse myself. I opened the door to find Lou and my aunt Jeannie.

My aunt's composure was thin, and it broke when she saw me, nearly breaking mine along with it. She looked like my mother, though a little bit older, a little bit different. She had the same dark hair and hazel eyes, the same smile, her appearance close enough that I imagined for a split second that it was Mom. I wondered fleetingly what she'd do if she were there, wondered what she'd say. She always knew just what to say.

My throat closed as she pulled me into a hug, standing on her tiptoes to reach around my neck as sobs shook her body against me.

"I'm so sorry, honey. So sorry," she whispered shakily.

I said nothing. If I spoke, I'd lose hold of myself completely.

She pulled away after a long moment, wiping tears from her cheeks. "How is he?"

I ran a hand over my mouth and swallowed hard. "He's okay. Come on in."

She cupped my cheek like I was a little boy as she passed, and I was about to turn to follow her when Lou leapt into my arms, surprising me.

"I'm so sorry. I just … I hope you're all right, Wade," she said, lips near my ear, voice sincere. "I'm always here for you if you need me."

I let her go, though she hung on a second longer, sighing sadly as she took my arm. We made our way into the house together, the physical connection of her hand in the crook of my elbow, confusing me. She seemed upset, and I wondered if this was just how she was dealing with it or if she was making a pass at me. I had to think it was the former — the latter seemed ludicrous by comparison.

I broke away from her once we entered the room, though not quickly enough for Elliot to have missed it. Color rose in her cheeks, her eyes full of regret and apology and pain before they darted away, finding Jeannie across the room.

Jeannie smiled at Dad and made a joke that elicited a relieved laugh, but the look on his face said he saw my mother too. It was something we'd always said — everyone who knew the two women noted their similarities — but now, knowing he'd be gone soon … the longing for her was a physical presence in the room.

Everyone in America could tell you where they were that day. Sophie and I were in elementary school, sitting together in the gym with all the other terrified kids as we wondered what had happened and why the adults were crying. Sadie was just a baby, at home with our nanny. Dad was in class, lecturing on Dickenson. And Mom was at work at the Trade Center.

She'd called Dad from the stairwell to say goodbye as the building burned and crumbled. I'd imagined that conversation thousands of times, what she said, what he'd said, her final words. But he'd never been able to tell us. He'd tried, but he could never form the words, never pass them on to us without the act breaking him down. So instead he would pull us into his arms and whisper, *She loved you more than anything, and that love will never die.*

I dreamed about her every night for nearly two years. Sometimes she'd be running down the stairs and the building would fall. I could see her pain, feel it, the nightmare waking me with her name on my lips. Sometimes in my dreams she would just disappear, vanish in the middle of some mundane task. Sometimes she held me and whispered in my ear with a warm, sweet breath that she was okay. She told me that she loved me. She said it didn't hurt.

And so I decided at age ten that I was going to join the Army. I would protect all the moms from dying, all the dads from hurting, all the kids from losing their parents. It was all I wanted, until I met Elliot.

I blinked back tears at the memory, the moments piling on higher and higher. There were all of a sudden too many people in the room. Too many things to say. It wasn't real, nothing was real or meaningful. Life was cruel, and we were caught in the web of it, helpless.

I turned to leave the room, breath shallow, needing air, needing clarity. Needing solitude. "Gonna go for a walk," I muttered to the room as I passed Lou.

"I'll go with you," she offered, and I couldn't say no. Literally, I couldn't speak, couldn't refuse, couldn't explain myself if she argued, so I just grabbed my jacket and walked out with her on my heels.

It was cold and gray, the winter sky pressing down on me as I hurried down the sidewalk toward Central Park.

Lou didn't speak, and neither did I, though I cursed her name in my mind, wishing for a second's peace, wishing for a way to stand my ground against the onslaught of emotions. I couldn't control myself, couldn't control the situation. I had no leverage, no purchase. I had nothing.

It was a long time before I finally slowed to a normal place. We were out of sight of the streets, surrounded by rustling winter trees, their branches naked, their bones reaching up for the sun, so far away, hidden behind the clouds. And I felt as naked, as stripped and cold, reaching for the sun that had disappeared.

I came to a stop at the edge of the reservoir, watching the rippling surface of the water, the reflection of the sky and trees upside down.

We stood there for a long while, her presence irritating and unwanted. I wasn't allowed to feel what I felt, not with her there. I had to say something, but I had no room for pleasantries or pretense. So I gave her none.

"Why did you follow me?" I asked with my eyes on the water.

"I thought you could use a friend."

My jaw clenched. It wasn't untrue, but a friend who knew me would know I'd have preferred to be alone. Instead, I found myself in a position of some social requirement to fake it, to survive the conversation when I only wanted to be selfish, when I only wanted to grieve without concern for anyone else. It seemed like such a simple thing to ask, but there we were.

"I know you're not okay," she continued when I didn't speak, "but we don't have to talk about it." She paused, watching the water too. "I just want you to know I'm sorry, Wade, for what it's worth."

"People keep saying that, and I don't really understand what it means. It's empty, meaningless, something to say when there's nothing to say."

She didn't answer, just glanced down at her shoes, shifting on her feet.

I sighed and ran a hand through my hair, huffing a swear word.

"It's okay. You're right. I don't know what to say other than I'm sorry. I'm sorry he's sick. I'm sorry this is happening to you and your sisters. But that doesn't make anything better."

"No, it doesn't." My eyes fixed on a far point of the pond. "I'm having a hard time pretending right now. I just wasn't looking for company."

"You don't have to explain yourself. I can go." She turned to do just that.

I breathed deep. "I'll go with you."

She placed her hand on my arm. "You don't have to do that, I'll be fine."

"I don't want you to walk back alone. It's getting dark."

"Really, Wade, you don't—"

"It's fine," I said sharper than I meant to. "I shouldn't have left anyway."

She nodded, and we began our walk back to the house, back to the truth and the fear.

"So," she started tentatively, "we brought more food for dinner, and Jeannie and I are going to get some groceries for you tomorrow. Just let me know if there's anything specific you need and we'll pick it up."

"Thank you." The temperature had dropped, taking my mood with it. "It seems like that's always the last thing to think about. Food. Something so basic, so essential, and I have no room to even consider it."

She shoved her hands in the pockets of her coat as we walked past a copse of trees, leaving the water behind us. "We're here to help with whatever you need. Should we, ah, plan for Elliot when we bring food?"

My jaw clenched. "Probably."

Lou nodded slowly. "Sure. And she's … Sophie's friend?"

"Her best friend."

"Oh."

I felt like I needed to explain her presence, and I didn't like the sensation. So I kept it as short as possible, hoping she would take the hint and leave it alone. "She and Dad are close — he's her mentor. She's been a part of the family for almost ten years."

Speaking about her felt too personal, too close to the edge of the chasm between us, and I backed away.

"This way." I gestured to a split in the path. "It's faster."

She rubbed her hands together and put them back in her pockets. "Good. It's a little colder than I'd realized," she said with a self-deprecating laugh.

I nodded, squeezing my numb fists in my pocket, not looking forward to facing them. Maybe if I'd had a chance to be alone, catch my breath. But as it stood I was only angrier, more unsure, more confused.

"Is there anything else we can do to help?" she asked. No hints would be taken from her.

I did consider the question, though, wondering if there was anything else I could delegate, but I couldn't think of anything. Not with my brain in the state it was in. "I don't think so."

"What will the next few days be like?"

"Dad's lawyer is coming tomorrow about the will, and we have to talk about the best way for him to give me the house to avoid us losing it to the taxes they'll place on it. A nurse will come three times a week and an aide every day to monitor him and his medication," I rattled off absently. "Otherwise, we're just …" *Waiting.* "… spending as much time with him as we can."

She nodded. "Any visitors planned?"

"Everyone's been calling, but I haven't had time to answer them all yet. It's on the list for tomorrow."

"You have to handle everything, don't you?"

"Yeah." The word was heavy from my lips and on my heart.

"It's a lot. I don't know how you're holding up as well as you are."

"Don't really have a choice."

"Well, I just want you to know that I think you're really strong. We're lucky to have you. Just don't forget that it's okay to lean on us, too."

I didn't offer anything else, just retreated into my thoughts, and mercifully she let me as we walked the distance back home.

ELLIOT

My voice was the only sound in the room as I read to Rick from Shakespeare's Sonnets. It's all I had done since Wade left, taking all the air in the room with him.

He'd felt what we all felt.

Hopeless.

The room had fallen quiet with his exit, but silence wouldn't do. Soon, silence would be all that we had. So I'd picked up the book of words that rested in my hands, and I read them.

No longer mourn for me when I am dead
Then you shall hear the surly sullen bell
Give warning to the world that I am fled
From this vile world, with vilest worms to dwell:
Nay, if you read this line, remember not
The hand that writ it; for I love you so
That I in your sweet thoughts would be forgot
If thinking on me then should make you woe.
O, if, I say, you look upon this verse
When I perhaps compounded am with clay,
Do not so much as my poor name rehearse.
But let your love even with my life decay,
Lest the wise world should look into your moan
And mock you with me after I am gone.

Sadie sniffled, and I turned to find her tucked into Sophie's side on the couch. But that didn't affect me as much as the vision of Wade standing behind them with his eyes cold and silvery, as solid as he was broken. He was on fire, and he was frozen. Lou was at his elbow, her brow furrowed with concern.

I closed the book, looking to Rick with my heart climbing up and up. "I'm sorry. This was a mistake."

He reached for my hand. "No, just too true. But we need truth." He looked over my shoulder, motioning to his children. I tried to pull away to make room for them, but he tightened his grip, telling me silently to stay as they appeared at my side, Wade the closest.

"Don't be afraid," Rick said gently. "Don't hide. I'm here." He let go of my hand and touched Sadie's heart. "I'm here."

Tears slipped down my cheeks, and Wade broke, his face bending, his hands fisted in the sheets as he dropped to his knees, his forehead pressed into the mattress.

"My boy," Rick whispered, cupping the back of his head. "I'm sorry to leave you."

Wade's shoulders shuddered, and I pressed my hand over my mouth, but the pain wouldn't stay down, stay in — it poured out of me, raw and burning.

"Don't be afraid," Rick said again as he looked us over, his voice thick and rough.

"Don't be afraid," he whispered to himself, eyes closed.

The girls bent to hold him, and I stepped back to give them room, to let them be, this family who I loved so much, unable to catch my breath, unable to see them through the curtain of tears. Wade hadn't moved, but as I backed away, he reached for me blindly, grabbing my hand, pulling me back. And I sank to my knees next to him, our fingers twined together; we existed only in our grief.

In that grief, time moved without purpose, an absent ticking from somewhere in the room, meaning nothing to us as we were swept away. The surge of emotion overwhelmed us, and when it ebbed, it pulled back through the sand with a whisper, taking us with it.

Wade didn't let go of my hand, just sat once he'd calmed with our hands tied together in his lap, his head bowed and shoulders bent. And when he finally looked up, his eyes held honesty and truth I wasn't prepared for. That moment broke my heart again, just when I thought it couldn't be broken any more.

He let me go, and we moved to stand, finding Rick smiling at us proudly with a quivering chin and eyes full of hope.

"You're what I give to the world, what I leave behind. I am proud."

He said it slowly, every word with intention, with concentration, as if it were the most important thing he'd ever say. "Now, we have truth. Hold onto it."

We nodded, smiling back through fresh tears.

"Now, ice cream."

Laughter burst out of us, Wade's coming through louder, clearer than the rest, warming my soul. And I realized how much he'd needed that, needed Rick, needed to *be*. It had set him free, if only for a moment.

Jeannie and Lou were in the doorway, hanging onto each other while they watched us. Jeannie moved her hand from her mouth, wiping her tears as we dispersed, moving for the kitchen, but Wade stayed behind, leaning in to speak softly to his father.

I closed the door behind us as we left, hoping he could say all that he needed.

"I wasn't sure if we should have stayed or gone," Jeannie said to Sophie as Sadie gathered bowls and Lou unpacked gallons of ice cream from the freezer.

"It's all right," Sophie answered. "I'm glad you stayed. You should spend as much time with Dad as you can."

"Thank you for that. I … This is almost as hard as when we lost your mom." She smoothed Sophie's hair. "I'm just so sorry."

Sophie breathed deep, grey eyes shining. "Me too."

We piled up bowls full of ice cream scoops, different flavors in different bowls for him. I arranged them on a tray as everyone made their own bowls, and we filed back into the room. Sophie and I sat on either side of Rick, taking turns giving him samples of all the flavors we brought. I was on his bad side, so I made sure I was swift enough not to let any fall from his lips.

He chuckled after swallowing when I'd caught a particularly drippy bite. "I'm like a baby."

I smiled. "You're far too handsome to be a baby, Rick." It was true

— he and Wade looked just alike, with a strong jaw, gray eyes, and dark hair, though Rick had shocks of gray at his temples.

"Nah. Need a bib. Reminds me of Sadie and the sweet potatoes."

Sadie rolled her eyes. "Oh, God. Not this again."

Wade laughed around a mouthful of ice cream, catching my eye with the spark in his, reminding me so much of days long ago spent just like this. I saw him, the boy I loved, in that moment.

"Man." He shook his head at Sadie. "I've never seen such a mess. I told you she didn't like them, Dad."

"You were right," Rick said.

Sadie pointed at him with her spoon, her gray eyes flashing. "Orange vegetables are unnatural."

Wade was still chuckling, poking at his ice cream with his spoon. "You were screaming like crazy, and Dad was doing the purple prose plane."

"What in the world is that?" Jeannie asked, amused.

Wade leaned on Rick's bed and crossed his ankles. "An airplane that runs on overly-descriptive prose. *Here comes the silvery jet on the wings of the storm, into the gaping maw of the giant!*" He laughed again. "Sophie hit the edge of the bowl with a screech, and it flipped around about a hundred times, slinging orange goop all over the kitchen."

"Hyperbole," Rick said. "Three times." He opened his mouth for another bite, and I heaped a spoon of double chocolate fudge in.

Wade shook his head, smiling into his ice cream. "Sophie just sat there with her mouth in a little 'o' and eyes as big as silver dollars, covered in orange slop, and then we all died laughing."

I switched out the bowl for mint chocolate chip and waited for him to finish his orange sherbet. Rick's brow quirked.

"Things taste different."

"Better or worse?" I asked.

"Neither, just … different. Farther away. Smaller." He opened up for a bite, and I fed him.

Jeannie stood and began collecting bowls. "Let me clean up, and then we should get going."

Rick smiled, and I noticed his lids were heavy.

"Tired?"

He looked to me when I spoke. "A little."

"It's been a big day. I should probably go too."

"Back tomorrow?" he asked hopefully, and I smiled.

"Of course."

He seemed comforted by that and refused another bite from Sophie. So we moved around straightening up in the library and kitchen. Jeannie and Lou left first, and I didn't miss Lou holding Wade close or touching his hand before she walked away. I said my goodbyes in the library, making plans for the morning before seeing myself out.

The sounds of the girls and Rick talking and laughing carried through the hallway and to me, setting a smile on my lips as I pulled on my coat and scarf. My hand was nearly on the doorknob when I heard my name softly, gently on his lips.

I turned and found Wade before me, but something had changed, something in his eyes. It wasn't forgiveness I found there, but layers of a newfound emotion, indiscernible to me. His hand lifted just a degree, and I imagined him reaching for me before it dropped again. He searched my face, the words he wanted to say warring behind his eyes.

"Thank you," he said after an agonizing moment. "Thank you for being here for Dad, for us. I know … I know it's not easy."

"It's not easy for any of us. I'm not alone in that."

"No," he said simply. "You're not."

"Thank you, too. For letting me be here."

His voice rumbled, velvety and solemn. "I wouldn't keep you from him, Elliot."

My name again, three syllables on his breath.

I nodded; my voice failed me.

He looked down at his shoes and back up, hands slipping into his pockets as he took a step back. "I'll see you tomorrow."

"Goodnight," I answered quietly and closed my hand over the doorknob, turning it to step into the cold night where I found a glimmer of hope caressing the moon.

SO EASY

Hurt is so easy,
Loss so simple
In its complexity,
And to fall into
The arms of the dark
Is effortless.

—M. WHITE

WADE

My sisters and I had spent the morning reading to Dad, hours spent in silence other than the cadence of verse and rhyme as he watched the window as if it held answers. I'd been reading Thoreau for an hour, comforted by the connection to Dad without the pressure of our own thoughts and fears.

The day before drifted in and out of my thoughts. He was home, and the anxiety of his homecoming was finally behind us after so much waiting, so much anticipation. We had all been left reeling. I hadn't expected to come home to Elliot's words, to the truth of the moment. It had opened me up, and I had spilled out, unable to find composure or control when my father held my face and called me his.

And she was there, by my side, as lost and broken as we all were, backing away, trying to disappear again when she held a place next to us. I couldn't let her do it, couldn't let her shrink away. So I stopped her, took her hand not knowing that it was me who needed her.

I didn't know until my eyes found her hands resting in my lap wrapped in mine, so warm, so soft, that connection to her like a breath of life.

When the moment had passed and were all smiling again, the ease and normalcy (that word, that feeling, a thing which I sought and feared) surprising me and somehow not surprising me at all. We slipped into it simply, the fight and anguish burned down and away.

I watched her leave the room last night, saw the gentle curve of her shoulder, the slight curl of her fingers, the tip of her nose when she turned for the hall. She was so familiar to me still, and I followed her almost against my will. There was so much I wanted to say. She'd brought me comfort while exposing a crack in the wall I'd built, and a sliver of light shone through, a warm slice of a feeling I hadn't been lucky enough to find since we'd parted ways.

I wanted to tell her that. I wanted to touch her face, breathe her in, feel her in my arms. But standing there before her with her eyes begging me to speak, the words left me.

The words I had weren't enough. They'd never been enough. They'd never be enough.

But I wanted them to be, always wished they had. She might have even forgiven me, but I didn't deserve her forgiveness.

The afternoon sun spilled in through the window as I read on, the words of Thoreau on my lips, sinking into my heart.

And each may other help, and service do,
Drawing Love's bands more tight,
Service he ne'er shall rue
While one and one make two,
And two are one;

In such case only doth man fully prove
Fully as man can do,
What power there is in Love
His inmost soul to move
Resistlessly.

Two sturdy oaks I mean, which side by side,
Withstand the winter's storm,
And spite of wind and tide,
Grow up the meadow's pride,
For both are strong

Above they barely touch, but undermined
Down to their deepest source,
Admiring you shall find
Their roots are intertwined
Insep'rably.

Dad took a heavy breath and released it, and I watched him.

"Want me to keep going?"

He turned his head to smile at me, looking tired. "Lunch?"

Sophie stood from the couch. "I'll get you some. Mac and cheese?"

"Bacon?" he asked hopefully.

She laughed. "Is there any other way?"

He chuckled back, and Sadie got up too. "Let me help you," she said, and they left the room.

I closed the hardbound book. "Feeling okay?"

He shrugged one shoulder. "Tired."

"Well, you should sleep after lunch. Once the nurse comes, it'll be impossible. All that poking and prodding."

"Like a science experiment." He smiled, swallowing before asking, "Know when Elliot's coming?"

I shook my head. "I think she's at work this morning. That's what Sophie said, at least," I added.

He nodded. "It's hard for you, with her here." It wasn't a question, but an observation, and I answered it honestly.

"It is. But it's all right. I'm all right."

"I know you'd never tell me otherwise." He reached for his water, glistening as the light shone through it, but it was just out of his reach. I stood and sat on the edge of the bed, picking up the water to bring the straw to his lips.

"You're probably right about that. But it's okay. It's getting easier."

"You still love each other."

My heart stopped painfully in my chest, restarting with a jolt. "I'm not who I was before, and neither is she."

"That's true. You've grown on your own, but Thoreau wrote: *Above they barely touch, but undermined / Down to their deepest source, / Admiring you shall find / Their roots are intertwined / Insep'rably.*"

Emotion surfaced like an oil slick, slinking with every color. "You're right. But please, don't ask me to dig through that, not right now. It's ... I don't know how to sort through her and me. One thing at a time."

He swallowed, gathering his strength to speak. "I won't ask, son. I won't force your hand. Just want you to know I understand. I see you, and her, and your pain."

His words trailed through that oily feeling again, the colors of my emotions swirling in their wake. "I don't want you to worry about me or Elliot."

He laid back, and I set the glass back down, moving the rolling tray close to his bed. "It's easier than thinking about myself."

We shared a silent moment, watching each other. I saw myself in him in large ways and small, counting every similarity as the clock on one of his shelves ticked incessantly.

"Are you afraid?" I asked quietly.

He nodded. "But there's nothing to be done, no way to fight. So, I'm resigned. I feel ... feel myself letting go. But I don't worry about me. When I leave, you'll stay. I know ... I ..." He struggled with the words, frustrated, wanting to communicate, so I waited patiently for him to find his strength. "Fifteen years have passed, and sometimes the pain is as fresh as the second she left us." He closed his eyes briefly and opened them again, reaching for my hand. "These days are about saying goodbye, and the luxury is one I want to take advantage of. I'm grateful for it." The words were labored by the end, his energy waning from exertion.

"So are we." The words were solemn, and grief struck me again, regret washing over me alongside it. "I … I'm sorry I haven't been here. I'm sorry I wasn't the son I should have been. I should have come home more, been present, stopped … stopped running away."

His brow dropped, eyes soft and full of understanding. "Wade, you are everything I wished for. I am proud of you, and not once have I resented you for finding your way in this world. Not once."

"I thought I had more time." My voice cracked, and he squeezed my hand.

"So did I," he said gently. "We all did. But do not regret that. That is one thing I *will* ask of you. *For of all sad words of tongue or pen, / The saddest are these: It might have been!* Stop running away so you don't spend the rest of your life wondering. Whittier knew this, and so do I. So should you."

I was left without words as Sophie and Sadie brought lunch in on trays, so I sat at his side, his words settling into my mind as I fed him.

Stop running. I had no choice. I was here. She was here. But I didn't know how to face my past. I'd been running for seven years, and there could be no full stop. There would be no sixty-to-zero, not without slowing down first or my brakes would catch on fire. But I thought about that crack in the wall again, and looking through it, I found the smallest hope.

We talked about nothing and everything, taking every small second where we could. And when he was finished eating, he fell asleep. When we left the room, we stood in the hallway without purpose, as if the hours of the day had been reset to mark the times when we could be by his side.

Dad would be asleep for an hour or two, and I didn't want to sit, didn't want to wait in that quiet room, didn't want to be still. I loathed the unscheduled time, the lack of structure I'd become so accustomed to missing, throwing me off kilter. I longed for the action of my body to distract me from the things I couldn't change, so I pulled on my coat and opened the door to find peace.

Instead, I found Elliot.

She wore her blue peacoat and yellow hat again, her eyes dark and wide with surprise at meeting me on the steps of the house.

"H-hi," she breathed, eyes moving behind me to the door. "Is everything okay?"

"He's fine, just resting."

I didn't offer more, and she looked away, the color rising in her cheeks. "Oh."

I cleared my throat, not sure what to do or say, caught in the stretch of the moment. "The girls are inside," I offered after a second.

She smiled politely. "All right, thank you."

But something came over me as she moved to walk past. "I'm going for a walk, if you'd like to come with me."

She stopped, her gaze meeting mine with shock, and I was sure mine reflected the same thing. "That would be nice," she answered softly, sweetly, and something in my heart thumped and rattled like a loose bolt with every beat.

I said nothing more, just started down the stairs and she followed. I wanted to be near her, but I was afraid of her, afraid for my heart. Indecision and uncertainty slipped over me like a fog as we walked quietly through the city and into the park.

The silence wasn't companionable; it was heavy with years and words between us, and it stretched on so long, there seemed to be no breeching it gracefully. It was the collective story of us in a twenty-minute span of footsteps.

We ended up at the Glenspan Arch, a place we had been a hundred times, what felt like a hundred years before. The small river ran gently next to us, and I could hear the steady hiss of the cascade just beyond the arch.

"Do you remember the first time we came here?" she asked, the words gentle and hesitant as we approached the stone bridge, nestled in the arms of the forest.

"You'd never been anywhere in the city, which was weird, considering you'd lived here your whole life," I mused. Once I'd met her family, I'd understood completely. They were self-serving, uninterested in participating in life outside themselves, and they'd do anything to drown out Elliot's light, to cull her spirit.

Those thoughts I kept to myself.

She nodded, smiling as her eyes drank in the world around us. "I thought we'd stepped into a fairy tale."

In a way, we had. I'd kissed her in the shadows of this archway, surrounded by the echo of the stream. I'd held her hand along this path, my world illuminated by her. It was a dream, a myth, a story from a long time ago.

"Do you come back often?" I asked, pushing the memories away, wondering why I'd brought us this way, although in the back of my mind I recognized that anywhere we'd have gone would have brought the past back to me.

Elliot shook her head. "I don't have much time these days, not without the kids. And bringing them here wouldn't really be relaxing." She chuckled. "I've come a few times to write, though."

Finally, ground I could stand on. "Sophie told me you got your Lit degree. Congratulations."

"Thank you. I don't know if I would have gone, if it weren't for

Rick. He's always believed in me, even when I didn't believe in myself."

"He does that. Decide what you'll do with it?" I asked as we slipped into the cool shade.

"I haven't had much time to think about it."

I made a noncommittal sound through my nose, which did little to hide my disdain at the thought of her family. "Because of your sister's kids?"

She nodded, face tilting down to her shoes, sending a wave of regret through me.

"I'm sorry, I didn't mean to judge. It's just …"

She smiled at me, lips together. "It's all right. I know how you feel about them. But those kids are the center of my universe right now. Mary needs the help, and I'm not sure what I want to do. Not much I *can* do besides teach."

"You could write."

"I do write."

"You could submit."

"I knew what you meant," she said lightly, her words echoing off the stone. "Those words are part of me, a real part of me, not fiction. They're my thoughts, my beliefs, my pain and joy. To subject my heart and soul to judgment is … well, it's terrifying."

"I can understand that."

"Maybe I'll be brave enough someday."

"You are brave. You're one of the bravest people I've ever known."

She laughed. I frowned.

"Braveness isn't always loud. Sometimes it's silent. There's braveness in sacrifice and kindness. It's in doing a thing that needs to be done, even though it's hard, and even though it hurts."

We stepped out of the arch and into the soft light of the forest, and she turned her face to mine, though I couldn't meet her eyes. If I met her eyes, I might say more, might say too much. And I couldn't do that. I told myself it was in the interest of self-preservation and not because I was afraid of her, of what it might do to me if I opened myself up and let her back in.

After a moment, she looked away.

"I suppose I don't really see myself that way."

"No, you never did. But that doesn't change the fact." The subject was dangerously close to the truth of my heart, and I turned it to something safer. "Dad's doing well today. We read to him, and he's able to speak better than he has yet. Longer sentences, more articulation. But he's exhausted. It's a lot for him."

"For all of you."

"For all of *us*. You're a part of this, Elliot."

Her name, a word still foreign, though familiar as if it were my own.

"The nurse will be here in a couple of hours," I continued, "and I think Jeannie and Lou are bringing dinner again. Will you be staying?"

She nodded as we approached the cascade. "If it's all right."

I pulled her to a stop across from the waterfall with my hand cupping her elbow, frustration and agitation mounting. She still wanted to disappear, as if she held no power. She didn't know she held all the power over me; my heart was in her hands as it ever was.

In her face, I found surprise tinged with regret and want. A mixture of wishes and apologies hung on her breath.

"Please, stop," I demanded.

"Stop what?" Her voice was quiet, the words trembling ever so slightly.

"Stop apologizing for your presence," I said, persuasion heavy in my words, in my heart. "Stop assuming you're not wanted. You have every right to be here with us, for us, for him. So stop disappearing. Stop hiding from what you wish for. Stop sacrificing yourself for everyone else."

Her eyes held their sadness close. "It's not so easy as that."

"It is." I'd pulled her closer without realizing it, unable to help myself. My hand was still on her arm, and before I could stop myself, she was pressed against me with her hand resting on my chest. "Elliot, it's always been that easy. That's what you never understood."

I let her go and stepped back, feeling the loss of her with the snap of cold air between us. The pull of her was undeniable, even after everything — time couldn't erase her from my heart.

When I looked her over, I realized I didn't know her anymore, and she didn't know me. I wondered distantly, as one watches the horizon, if I was only in love with the idea of her, a version of her that existed in the past. Or maybe it had never existed at all outside of my mind.

I was in love with a girl who had dreams, a girl who loved quietly and without expectation. But the girl before me had her dreams dashed, and she loved submissively, putting everyone else before herself until she found herself buried and gone.

Maybe she had vanished after all, the seven years had passed by, erasing the features I had loved so well.

I walked away, and she stood rooted to the spot for a few heartbeats before moving her feet. And feeling her there by my side, I knew I was wrong. I loved her still, and that love was real. And I only wanted her happiness, but I had no rights, no means to provide it.

We circled back, walking the edge of the pond called The Pool in silence, waiting for the moment to be behind us, waiting to get back to the place where we could pretend. Waiting for the polite pretense that covered the truth where we couldn't see it. Didn't matter that we could still feel it.

But I didn't want to feel it, not now. I didn't want to feel her there, the pull so strong that I could barely fight it. I hoped I could find the strength to hold up the wall between us, wondering for a beat what would happen if I let it go, let it fall. Let myself fall back into her. Would she catch me, or would I tumble to the ground?

A flash of relief hit me at the thought of submission; I imagined yielding to her would be to breathe again, knocking the dust from my lungs. Just the illusion of that comfort was transcendent.

But it was just that — an illusion, a falsity, fictitious and fabricated by my desire to find my way back to the fantasy of her.

BRING IT ON HOME

Home is not a place,
Not a smell,
Not a face,
But a space
In your heart.

—M. WHITE

ELLIOT

My hands were ice in my pockets as we walked in silence, his thoughts rolling off him in waves as we walked through the park, saying nothing.

He was right, and he was wrong. True and false. Yes and no. The words warred through him, through me.

The fight was the same as the last we'd had, and the years had changed little about it. He was the same as he always was; there was nothing I could say to change his mind. There never had been, though I wished I'd given him the answers he'd wanted so long ago. But the ship had sailed and left me on the shore. And his words now were right, and they were wrong.

He was still angry, still hurt, and even as he spoke of the ways he wished me to change, he pulled me closer. Hot and cold. One extreme or the other.

I was left reeling.

My breath was shallow, my chest hollow, my pain dull and aching. I could think of nothing to say; there was nothing to defend. But I found no words of agreement either.

Same fight, but everything else was different, somehow more true than it had been the first time, his words an arrow, sharp and barbed, running me through.

How could I explain that when he'd left, he'd taken me with him? How could I tell him he was all I wanted, and when he was lost to me, I lost all hope?

I couldn't. I could barely whisper the words to my own heart, never mind where his ears would hear.

So I walked next to him in the cold, feeling ashamed and wrong, feeling that I'd been put back in my place. I accepted it, shrinking back into that small space where I could hide, disappear, even though he'd asked me not to while he pushed me into the role with his own hands.

I didn't know how to exist any other way, not anymore. My light had gone out when he left me years before.

I was turned so inward that I didn't feel that his frustration had ebbed, softened, though the tension between us snapped as we approached the steps to his house.

He stopped in front of me, bringing me to a halt.

"Elliot, wait."

My heart thumped in my throat as I waited for him to speak, looking up into his hard face.

He grappled with something — I could see it behind his eyes as they searched my face, in the set of his lips as the seconds ticked by. He didn't know what to say any more than I did. But at least he was strong enough to try.

"I … I'm sorry. I didn't mean to upset you. Your choices, your wishes are none of my business, and they haven't been for a long time."

The heat in my cheeks spread. "You weren't wrong."

He looked down. "I'm not right either."

I could feel his regret, his hurt, and I only wanted to take it away. I only wanted to make him whole again.

I only wished I knew how.

"Wade, really," I soothed. "It's all right. This … this isn't easy for any of us. Least of all you. Don't worry about me."

He met my eyes, gray and cool as snow. "I always have. Can't stop now."

I opened my mouth to speak, but he turned and started up the stairs.

"I really am sorry. For all of this," he said with his back to me, and then he opened the door, leaving me standing on the step, my soul staggering.

After a breath, I gathered myself up and walked in behind him, hearing a new voice from the library.

"Ben?" Wade muttered, hanging his jacket hastily before striding away with bewilderment on his face.

I watched his profile as he stood in the threshold of the room for a second, face illuminated by the sunlight streaming in the window, and he lit up from the inside with pure joy.

I didn't move until he bolted into the room, laughing.

I hung up my coat and hat and stepped into the room to find him embracing a man whom I'd never seen before. He was as tall as Wade, with dirty blond hair cut almost identically, and he smiled a big, gleaming smile as they clapped each other on the back before pulling away.

"What the hell are you doing here?" Wade asked, grinning like a little boy on Christmas morning. I found myself smiling too, infected by their happiness, by the lightness in the room.

Ben smirked and shrugged, stuffing his hands in his pockets. He looked dashing, cavalier, without a care in the world, though his eyes hid a heaviness and sadness behind their twinkle and spark.

"Thought you could use backup. That, and I'm a terrible listener."

Wade laughed again, shaking his head as he looked Ben over. "Goddamn, I can't believe it. I mean, I can believe it, but I didn't think …"

He was still smiling, though it shifted, colored with unsaid understanding. "Good to see you too."

Wade stepped around him to display him to the crowded room.

Sadie sat at Rick's feet on the bed, and Sophie sat in an armchair. Lou waited on the couch, apparently next to where Ben had been. Consequently, she was looking at him like he was a warm chocolate chip cookie.

Selfish relief slipped over me at the thought of her being interested in Ben rather than Wade.

"How long have you been here?" Wade asked Ben. "Have you met everyone?"

"I just got here a bit ago, and I've met everyone but you," Ben said as he turned to me, flashing his friendly smile as he approached. His eyes were dark and his face boyish, full of mirth and levity, a breath of fresh air in a room stifled with the weight of the world. "I'm Ben," he said, extending his hand.

"Elliot." I took his big, strong hand and smiled. "Lovely to meet you."

Recognition flickered behind his eyes. "Same to you."

"Do you work with Wade?"

He stepped back, eyes cutting to Wade, the smile still on his lips. "I do, off and on since our first tour in Afghanistan. I've been following him around ever since."

"It was good of you to come," I offered, and Wade nodded, still beaming. I glanced around the room, realizing there wouldn't be enough seating for all of us. "Let me go grab a few more chairs."

"I'll help," Sophie said as she stood, giving me a meaningful look, falling into stride as we walked out of the room.

Once in the hallway, she sighed.

"Everything okay?" I asked, taking her arm.

She nodded as we walked into the dining room. "It's fine. I mean, relative to everything, it's fine. Things feel better, but it's so strange. I'm glad he's home, but it's underscored by the waiting. Sadie's trying, but she's so young and leaves whenever she can to be with her friends. I think … I think she doesn't know what to do. None of us know what to do."

"How could you know?" I asked quietly, looking into her eyes.

She glanced away, shaking her head, her brow heavy with worry. "I don't know. And Wade … I think he's struggling more than any of us, but he insists he's fine. I just wish there were something I could do."

"You know how he is. When he needs you, he'll ask, and if you try to force it out of him, it'll backfire." The words were matter-of-fact, a truth.

"I just hate it. All of it. Everything. It's not fair, Elliot." The words wavered, and I held her at arm's length, searching her face until she met my eyes.

"You're right. It's not fair. It's cruel and ugly and unjust. But we'll endure it for your dad because this is the sum of what we have to offer him — our love."

She pursed her lips and nodded, eyes shining. "I'm just so glad you're here."

I pulled her into a hug. "I know. And I'm not going anywhere."

She held on to me for a moment before breaking away, sniffing once as she turned for a chair. "I can't believe Ben came just to be here for Wade. The room already feels lighter, doesn't it?"

"It does. Wade's face! Did you see his face?" I beamed at the image in my mind.

Sophie mirrored my expression. "I haven't seen him smile like that in ages."

"They must be close."

"They are. He just hopped a plane, used his leave to fly here because he knew Wade needed him." She shook her head and sighed. "I'm so glad Wade has him. He needs someone so badly."

My chest ached, deep inside where she couldn't see.

Sophie picked up a chair and smirked at me, changing the subject. "Did you see Lou?"

I chuckled as we hauled the chairs out. "Hello, nurse."

She laughed. "Seems like she's already given up on Wade."

"*Thou art not false, but thou art fickle,*" I recited.

"Byron?"

"He knew his stuff."

"Well, good riddance on that front anyway. Cousins dating? That's straight out of an Austen novel."

I laughed again, surprised at how quickly we all found relief, as if we'd been waiting on something to bring us back up to the surface.

When we entered the room, Wade approached, taking the chairs from us, changed once again. The heaviness of our exchange during the walk had dissipated, gone without a trace. I marveled over him smiling at his friend as they sat.

Ben laughed. "I don't know why you look so surprised to see me."

"Me neither, but I sure am glad you're here."

"Me too, brother."

Rick shifted to sit a little straighter in bed. "How long are you here, Ben?"

"Two weeks, or until I run out of money."

"You'll stay with us. No arguments."

Ben's smile slipped when he and Wade shared a look: Ben's was one of uncertainty and Wade's told him to just accept it. "I booked a room, so you don't have to worry about me."

"Indulge me," Rick insisted. "We've got room. Stay."

Wade nodded. "You should stay. It's all right."

Ben nodded once in return. "As long as you promise to tell me if you need me to go."

"Deal."

Lou perked up in her seat next to me on the couch. "We'll add one more to the list for dinner then."

Ben's brow rose, and he rested a hand on his flat belly. "Home cooked meals too? You guys are going to spoil me."

Rick laughed. "Get used to it. They're all in spoil mode. Watch out, or you might even get sponge baths."

"Only if I'm lucky," Ben said with a smirk.

"So," Lou started, crossing her long legs, "you two were stationed together in Afghanistan?"

Ben nodded, leaning back in his seat. "Deployed, for three years at a tiny base in an outer province. I never missed civilization so much."

"What," Wade cut in, "not a fan of packs of wild dogs?"

Ben snorted. "Yeah, nothing like thirty starving dogs running after you. I thought I was done for a couple of times."

"Wild dogs?" Lou asked, brows up.

"It's the wilderness. Not for the faint of heart. Life on a FOB isn't exactly glamorous," Ben said with a chuckle.

"FOB?" Sadie's brow quirked.

"Forward Operating Base," Wade explained. "We built huts out of wood for those who thought they were too good for a tent."

"You didn't have beds or anything?" Her words were disbelieving.

Wade shrugged. "Just threw a sleeping bag over a shipping crate, or some of us built beds, but for the most part, nah."

Ben shook his head. "I still have nightmares about veggie omelet MREs."

"Psh, those aren't near as bad as Captain Country Chicken."

Ben made a face. "I only had one of those once, and you're right. It was the worst, only because it would burn your colon to the ground."

"Remember when Billings showed up as our new 'Terp? You fed him an omelet, and he only made it three bites before puking."

"Oh, man," Ben said with a laugh. "I forgot about old Billings. He was a damn good interpreter."

"Was?" Sophie asked, and Ben's face tightened.

"IED."

My stomach sank, and my eyes found Wade, imagining all the things he'd seen, all that he'd been through, the normalization of war. But his eyes were on Ben as he changed the subject.

"Germany is easy though. Feels like the Ritz compared to life on a FOB."

"So much beer. I actually had to start working out again because my pants were tight." He leaned back and patted his stomach for emphasis.

"Ah, to live in Europe, though," Rick said wistfully.

"Where would you have lived?" I asked Rick with a smile.

"Well," he looked up to the ceiling in thought, "Rome, I think. For a while at least. I'd have liked to move around, a city a year. Abby and I went after we graduated. Best summer of my life."

An idea sparked in my heart. I prodded for details. "What other places do you wish you could see again?"

He sighed, still smiling, and Wade caught my eye, his face full of curiosity. "So many. Fiji — we went there on our honeymoon. Or the Adirondacks. We had a cabin there, do you remember?" he asked his children, who brightened at the mention.

"We haven't been there in so long," Sadie said.

"I remember camping in those woods as a boy," Rick continued. "Some of my most cherished childhood memories were made there."

The doorbell rang, and Wade stood to answer it, coming back with the nurse, effectively clearing the room while she went about her business. I made my way into the kitchen to make coffee, and everyone followed, none of us knowing where else to go. But I was giddy as the idea not only formed, but bloomed.

Sadie pulled down mugs as I filled up the pot.

"I have an idea," I said quietly, smiling at the prospect of what I was about to propose.

"What's that?" Sadie asked as Wade and Ben sat down at the island next to her.

"What if we bring all of his favorite places to him?"

A slow smile spread across Sophie's face. "Elliot, you're a genius."

"We can bring Italy to him. Fiji. Camping. We can get a tent, roast marshmallows. Recreate his memories. Make new ones. Do you think he'd like it?"

As I looked everyone over, Wade smiled at me, and I found I couldn't breathe. "It's perfect," he said.

I felt bright, as if I were shining. "Then let's start today. We'll need a few days to plan it, I think. We can get a planetarium to project stars. Oh!" I straightened up with excitement. "Christmas trees."

Sophie nodded enthusiastically and hiss-whispered, "*Yes!* I bet we can find some plastic trees on clearance from the holidays."

I leaned in, smiling conspiratorially. "We'll bring him a forest."

Sadie beamed. "He's going to be so surprised. It's brilliant."

"I hope he loves it. I hope it makes him happy," I said, already tallying the things I'd need in my head, excited to have a way to celebrate him, to bring him joy while we could.

We sat in the kitchen, drinking coffee and making plans. Wade was happy and smiling, the afternoon forgotten, his apology lightening my heart. His laughter, his joy at Ben and the camping trip — it reminded me of a time years ago when he was like this every day. I wondered again over all the things that had changed him, hardened him, wondered just how bad it had been to erase him so completely.

The nurse came in a little while later to let us know she was leaving and Rick was resting. With my new objective, I decided to leave, anxious to get started so we could give him our gift as soon as possible as the little voice in the back of my mind whispered, *Time.*

I felt lighter, happier as I walked home. What a strange day it had been — I recounted the moments. Meeting Ben. Our surprise for Rick. Wade. Walking with him, touching him, being seen by him in a way that no one had in years, even if it was hard, even though it hurt.

The invisible girl, visible again, but only to him.

Of course, the second I opened the door to Mary's, I was invisible again. I found everyone in the living room, sisters and father on the couch talking while Charlie sat in his armchair, chatting with his friend Jack, who lay on the ground on his back covered in giggling children.

I smiled at the scene, and Sammy chanted *Uncle Jack!* until Jack tickled him. Dad shot him a look at the burst of noise, but Jack didn't seem to mind, making punching sounds as he tickle-assaulted the little boy. Jack smiled when he saw me.

"Hey, Elliot."

Maven squealed and ran over to me, and I picked her up.

"Hi," I said before kissing her on the cheek. Jack sat up, and Sammy proceeded to climb up his back.

"How's Rick?" Charlie asked, and my sisters and father quieted down to listen.

"He's good. His speech has improved, and there was a lot of excitement today. A friend of Wade's flew in from Germany to stay for a while and help out. Rick seemed so happy to have everyone there."

Jack's eyes softened. "I'm really sorry to hear what happened, Elliot."

"Thank you," I answered politely as I took a seat on the floor with Maven, who toddled off, picked up a Barbie from her little toy box, and brought it to me with a new dress to wear. Dad started talking to Mary again, still without acknowledging me, and I was thankful for Charlie and Jack's company at least. "What are you doing over, Jack?"

He smirked at Charlie, eyes darting to Mary for a flash before landing on me. "Charlie called in the cavalry," he said under his breath.

"Ah," I said with a chuckle. "My condolences."

"The things I do for love."

He smiled a handsome smile from his long face, his blue eyes twinkling. I'd known him for years, and though he'd never paid me much attention, he'd always been kind, providing friendly conversation and sometimes a safe haven from the exhaustion of socializing with my sister. When it was the four of us, it was easier — Mary was outnumbered. Rather than argue with us, she drank.

"So your friend's dad, he's really doing okay?"

"He's in good spirits," I answered as I worked the Barbie's stiff hands through blue, sparkly dress sleeves. "We're just spending as much time with him as we can. We came up with a plan today to bring the world to him, starting with an indoor camping trip. I've got a list of things to get for it."

Jack perked up. "Oh yeah? I've got a ton of gear, what do you need?"

"A tent, sleeping bags, camping chairs, that sort of thing. I want to get some other stuff too, like there's a shop that sells candles that smell like pine trees, and I need to find a star projector for the ceiling. We want to turn the library into the Adirondacks."

Jack smiled with appreciation. "That's brilliant. I've got a lot of the gear, and I think I know where we can get what I don't have. When were you wanting it by?"

"Tomorrow is the day to get everything together, if we can. Then I think we're planning on actually setting it up the next night."

"Well, I'm off work tomorrow. Want to go together? We can go shop, then swing by my place and grab everything."

"Oh, that would be so great." Relief settled in at the thought of having a little help and company.

He winked at me. "It's a date. I'll be here at ten."

I felt myself blush with surprise, certain he didn't mean it like it sounded. "Thanks, Jack."

"Anytime."

Dad and my sisters were quiet, listening to us. Dad looked approving with wall-eyed Rodrigo on his lap shivering, and Beth looked at me like she couldn't understand why anyone would even be talking to me. Mary had an unreadable expression on her face, which she hid behind her wine glass as she took a long pull.

Jack cleared his throat. "Well, I really should head out."

Charlie shot him a look. "Please. Stay for dinner."

"Oh, I don't know. I wouldn't want to impose." He flipped Sammy over his shoulder and into his lap to commence his tickling again.

"It wouldn't be an imposition," Mary added sweetly. "We're having roasted chicken, and I'm sure we'll have leftovers for days if you don't stay and eat."

He shrugged. "Twist my arm."

Mary smiled. "Great. Elliot, since you're home, do you mind cooking?"

I smiled back, ignoring the fact that she'd placed that responsibility on me deliberately. I was grateful for another room I could occupy, complete with four walls and no father. The no father part was certain — I didn't think he even knew how to use an oven.

"I don't mind at all," I said as I stood, depositing Maven in Charlie's lap.

"Need some help?" Jack asked.

"Oh, I'll manage."

"You sure? I make a mean herb rub, and I love to help."

I laughed. "Well, if you really want to rub herbs, I won't be the one to stop you."

"Thank you for not dashing my dreams. Lead the way." He extended his hand for me to go first as my immediate family watched, gaping, even the dog. Well, all except for Charlie, who looked pleased as punch.

The kitchen was quiet, and I turned on music as Jack retrieved the chicken from the fridge, making it do a little dance once he got it into the dish. He rolled up his sleeves and melted butter to go along with those mysterious herbs, chatting with me as he rubbed the bird down, all while I peeled potatoes and carrots.

It was nice, the time spent not thinking about Rick, not thinking about my family, just making dinner and laughing with a friend. It had been a long time since a man had been so companionable, putting himself in my space with intention, though I didn't know what exactly that was. I hoped it was just that he knew I needed a friend, because I did. I was certain it was nothing more than that, and that was lucky — I didn't know how to give of myself just then. But deep down, I reveled in the thought of being wanted, of being seen by someone who wanted to see me, who saw me without pain in his eyes. And in that, the moment was a rare gift.

WADE

I stood in the guest room on the lower floor, unable to stop smiling as I shuffled things around to make room for Ben, my surprise over his arrival still fresh hours later. He seemed to be pretty proud of himself for pulling the whole thing off, and so was I. My burden had been lifted by his presence alone.

He looked around the room. "Well, I've gotta say, this is way better than the Airbnb I booked."

"And this way, you're close."

"And fed," he added.

I chuckled as I pushed a couple of boxes into the hallway. "Yes, and fed."

Ben sat on the bed and bounced a couple of times before inspecting the comforter. "So, Elliot's pretty."

"Just gonna jump right in, are you?"

He shrugged. "Would you expect anything else?"

I sighed as I leaned against the doorframe. "No, but I can hope."

"Were you guys somewhere together when you came home or

was your showing up together just a coincidence?"

"We were on a walk. An uncomfortable walk."

"Why'd you agree to go if it was so uncomfortable?"

"I asked her in the first place."

One of his eyebrows rose in question.

"I don't even know why I asked her to walk with me. I just …" I pursed my lips, wetting them from the inside. "Everything is just so *intense*. With Dad, with her. So much has happened, and I can't sort through how I feel about any of it, partly because it changes from one second to the next. Things with her are …" I fumbled for the words again, frustrated that I couldn't verbalize how I felt. "Things are changing, which I knew was inevitable. It's part of why I don't want to be around her. How am I supposed to deal with how I feel about her right now?"

"I don't know, but it doesn't look like you're ignoring them very well either."

"No, I'm not. I want to be around her, but I don't know how. I want to ignore her, but I don't know how to do that either. So I asked her to walk with me and it was a disaster."

"Define disaster. Like, trip-and-fall-with-a-side-of-accidental-groping disaster? Or like a why-did-you-break-my-heart-and-ruin-my-life kind of disaster?"

"Closer to the latter, though with less honesty." I ran a hand over my face, feeling the unfamiliar scratch of stubble against my palm. "I don't know how to hold up the versions of who she was, who she is, and who I remember against each other to figure out what's real."

He nodded thoughtfully. "That's fair. So take it one day at a time and sort it out as you go."

"But today I pushed her. I hurt her. I said too much because I don't know how to be around her. I have too many feelings and none of them agree with each other."

"But you did say you want to be around her, right?"

I thought back to her hands in mine last night, even back to that afternoon when she was pressed against my chest, my words sinking into her heart as I spoke them. "She brought me comfort in a moment when I needed it very much. I can't deny that I still care about her —" The word love was on the tip of my tongue, too strong, too real. "— but I'm still hurt and angry and …" I huffed and ran a hand through my hair. "Nothing makes sense. I'm winging everything."

"You've got to just talk to her."

"Easy. I'll get right on that."

"I mean it, Wade. All that stuff you don't want to say, you've just got to say it, and then you've got to listen to her say all that stuff you don't want to hear."

I squirmed, shifting to offset the feeling. "I don't know how. I've bottled it all up for so long that I don't even know where to begin."

"Well, then you just have to jump." The honesty in his face was a small comfort. He believed his words, and he believed in me, even if it wasn't warranted.

He had faith. I didn't.

"We'll see, I suppose."

"Look, it's the perfect opportunity. She's busy tomorrow, so you've got a whole day to psych yourself up, and then she'll be here the whole day after. There will be time at some point." I must not have looked convinced, because he added, "Just think about it."

I didn't agree, but I didn't disagree, just switched gears to making sure he had what he needed before I ducked out of his room to ascend to mine. As I lay in bed in the dark, I imagined saying all the things I wanted to say, imagined every scenario, and one decision rose to the top of them all: it would have to be said, and it would have to be heard. And I held the power to take that step, even if it took me over the edge and into the sweet darkness of nothing.

NEVER
PREPARED

And when you think
That you have found
Your feet planted firmly
And your heart sound
That is when the moment
You trip,
Fall,
And hit the ground.

—M. WHITE

ELLIOT

I *was in my room when* I heard the knock on the door at ten sharp, right on time. I smiled to myself, glad I'd have Jack's company while I ran my errands, thankful to know I wouldn't have to talk about Rick or bear the responsibility of anyone else like I did when I was at the Winters' house. It was just a simple morning with a friend.

I grabbed my bag and headed up the stairs, surprised to find Mary in the doorway, hissing at Jack, who straightened up and smiled when he saw me. Mary turned around, her face hard.

"I need you home tonight," she snapped. "I'm on the night shift, and Charlie's got work to do."

I nodded. "No problem, I'll pick up the kids and take care of dinner."

She was scowling at me, but I barely registered it, just stepped past her and onto the stoop.

"Morning," Jack said with a smile. "You ready?"

I smiled back. "I am, thanks."

He looked over my shoulder at my sister. "See you around, Mary."

"Whatever," she popped and shut the door.

"Wonder what's gotten into her," he said as we walked down the steps.

I chuckled and adjusted my hat. "Who knows."

"She treats you like that a lot."

"Most of the time."

He shook his head, eyes on me. "Why do you put up with it?"

I smiled over at him, not minding the judgment. "Charlie asked me the same thing the other day."

"Well, he's a smart guy."

I sighed, knowing it was futile to try to explain but trying all the same. "Mary's harmless. She's demanding, sure, but … well, she's just *Mary*. I don't take it personally, though everyone else seems to on my behalf." I gave him a look, softened by a small smile.

"Can you blame us for being concerned for your well-being?"

"No, and I appreciate it. It reminds me that I'm cared for, but you have to understand that this is how my life has always been. So I've learned to find joy where I can."

"That makes me sad, Elliot. To think that you endure people who treat you with no respect just to be noble."

I frowned. "That's not why. I barely interact with Mary most of the time — I'm working at the bookstore or alone with the kids every day, caring for them in the evenings, and then writing when they're asleep."

"Sounds lonely."

It is. I brushed the thought away. "I have Sophie and my friends at the bookstore. And anyway, I don't have to *endure* much at all usually — it's not so bad when my father is gone. Mary is easy enough to ignore. All of them are, really, if one puts one's mind to it."

He chuckled at that.

"You have to believe me when I say that they've always been this way. Unhappy. Dissatisfied."

He considered my words. "But you're not?"

"I am right now, but not because of them."

Jack nodded. "He means a lot to you."

Wade. But Jack couldn't know about Wade. "Rick?" I clarified anyway.

"He's your mentor, right?"

"You could say that. He's inspired me, believed in me always. Convinced me to go to college and get my degree, though I still have no real use for it. He's the reason I write."

"Poetry, right? Ever published anything?"

I brushed my hair from my face. "No, not quite brave enough for that yet."

"Do you let anyone read it?" he prodded with a mischievous look on his face.

"Sometimes."

He smiled playfully. "Would you let me read it?"

I smiled back. "Maybe someday, if you prove yourself to be trustworthy."

"Me? Untrustworthy?" he asked with mock drama.

I laughed. "I've seen you play cards."

"That's fair," he said with a smirk.

"So, where to first?"

"Well," he started, "there's a toy store where I think we can find your planetarium. I've got most of the gear, which we can get at my place, but there are a few things I don't have. So let's hit up the little shop where I get my gear."

"Sounds great."

"Maybe we can grab lunch too. I should feed you, since we're on a date and all."

I laughed, but he didn't, he just kept smiling at me. "You're serious."

He shrugged. "Why wouldn't I be?"

I blinked, feeling a flush in my cheeks. "Well, I don't know. I've known you for years and you've never …"

"Hit on you? Well, I had a girlfriend before. But I've always noticed you, Elliot."

Discomfort niggled at me on the wings of surprise, and with a lack of anything better to say, I deferred to my manners. "Thank you."

"You really are beautiful. I don't think you know it. You look a lot like Mary but smaller, softer. Kinder."

More blinking. "That's sweet, Jack, but—"

He sucked in a breath. "I'm about to get shot down, aren't I?"

My cheeks were warm, and I opened my mouth to speak, but he saw me coming and headed me off.

"How about we don't label it? Let's just hang out, grab some lunch, and pick up what you need. Everything else will sort itself out. What do you say?"

He looked so hopeful, so sweet that I couldn't say no. Instead, I smiled and gave him the only answer I could.

"Deal."

The day went by quickly, full of easy conversation. I'd always liked Jack but had never really thought about him in the way he seemed to be thinking about me. I wasn't sure I was thinking about him that way now, but he was so charming. So easy.

But as we walked from store to store, from café to coffee shop, I tried to consider him, tried to think about what it would be like to date him. It wasn't hard to imagine; he insisted on buying my lunch, guided me through doors with his hand on the small of my back, smiled at me like I was the only girl in the world. But that consideration kept bringing me back to Wade, and the comparison of the two left me in a lurch. Wade could walk into a room and command my heart and soul without speaking a word. I'd been around Jack a hundred times, and now for an afternoon where he touched me and smiled at me, and still I hadn't found myself with feelings for him other than the fondness of a friend.

At one point in the afternoon, I found myself frustrated, wondering why I couldn't just go for him. On paper, he was perfect: a successful entrepreneur, charmer, and overall beautiful man. In my heart, he was lacking; there was no spark, nothing to inspire my feelings for him to grow.

Maybe Wade had broken me more than I'd even known. Maybe I wasn't capable of love.

Even with my mind drifting, we spent an amiable day together, finding everything we needed. Jack wouldn't let me buy anything from the camping store and paid for it himself, insisting that he'd use it that spring. And by the time we were finished there, it was nearly time to pick up the kids.

We weren't far from the school, and Jack was in the middle of a story that had me laughing up at him. When I turned to look ahead of me, I slowed, stumbling a little.

Wade stood in front of us, hands deep in the pockets of his wool coat, collar flipped and brow low. He looked angry, angry and hurt and silent as stone.

"W-Wade," I stammered, my cheeks flushing as we approached him.

He nodded, jaw flexing as his cool eyes landed on Jack.

"We, ah, we were just shopping for tomorrow night," I offered, feeling strangely ashamed, as if I'd been caught, as if I owed him an explanation.

"Same thing," he said, two gruff words. "Had to pick up a few things."

He watched me with the weight of a thousand years, and no one spoke for a long moment.

Jack smiled amiably and extended a hand. "How's it going? I'm Jack."

Wade took his hand, gripping it hard as he pumped once and let it go. "Wade," was all he offered.

Another awkward moment passed. "So, I'm guessing you're Sophie's brother?" Jack asked.

He nodded, a single bob of his chin. My heart thumped its warning; the softness I'd seen in him yesterday had vanished, taking my hope with it, leaving behind a cold shell of a man, hardened to steel.

"I'm sorry to hear about your dad," Jack continued as if everything were normal. Maybe to everyone but Wade and me, it seemed that way. "Hopefully the stuff we got today will bring him some happiness."

"Thanks," Wade said, the word flat, colorless. "I'd better be going." He turned his gaze to me, the chill slipping all the way into my marrow. "See you tomorrow, Elliot."

"See you," I echoed feebly as Jack touched the small of my back.

"Nice to meet you," Jack said, but Wade's eyes were fixed on Jack's arm.

He said nothing, just gave another curt nod before blowing past us.

Jack watched him over his shoulder, guiding me forward with his hand on my back, a protective gesture that gave me no strength. "Well, isn't he cheery."

"His father's dying," I said quietly.

His eyes were still on Wade's back. "That's not really an excuse to be rude."

I didn't have the heart to say that it was because of me. The moments we shared, those glimpses of him that I caught when he let me in, let me through, it was all erased in an instant. We'd barely spoken, had barely seen each other, and now he acted as if he held claim to me, as if I'd ruined him all over again. As if I still held the power over him that he held over me.

And the worst part of it all: after an entire day with a handsome, charming man who wanted me, with a single sighting of Wade, I realized I would never get over him. Not as long as I lived.

$$\boxed{\text{W A D E}}$$

I couldn't stop walking.

My tasks were forgotten, my list forgotten, wiped out at the sight of Elliot with him.

Jack.

The word was a curse as I walked aimlessly around the Upper West, replaying the meeting over and over again as if I could will another outcome into existence. As if I could erase the image of her smiling at him. As if I could eradicate the sound of her laughter. As if I could break the hand that touched her back.

Coming home to find Ben had shifted something in me, given me hope, given me strength. Given me purchase against the shifting ground I found myself on. All night, I'd thought about the possibility of her. All day, I'd considered what I would say. I'd let myself hope, hope that was dashed by the sight of her by his side.

She'd moved on, and the realization left me reeling.

I was stupid to think she'd never gotten over me like I hadn't gotten over her. It hadn't even crossed my mind that she could have a boyfriend, that she could have been dating someone. That someone could be interested in her, and she in him. Because the way she looked at him, the way he was smiling at her — it all spoke of happiness, togetherness.

It never even occurred to my one-track mind because I'd never moved on, never imagined I could or would. Never even tried. And now that it had occurred to me, I couldn't shake the maddening thought of her with another man.

Maybe he was better for her. He was here, after all, available. I was unavailable, and I would be leaving again. Always leaving. If she cared about him, I'd let her be. There would be no telling her how I felt, not if she was happy. I wouldn't get in the way of her happiness.

But that didn't mean I was happy about it.

I turned the corner and found myself on my street, my feet carrying me home on their own, and I stormed into the house, not sure what else to do. It was quiet — I found Sophie on the couch next to Dad, both napping. Sadie was nowhere to be seen, and I heard voices in the kitchen … Lou and Ben, I realized as I approached.

Lou was laughing, and she laid a hand on Ben's arm where it rested on the island counter. He leaned toward her, smiling, and relief slipped over me at her redirected attention.

She caught sight of me as I walked into the room and pulled her hand back, cheeks flushing. "Wade," she said, and Ben looked over his shoulder, frowning when he saw me.

"You okay?"

I ran a hand through my hair. "Yeah."

He gave me a look that said he knew I was full of shit.

Lou slipped off her stool. "I should get going. Dinner's in the fridge with heating instructions. I'll, ah, see you tomorrow?"

I gave her a nod and pulled open the refrigerator door, reaching for a beer.

"Let me walk you out," Ben said as he followed her out, hand on her back.

I twisted the cap off and took a long drink, leaning on the counter with damp hands for support.

They chatted in the entryway for a minute before I heard the door open and close, and seconds later, Ben was getting a beer of his own. He didn't say anything until he was seated across from me.

"What happened? Is … is this about Lou? I didn't think … I mean, if you're into her, I'll back off, no questions."

I huffed and rolled my eyes. "My cousin? No. This isn't about my cousin."

He looked relieved, pointing the neck of his beer at me. "Cousin by marriage. That was a reasonable question."

I took another heavy drink, nearly draining it before setting it on the counter. "I'm not interested in Lou. She's all yours."

He smiled. "Thank you. I haven't wanted to bring it up with everything going on, but ..." He rubbed the back of his neck, his cheeks flushing. "I'm into her. Really into her."

I blinked, surprised.

I could tell when he started rambling just how bad it was. "I asked her early on about you — I thought you guys might have had a thing by the way she acted around you. But she said it was just a crush, that she didn't really get it before me." He paused. "Do you believe in love at first sight?"

I nodded, feeling my lips flatten at the memory of Elliot, at the memory of hope. "I do."

Ben shook his head in wonder. "It felt like that. Like I'd been zapped by electricity. Like there was no one in the room but me and her. I didn't think it was real, but now I'm almost certain I was wrong."

"I'm happy for you and Lou."

He sighed. "Thanks. It feels good. I only wish I didn't have to leave so soon." There was pain and worry behind his eyes that I knew all too well.

"I have a feeling you'll make it."

His smile was earnest. "I hope so." He leaned on the surface of the bar, his smile falling as he spoke. "So if you're not upset about Lou ..."

My jaw flexed, teeth clenching almost painfully. "I saw Elliot."

He waited. "You've seen her every day this week."

"I saw her *with a guy*."

"Ah," he said knowingly and with lament. "Boyfriend?"

"I don't know. Seemed that way."

"Did Sophie mention she was seeing someone?"

"We don't discuss Elliot. Ever." I killed my beer and walked over to the fridge for another.

"Well, maybe it's nothing. Maybe he's just a friend."

I twisted the cap and dropped it on the counter with a clink as I took a swig, wishing I could drown the part of me that cared.

"Doesn't matter," I said, wishing it did.

Ben watched me, and I avoided his eyes, fixing my gaze across the room at nothing in particular.

"If it doesn't matter, why are you upset?" he asked.

"Because." I paused, wishing I could leave it at that, but there was no hiding from Ben. "I thought … I thought she felt like I did. I thought she couldn't be with anyone else." The words were quiet, my eyes still distant. "But it was just me. She found a way to move on. Why couldn't I?"

He didn't answer for a moment, and I'm not sure I expected one as I dug through my feelings, the sensation like cold hands through muddy earth.

"You loved her, and you still do. What you've been through, what *we've* been through, the war, the isolation … it changes us, makes it harder to let go. It's rigid, our lives. And you never stopped loving her."

I leaned on the counter and dropped my head to my hands, slipping my fingers into my hair. "I don't know how to stop."

"But you don't want to be with her?"

"What I want isn't an option. What I want died seven years ago. What I want doesn't want me. I made sure of that a long time ago."

His brows knit together. "You don't know that for sure because you still haven't talked to her."

I didn't answer, just pulled in a long breath through my nose and let it out.

"Ask Sophie about the guy."

"And what good does that do me?"

"It'll ease your mind. Or not. But then you'll know for sure."

I lifted my head to meet his eyes. "And then what do I do? Ask her out on a date?" I shook my head at the ridiculousness of the thought. "Two issues: There are too many problems between us and not enough solutions, and I'm not here for her. I'm here for him." I pointed toward the library. "I shouldn't even be thinking about her. I shouldn't want her, not now. It's impossible, Ben."

"Nothing's impossible. Do you really think there's no way to bridge the gap here? You haven't spoken to her in seven years. The last real conversation you had, you broke up. You were eighteen. You don't think there's even a slight chance you could talk? Forgive each other? Make amends?"

I shook my head, eyes on the surface of the island. "You don't understand. It's not just what she said or what I said — it's deeper than that." I paused, gathering my thoughts. "It wasn't what was done, it was what wasn't done. And now I've changed, and so has she. There's no going back."

"Then go forward."

I shook my head, looking away. "It's not that easy."

"Sometimes it's exactly that easy."

I blinked at him, hearing echoes of Elliot's voice, wondering for the first time if I should take my own advice.

LIMBO

The in-between
The purgatory
Of floating
Like vapor
And mist
Uncontained.

—M. WHITE

ELLIOT

The next morning, we sat on the floor in the living room as Sammy and Maven laughed from Jack's back. It was early, but Jack had insisted he come over before I took the kids to school to bring everything for the camp-in tonight, since we hadn't had time to pick it up the day before.

I couldn't help but smile as Jack whinnied, crawling around in circles. Dad laughed before taking a sip of his gin, then glanced at me meaningfully.

"I like him, Elliot." The words were pointed and direct, obvious and embarrassing.

But I smiled through the flush in my cheeks. "I guess he's not half-bad."

Jack shot me a smile and a wink before he neighed, raising his arms, and the kids squealed.

Dad sat there on the couch in his bathrobe, nursing his gin at eight-thirty in the morning, scheming — I could see it in the arch of his brow and the tick of the corner of his lips. I had to admit, I was surprised he'd nudge Jack to me before Beth. It was all an enigma to me. They all were, really.

I found myself longing for simple relationships like I had with

Sophie and Rick. I knew it didn't have to be so hard, but I struggled to find anyone whom I could be myself with, freely and without apology, friends without strings or expectations or motives.

I also longed for Dad to go back to Miami.

"Have you been enjoying your visit, Dad?" I asked, wondering if I could get any information out of him on the matter.

"Very much," he answered, two sugary sweet words that held an edge of some meaning I couldn't quite grasp.

"Have you decided how much longer you'll be here?"

He scowled at that, glaring at me. "Why? Already tired of me? We've only just gotten here, and you're already pushing us out the door. And it's not even your door!"

Mercifully, Charlie walked in, dressed in a suit with his coat hung over his arm, defusing the situation with his presence. He smiled, surprised when he saw his friend. "Jack? What are you doing here, man?"

"Came by to bring the gear for Elliot."

"Aren't you chivalrous?"

He flipped Maven off his back, setting her on her feet, then Sammy just the same. "I'm a regular old hero."

Dad admired Jack as he stood. "So tall. And handsome. Tell me you're rich, too."

Jack laughed awkwardly and ran a hand through his hair. "Thanks, Mr. Kelly. I do all right."

"Mmm. Quite a catch." Another look at me over the top of his glass.

I ignored him. "Come on, kids. Ready for school?"

They cheered and giggled, following me into the entryway.

"We still on for drinks tonight?" Charlie asked as I put coats on the kids.

"At six, right?" Jack pulled on his coat, glancing at me. "Can you get away with Elliot gone?"

"Mary will survive."

Jack laughed just as the front door opened. "I want to be in the room when you tell her that."

"Tell me what?" Mary asked, looking haggard as she walked into the entry. Her eyes narrowed when she saw Jack. "What are you doing here?"

"Good to see you too," he answered happily and brushed past her to stand next to me. "I was just bringing some stuff by for Elliot and was going to walk her and the kids to school."

She glanced at me with a look that would have withered anyone else, but I went about my business, immune. They say that when you care, it gives them power. And she had no power over me.

She didn't have a chance to respond before Charlie jumped in.

"We were just talking about tonight. Elliot was here last night, and she's got a big thing at Rick's tonight, so she's off the clock. Jack and I are getting drinks, so you've got the kids this afternoon and dinner tonight."

Her cheeks flamed, her eyes hard as she glared at Charlie. "I just worked all night and you dump this on me as soon as I walk in the door? What the fuck, Charlie?"

Sammy jumped in a circle saying *fuck* over and over again. I bent down to whisper in his ear that it was bad manners for a little boy to say that word, and he nodded, quieting down.

Charlie fumed, brows low. "We had plans already, all of us. So handle it."

She turned on her heel and stormed away. "This is so fucking typical. Selfish assholes," she said as she blew by, and Charlie followed her in a gust of heat and anger.

"*We're* selfish?" he asked as he made his way up the stairs on her heels.

"Yes, *you* are selfish. Elliot's selfish. You don't give a shit about anyone but yourselves." Her voice grew thin as she walked into her room.

"That's fucking rich, Mary," Charlie slammed the door, muffling their argument, and Jack and I shared a look.

Dad stood, one eyebrow up. "How unsavory. Trouble in paradise, I suppose."

"I suppose," Jack echoed before picking up Maven. "You ready, princess?"

"Weady!" she cheered, and we filed out the door, leaving the mess behind us.

I breathed easier as soon as the door was closed.

"You okay?" Jack asked.

"Fine, thanks."

"They fight like that much? I've never seen it like that before."

I shrugged, not really wanting to talk about it. "Sometimes. Mary's just tired. She's the worst after she works a night shift."

He made a noncommittal sound.

"You work today?" I asked, anxious to change the subject.

"I do. Heading there after this."

"It must be nice, having your own business, making your own hours."

He chuffed. "That's one of the perks, but running a business is way more work than anyone tells you. But I have a problem with authority, so this is pretty much my only career option."

I chuckled.

"What about you? Planning on nannying forever?"

"God, I hope not," I said with a laugh. "My dream is to write, have my work published, but I'm not ready yet. I'm kind of … in limbo. Pretty much the only thing I can do with a literature degree is write or get certified to teach."

"I think you'd be a great teacher. You're patient, kind. I'd murder a room full of kids — wouldn't last a week."

"Oh, I don't know about that. You're great with Maven and Sammy."

He shrugged. "Just 'cause they're cute. But really, I'd rather be at the bike shop amidst the smell of rubber and grease."

"Kinky."

He laughed — it was such a nice sound — and looked down at me, smiling. "Go to dinner with me, Elliot."

My cheeks warmed, and I looked down at my feet as we walked. "Jack …"

"You keep surprising me, and I'm not easily surprised. But you … you're unexpected. I know … well, I know now's not the best time, but humor me." He slowed to a stop, grabbing my hand to stop me too. "Say yes. It's just a meal. I promise, I won't even try to kiss you. I'll wait for you to make the first move — I'm a patient guy."

I sighed, trying to find the right words, wishing I felt the undeniable need to give him the answer he wanted. But I didn't. "Thank you for the offer, but with everything going on with Rick … I just can't right now."

He nodded, looking only a little crestfallen. "I get that. But like I said: I'm a patient guy. I can wait."

I wished I could have told him the truth about who possessed my heart, but it was too true to admit to him, too real to say out loud.

He ran his thumb over my knuckles. "In the meantime, I'll help you scavenge things for Rick and be around if you need to be rescued from your sister."

I smiled at that. "Thanks, Jack."

"You've got it, Elliot." He let go of my hand, and we walked for a moment in silence. "So, I guess broody guy will be there tonight too."

I tried to focus on the rhythm of my feet on the pavement and Sammy's small hand in mine. "Yes, Wade will be there."

"I asked Charlie about him — he said you guys used to date?"

"That was a long time ago," I answered softly.

"Was he always like that? So … angry?"

"No. Not before. But he's been through so much. War. His dad." *Me.*

Jack shook his head. "You excuse everyone for treating you the way they do, did you know that?"

A defensive wind blew inside of me. "Because there are reasons, valid reasons, and I'm not so self-important as to think that I'm above their feelings."

"But what about your feelings?"

"It's not about me. That's my point."

He clenched his jaw, his voice hard. "But they treat you like you're not important at all."

"That's not entirely true. But I don't need their validation."

Another shake of his head. "I just hate that they treat you the way they do."

I stopped in the middle of the sidewalk, fuming. "Are you suggesting that I'm a doormat?"

He flushed and rubbed the back of his neck. "No, I didn't mean it that way."

"It sounds that way. It *sound*s like you're saying that because I don't stand up to them that I'm weak. But here's the thing — there's no point. Arguing will not change their behavior, and it helps no one, especially not me. I don't suffer very often because I don't let them hurt me. My being present is a choice. My enduring their judgment is a choice. *My* choice, and therein lies my power. I stay for the kids. I stay because, believe it or not, Mary and Charlie have helped me, and I repay that gladly. So my sister is condescending and demanding, just like my father. They've always been this way, and I've always been the way I am. I have my reasons, but I want you to understand that this is my choice. I endure enough judgment from them — I would really rather not receive it from you too."

His face was long, eyes sad and apologetic. "I'm sorry, Elliot. You're right. It's none of my business. I think … I think I just wanted to know that you had fight in you, and that if you wanted to use it, you could."

"Thank you." My heart hammered against my ribs at the confrontation. We started walking again, and I felt strange, better, stronger for having spoken up.

I wondered over why I'd said it, a brash rush of emotion that I'd normally have felt and let pass through me. Was it because he wasn't one of the alleged oppressors? He was unaffiliated, safe. I wasn't blind to his points — in fact, they were completely valid, things I'd considered myself so many times over the course of my life.

Did my family weaken me? Possibly. Did they take advantage of me? Definitely. But I imagined arguing with Mary, and the thought held no promise. She would never change — none of them would. It was one thing to defend my own choices to someone sort of unaffiliated, like Jack. It was another thing entirely to convince Mary she'd done something to hurt me — she'd only blame me, tell me I was wrong for feeling the way I did. It was pointless, a waste of energy for an affirmation I didn't need.

The thought crossed my mind to leave, to remove myself from the situation entirely, because I knew it was toxic, whether I let it get to me or not. But imagining walking away from the kids set my heart on fire. Who would they turn to? Who would tuck them in and sing songs in the bathtub with them? I couldn't leave them with Mary alone to show them love, and Charlie would try, but he couldn't devote the time to them that I could. That was, if I even had somewhere to go, which I didn't.

And just like that, I was reminded of the corner I'd painted myself into.

Jack and I chatted a little before reaching the school, and we parted ways with my promise to text him to let him know how the camp-in went. And once the kids were safely in school, I was alone with my thoughts once again as I walked the blocks to the bookstore.

I smiled at the familiarity of the store when I walked through. An old Shins album played over the speakers, and I headed to the back to put my things away, stopping in the office for my register drawer. Cam smiled up at me from her desk.

"Hey, Elliot. How's everything going?"

"Good, thank you."

She handed me the plastic drawer full of money to count. "And your friend's dad?"

"He's well. We're throwing him a camping party tonight," I said with a smile, imagining the look on his face when he saw what we'd done. "Roasted marshmallows and stars and everything."

Cam smiled, propping her head on her hand. "That is a stellar idea."

I chuckled at the pun. "Thank you. It should be fun."

"Well, once things settle down, I'm going to hound you until you come to a singles night. The next one is an Austen party. We're having a costume contest and everything." She beamed, and I chuckled.

"I'm sure there will be *hordes* of men at this Jane Austen costume party."

"That's why it's also Viscount's Night — guys drink free before ten if they come in costume."

"That is genius."

"What can I say," she said theatrically, shaking her head like it was her burden. "This is my gift to the world. Well, this and getting people to tell me their secrets. Just yesterday I learned way more about Beau's foot fetish than I ever needed to know."

"Oh, my God," I said with a laugh.

"So, you're coming to the next one." She eyeballed me over the top of her glasses.

I sighed and turned my attention to the cash drawer. "We'll see."

She watched me for a second, assessing me. "Question."

"Answer."

"Who broke your heart?"

I blinked at her.

She waved a hand. "I'm sorry. You don't have to answer that. I'm also notorious for asking questions I don't need the answers to. It's just that I've been hurt too, and it took me a lot to get past it. I was … resistant to relationships for a long time, so … I get it. I mean, if that's what happened to you." Her hand waved again. "I'm rambling."

"It's okay. You're right," I said, surprising myself, still brave from finding my voice with Jack. "I was engaged a long time ago."

Her eyes widened. "I had no idea."

I nodded. "We were young, in high school, and my father didn't approve because of our age. We broke up when he left for the Army, and I didn't see him for a long time. Until just last week, actually. He's my best friend's brother. It's his father who's dying."

Her mouth popped open in surprise, and she covered it with her hand. "Oh, Elliot."

"And I think I'm still in love with him." The words were quiet, and I didn't know why I said them, the things I never said aloud. But she was safe in the sense that she was completely separate, unaffected, with only my best interest at heart. It hurt just as badly as I thought it would to speak the words, but I found comfort in the admission, an acknowledgement.

"Does he know?"

"I don't know. But it doesn't matter. There's just too much between us. Pain. Time. Change."

"Does he love you?"

I shook my head, my heart aching. "I can't know. Sometimes I think he does, and others …"

Her brows pinched together with sadness. "Elliot, that's …"

I tried to smile. "Honestly, it's all right. I wish things were different, but they're not."

She watched me for a beat. "You should talk to him."

A small laugh passed my lips. "I wrote him hundreds of letters when he left, and he never responded. That silence was my answer. And when we've tried to talk since he's been back, it's only devolved and dissolved into us hurting each other. It's over and done, years ago."

"But you love him. Maybe you're wrong. Maybe he loves you too, and if you guys just talked about it, everything would be fine. You could be together."

"It's so much more complicated than that."

She stood, her face quirked with purpose. "You've just got to find a way to tell him how you feel, that's all. At least find out for sure how he feels. Because look, what if you're wrong? What if there *is* a way and you just haven't found it yet? You can't give up, not if you really love him. You've got to fight for him."

Out of nowhere, I felt exhausted, weighed down by the futility of Wade, of Rick, of my life. "I don't know how much fight I've got. If I fight and lose—"

"But what if you fight and win? Isn't it worth knowing?"

"Of course, but … Cam, it's not the right time."

She took my hands. "Just think about it, okay? Be open to the possibility, and take the opportunity, if it arises. Does that seem reasonable?"

I squeezed her hands, thankful for someone who believed in me more than I believed in myself. "Very reasonable."

She smiled. "Good. And see? People love telling me their secrets."

And I couldn't help but laugh.

TRUTH IN DARKNESS

In the darkness
In the cold grip of night
When the light disappears
And the shadows swallow the
sharp edges
This is where
The truth lies.

—M. WHITE

WADE

"**H**ere," *Sophie whispered as she* handed me a tent and a couple of sleeping bags. We stood in the foyer, Elliot passing things in from the stoop that she'd brought, all my concentration spent on keeping my eyes everywhere but on her. "Take this into the living room. We'll put it together there."

"I'll bring up the trees, too," I whispered back, and she nodded, smiling.

It was too much to resist, and I looked at her, but she wouldn't meet my eyes — hers were on the ground as she brought in a couple more sleeping bags. I walked past her to deposit everything in the living room. She looked fresh and crisp, her cheeks rosy, dark hair falling over her shoulders, and I watched her as I passed through the room again, willing her to look at me. But she wouldn't, just kept her eyes on her task or on Sophie as they moved things into the living room quietly.

She had every right to ignore me.

I trotted down the stairs and into the basement, grabbing the first Christmas tree I came to. We'd bought half a dozen on clearance the day before, and I'd hauled them all downstairs so they'd stay out of sight.

I kept on wishing things between us would get easier without effort, kept on hoping maybe she'd walk through the door and somehow I would be able to find the words. If nothing else, I hoped for cordiality at least, to be polite, pretend. It was so much easier to pretend.

And then again, it wasn't. Being around her sent me into a tailspin, my sense of direction lost, the horizon constantly moving. Still she called to me without saying a word.

Elliot.

My heart flinched at her name in my mind, thinking about the day before, thinking about how angry I'd been and how bad I'd been at hiding it. She hadn't forgotten about it either — she seemed smaller today, and it was my fault. I wanted to apologize, wanted to make it okay. But I kept hurting her.

The best thing I could do for her, the only way to protect her, was to keep my thoughts to myself. As if I could verbalize them anyway.

Time had burned my anger down to an aching smolder — as much as I hated seeing her with him, she wasn't mine. The takeaway: I had no rights to her, and being angry or jealous about it wouldn't change that fact. But Ben's words echoed in my thoughts. We hadn't talked, and I hadn't asked Sophie who Jack was or what he meant to her. It could be nothing. It could be everything.

The more striking thing about the moment was the overwhelming desire to be the one to make her laugh. I wanted to be the one to touch her back with possession. But the world in which that possibility existed seemed like fiction, so far beyond me, so far out of my reach.

Futility. That was the thing I felt the most.

I trotted up the stairs and set the first tree under the window in the living room, and Ben headed down to grab another. I followed, finding him waiting for me, standing in the middle of the space with an accusatory look on his face.

"Tell me you're going to talk to her."

I moved past him and picked up another box. "I don't know, Ben," I answered impatiently.

"Because *that* was ridiculous. You two aren't fooling anyone into believing that you don't care that the other one's in the room." He stepped in front of me as I tried to pass him. "You didn't ask Sophie, did you?"

"No, I didn't." I sidestepped him, but he blocked me again.

"Wade, you have to talk to her."

"*Ben*, it's no use."

He still wouldn't let me pass. "You have to at least *try*."

My teeth clenched and released as I put the box down, since I'd clearly not be leaving until I heard him out. But I didn't want to talk about it, and I didn't have to. "And say what?"

"You could start by apologizing."

I folded my arms across my chest. "Who says I need to apologize?"

"You're telling me you were the picture of politeness when you got Shanghai'd yesterday? Because if I'm going by her body language, I'd say you weren't pleasant."

I scowled at him.

"That's what I thought. Just talk to her. You don't have to profess your undying love, but an apology might be a good place to start."

I just stood there, scowling.

"Maybe it's nothing. Maybe that guy's nobody."

I still didn't budge.

"I'm serious." He kept going, wanting me to argue, but I could see I was wearing him down. "I mean, the tension between you two takes the temperature in the room down thirty degrees." He paused, waiting. Then, he sighed. "Do it for your dad then, if not for yourself. You wouldn't want your dad to be cold, would you?"

I narrowed my eyes. "Are you done?"

He rolled his eyes and moved for another tree. "Yeah, I'm done."

"Good," I said as I picked up my box and headed back up the stairs.

As I hauled the unwieldy boxes up the stairs one by one, I

acknowledged that he wasn't wrong. I also acknowledged that an apology — one which I owed her — might make her feel better, safer. When I considered apologizing for her, not for myself, I thought I might be able to do it. I longed for the hope I'd felt in bursts, wishing I could just hang on to it for a moment, wishing I could find a way to keep it.

I walked in with my last box to find Elliot struggling with the big bottom section of a tree. It hung on the box flap as she lifted it with all her strength and weight, and I set my box down, moving to her side. I took it from her, lifting it easily, and she blushed up at me, the expression hitting me in the heart — it wasn't longing I found in her face. It was regret.

"Thanks," she said softly.

"You're welcome." I moved to the base, placing it in the slot, and she began fluffing the branches as I watched, wondering if now was the time to speak or if I should wait. Uncertainty gripped me, fear skimming the edges. *Just jump.*

I opened my mouth to speak.

"What are you guys scheming?" Dad called from the library just down the hall.

Sophie smiled, shooting me a glance as she grabbed Sadie as she left the room. "Nothing, Dad. Need company?"

Ben set the last tree down next to the others and hung his hands on his hips, assessing the room. "I think we're going to need some coffee for this. I'll put a pot on."

And with a scheming smile, he left me there alone with Elliot.

She arranged the bottom branches as I reached into the box for the middle piece of the tree, popping it into the bottom piece with a snap, not knowing what to say, not sure how to broach anything with her anymore. There used to be a time when I could tell her anything. I wondered if I would ever know that trust again, and the thought gave me hope, the elusive, shimmering notion I wanted to feel so badly.

I picked up the tree top and stated it simply, since pretense escaped me. "I'm sorry. About yesterday." My voice was low, earnest.

She looked up at me, her bottomless eyes full of things I couldn't read.

I broke the connection when I placed the top of the tree in, pretending the scratchy plastic branches in my hand were difficult and fascinating to assemble. "It's been hard to know the right way to handle things, even small things, even things that have nothing to do with me. Especially when I'm caught off guard."

Her face was turned up to mine, but I kept my eyes on my hands, moving the branches around with no purpose. But when I finally got the courage to look at her, she'd turned her attention back to the tree.

"It's all right. I understand."

Do you? I thought to myself, wishing I could say it out loud.

Did she know I was sorry? Not just for yesterday, but for all the days before? Did she know I loved her still? I didn't know if I was prepared for the answer. I didn't know if I was ready to deal with the consequences of knowing.

"So, is Jack your …" The word *boyfriend* lodged itself in my throat.

"Friend," she finished for me.

Relief washed over me, but it was heavy with caution. I'd seen the way he looked at her, and it wasn't like that of one friend to another. Did she know he had a thing for her? Did she have feelings for him? Too many questions, and I couldn't ask a single one. It wasn't my place.

I cleared my throat, still working on the branches, and she stood and moved next to me.

"Here, let me show you how to do it so the tree looks more full." She demonstrated while I watched her, my eyes on the line of her small nose, the swell of her bottom lip, the curve of her chin.

I wanted her still, that fact was suddenly unbearable, now unburdened by the prospect of another man.

The only way I could have her was to beg for her forgiveness, apologize for pushing her, for leaving, for disappearing. But could we build on top of the wreckage of our past, or would it all fall apart, unstable and broken?

There was only one way to know — I had to try.

"Like this, see?" she said, her head tilted as she arranged the foliage, and I smiled at her, though she didn't know.

"Yes, I see."

The sunlight had shifted to hues of orange and red as we crept around the library, the air filled with classical music as Dad slept. The black sheets were nearly all hung around the room, and the furniture had been moved out and the trees moved in. The tent was in the other room, already assembled and waiting to be brought through the double doors when he woke.

Sophie and Sadie had brought in a tray of supplies for s'mores and hot dogs, downloaded a looping track of forest sounds to play, and Elliot brought wood for the fireplace and candles that smelled like pine, sleeping bags, and the planetarium. And as the sun dipped below the horizon, we were all set.

Elliot and I moved around each other silently, sharing moments: her hand brushing against mine, her lips blessing me with the smile I'd wished so much to see, and my heart squeezed and tightened and ached. Something had changed — Was it me? Was it her? — and I felt caught up in her at the prospect of forgiveness. I knew everything that stood between us, and yet it felt inconsequential, simple, a crack rather than a chasm.

I found myself watching her from a few feet away as she stretched onto her tiptoes on the ladder to reach the top shelf, sheet between her fingers. She wobbled, nearly losing her balance — I was at her side, hands circling her waist to steady her. The curve was slight, and my hands rested in it as if they belonged there, the feeling of her against my palms and fingers sending heat through my chest. Another smile, the kind she'd always saved only for me, and as I looked up at her, I imagined her touching my face, kissing me sweetly, telling me—

I let her go and stepped back, not trusting myself.

Dad stirred, and I moved to his side with Elliot by mine. He glanced around, confused. "What's all this?"

"We have a surprise. Hang on."

I grabbed everyone, and within a few minutes, we'd brought everything in, the trees, the tent, all while he watched us with tears in his eyes, lips parted as he took it all in.

I held out my hands in display, our joy so bright, so strong, it filled the room. "You can't get to the Adirondacks, so we brought them to you."

"A camp-in?" he said with a laugh.

I nodded. "Complete with a campfire and stars. The works."

He reached for my hand with glistening eyes. "I'm so fortunate to have you."

I squeezed his fingers and said softly. "No, Dad. We're the lucky ones."

Elliot made quick work of lighting the fire as I sat with him, and Sophie lit the candles, placing them all around the room as Sadie turned on the track of rustling trees and crickets.

Dad looked around in wonder. "Smells like pine and smoke."

"But here's the best part." I killed the lights and clicked on the projector, throwing stars all around the room.

He sighed and laid his head back, eyes tracking the ceiling in wonder.

Elliot was at my elbow, watching him with the same awe I felt, but I found myself watching her. She struck me in that moment, a quiet moment, a moment of reverence.

She was all I'd ever wanted, and she was here, right here. All I had to do was reach out and touch her. All I had to do was ask.

My sisters laid out sleeping bags around the fireplace, and we turned Dad's bed, careful of the machine wires and tubes. And then we sat, telling stories, reminiscing. I watched Elliot as she roasted marshmallows, her face illuminated by the fire, the sound of her laughter filling my heart. I listened as she read Emerson's "Song of Nature," the words floating from her lips like a spell.

It was very late, the fire burned down to embers, and the house was quiet, everyone asleep but me and her, the lot of us lying scattered through the room in sleeping bags. And I found myself in the dark, found her in the dark. I found light and truth in the darkness, hiding there where I couldn't see, right in front of me the whole time.

And all I had to do was reach out and touch her.

E L L I O T

The room was quiet other than the chirping of crickets. Everyone was asleep except me, and I lay with my eyes on the ceiling, watching the stars next to Wade.

We were so close, close enough that I could reach out and touch him, but still so far away. Something had shifted though, the air between us charged with things he wanted to say — I could feel them in every word, every motion, as if the ice between us had begun to melt, and the boy I used to know was visible once again, though still distorted by the crystalline ice.

He was an enigma to me, every day providing a new challenge, a new fight. I never knew what I'd get. Angry and hot. Solemn and cold. Or warm, like today.

Today, the sun shone. Today, I saw him, saw the tenderness I'd longed for, dreamt of. Today, tonight, was magic.

My eyes were trained on the ceiling as I lost myself in my thoughts, and I was so intent that I didn't realize he wasn't asleep at all, not until his hand moved, reaching for mine in the dark. His fingers slipped into my palm and opened up, winding through my own, our hands clasped as if they were made to touch, as if they'd found their way home.

I turned my head to find him looking at me, his eyes catching the dim light of the room.

"I'm sorry," he whispered so softly, I wondered if I'd heard him at all.

"Me too," I whispered back, my voice too small.

His thumb shifted, stroking the back of my hand gently, and I was overcome, overwhelmed as I wondered if it were a dream. There were no words to speak aloud, the thousands of words we needed to say hanging in the air. But I didn't want them, not in that moment, that perfect, painful moment. I existed in the space between our hands, between the beating of our hearts, between the breaths we slowly sipped, savoring the moment I'd imagined for so long.

There was no certainty in what would come next, when the words found our hiding place and made themselves known.

Minutes passed, the clock on a shelf in the room ticking as we looked into each other's eyes and forgave and begged and hoped. And then, our twined hands weren't enough. He released me to drag my sleeping bag closer, and when he reached for me, when he pulled me into his side, I melted into him. His arms wrapped around me, and I closed my eyes, sure now that it was a dream, a beautiful dream.

I was whole again in his arms.

He held me tight, and I thought he might feel it was a dream too, as if we could hang on to each other and make everything all right, erase the past. I'd imagined it a hundred times, remembered a hundred moments like this, but different; this moment was pure, the honesty breaking me and healing me as we lay beneath the stars, spinning silently in the center.

"I'm scared," he whispered, his breath stirring my hair where his cheek pressed, warm and alive.

"I know," I answered, because I was scared too. And he held me in the dark in the silence until our hearts beat together and our minds slowed, slipping away into the solace of sleep.

WADE

The sun hadn't yet risen when I woke, but she was still in my arms, her body pressed against mine, our legs wound together. It had been so long, so very long, and I didn't want to breathe, didn't want to move for fear I'd wake her and the moment would end.

We'd said nothing, and we'd said everything, and I knew she understood me, understood how I felt, what I wanted, what I needed. We were connected, as much now as we'd ever been. Because with her in my arms, I knew she was all that mattered.

She had to know that I loved her, must have felt that love in the same way I'd felt her love for me, transmitted through her touch, through every breath.

But I wanted to tell her, wanted to speak the words, and as I held her in the early rays of dawn, I formed them in my mind, imagined the admission, reciting the things I needed to say. The things she needed to hear.

She stirred against my chest and sighed, and I squeezed her, slipping my hand into her dark hair, holding her against me.

We lay that way for a while, quiet, still until light slipped slowly into the room, and Dad coughed from behind us.

Elliot pulled away slowly and met my eyes, a flash of understanding in their depths with a smile full of promises before she stood and moved to his bed. He was still half in sleep, eyes listing lazily as he took in his surroundings and smiled.

"You took me camping, Elliot," he said, reaching for her face to cup her cheek.

"We did. And that's not all."

He smiled wider. "More surprises?"

"More surprises."

"Something to look forward to."

I stood and moved to the bed to sit on the edge. "Morning, Dad."

"My boy. Thank you."

"Did you sleep well?"

"I liked having you all here with me. Made the night less lonely, less foreign."

My chest ached. "Well, maybe we'll make a habit of it."

"I wouldn't complain."

Elliot checked her watch and her bottom lip slipped between her teeth. "Would you mind if I ran home and helped out with the kids for a bit? I'll be back around lunch."

"Not at all," Dad said, patting her hand. "We'll be here."

Her eyes met mine and looked down, her cheeks flushing, sweet lips smiling gently, innocent and beautiful. "All right. I'll be back in a few hours, okay?"

"Can't wait," he answered and yawned.

"I'll walk you out." I followed her as she collected her things, pulling on her coat and hat as we stood silently in the foyer.

All of the things I wanted to say piled up in my throat, and my fears seeped in again, exposed by the daylight. It wasn't the right time or the right place. I should have told her last night, I thought, chastising myself for wasting my chance as she took her time situating her hat, waiting for me to speak.

But I couldn't. There would be time, but that time wasn't now, in the hallway, as she was trying to leave.

"I … I'll see you in a little while, Elliot." I hoped she heard the meaning, the promise in my words.

She nodded and smiled, the tension between us almost unbearable as she turned for the door. "All right, Wade."

She walked out the door, and I'd lost the chance completely, stupidly, cowardly. But I was already planning the moment when I could tell her how I felt, when I would tell her everything.

I only hoped she'd forgive me.

CHASM

The wind
That blows across the chasm
Between us
Pierces my soul.

—M. WHITE

ELLIOT

sat with the kids as they ate lunch, musing over all that had happened in a lovely haze.

The night before was still on my mind, in my heart, occupying my thoughts. I had the shining sensation that everything would be all right, somehow, some way. He touched my hand and wiped away the past. He wrapped his arms around me and pulled me back into his heart. He whispered to me in the dark and gave me hope.

I hadn't wanted to leave, but I'd been away from the kids and knew the little window would do Wade and me good. It was too much to process — I needed time to collect my thoughts, my feelings, so we could talk. Maybe we could go for a walk, go back to the cascade. Maybe he would kiss me under the bridge. Maybe everything would be all right.

My heart skittered in my chest at the maybes, the hopefullys, the daydreams of a future after I thought all I'd wanted was lost.

So I'd floated through the morning with the kids in the quiet house. Charlie was locked in the office working, and Mary was shopping with Dad and Beth. The little bit of normalcy was welcome.

The kids were almost finished eating when someone knocked on the door, and Charlie trotted up the stairs from the first floor to answer it. I heard Jack's voice when the door opened, and my heart jumped anxiously. I'd forgotten about him completely — the whole of me was focused on Wade.

They walked into the kitchen, laughing as they passed the threshold of the room, and I smiled at them as I cleaned up.

"Hey, Elliot," Jack said, smiling sheepishly with his hands in the pockets of his coat.

"Hey," I echoed as Charlie walked by, grabbing a grape as he passed the dish on the counter. He tossed it up in the air and into his mouth.

"Heading back to Rick's?" Charlie asked.

I nodded. "I was going to put the kids down for a nap first."

He waved a hand. "Don't worry about it. I've got it."

"Thanks, Charlie." I dunked a bowl into the bubbly sink water and scrubbed it.

Jack pulled off his coat and walked over to the sink, grabbing a dishtowel. "How did it go last night?"

My only thoughts were of Wade, of his hands and skin, the smell of him mingled with pine and campfire. "Rick was so surprised, so happy. It was a good night."

"That's great." I could hear him smiling as he spoke — my eyes were on my hands.

"Thank you so much for lending your gear." I rinsed the bowl and passed it to him to dry. His fingers grazed mine, and my stomach flipped with surprise at the contact. "I didn't know you'd be stopping by or I would have brought it back with me."

"Oh, it's fine. I didn't expect it back just yet, just wanted to stop by and see how the night was."

"Thanks to you, he had a wonderful time. I haven't heard him laugh so much in a long time."

The front door opened, followed by chatter and the rustling of bags and footfalls.

I exchanged a look with Charlie, who grabbed the baby wipes and began the task of wiping the kids up.

"Hello?" Mary called.

"In here," Charlie answered, and a second later, there she stood. Her smile fell as she looked over the room, her calculating eyes falling on me last.

"What are you doing here, Jack?"

I passed him another bowl, and he took it cheerily — Mary's frost clearly had no effect on him. "I came by to see how the party went for Rick."

"I don't know why you're so invested in the whole thing. You don't even know him." I shot her a look, but she'd already moved on. "Charlie, we need help with the bags."

He dabbed at Maven's cheeks. "I'm busy."

She huffed. "Elliot can do that. I need your help."

"Elliot's leaving, so figure out your shopping bag problem on your own."

Jack wiped off his hands. "I'll help."

Mary scowled at Charlie. "At least *someone* cares. Come on, they're in here." She turned on her heel with her nose in the air.

Jack smiled down at me with a wink. "I'll be right back. Don't leave without me — I'd like to walk you back to Rick's, if that's okay."

"Sure." I smiled back politely, hoping in the back of my mind it would give me a chance to tell him the truth about how I felt about him. Or, more importantly, how I felt about Wade.

Once Charlie and I were alone, he scoffed. "God, she's gotten worse since your dad has been here, don't you think?"

I sighed, washing the spoons. "It always happens this way. It's like they feed off each other."

"How did you survive as a kid? It's like a sheep in the wolf's den."

"I had books. Lots and lots of books."

He laughed at that and sent the kids out. "You know, I really like you and Jack together. I've been trying to make that happen for years, did you know?"

I kept my thoughts to myself, washing dishes like my life depended on it. "No, I didn't."

"He's a great guy. One of the best."

"Oh, are we talking about Jack?" Dad said from the hall as he entered the room with his quivering Chihuahua under his arm. He looked like a vulture: hungry eyes, the skin of his neck sagging just enough to betray his age, his camel coat hanging from his shoulders, lined with the slightest bit of fur, fashionable if not ostentatious.

Charlie smiled. "Yeah. They've been spending a lot of time together lately."

"Well, I approve," Dad said.

"Me too, Walter," Charlie added.

"He's quite a catch, Elliot. You're not likely to find another man with money and looks who's interested in you. Maybe if you put in a little ... effort you'd have more prospects, but Jack ... Jack is something else, all right." He smiled, lips curling up at the edges.

Charlie cleared his throat. "Let me finish that up, Elliot, if you want to go."

I turned, wiping my hands on a dishtowel, grateful for him. "Are you sure? I can stay a while longer."

"I'm sure. Go on, and good luck over there."

Dad stopped me as I passed. "Don't spend too much time over there, not if you've got Jack interested. I'd hate for the Winters boy to interrupt anything between you and him."

I didn't acknowledge his words. "I'll see you later, Dad."

He nodded, looking pleased with himself, and I walked out, wondering more and more what I was doing there. I heard Jack and Charlie and *everyone* in my mind, and for the first time, I didn't feel defensive. I heard their truth.

I pulled on my coat and hat in the hallway, and just as I finished, Jack walked in with Mary on his heels. He smiled. She scowled.

"Ready?" he asked, reaching for his coat.

"I am," I answered.

"Then let's go." He placed a hand on my back, and I felt myself flush. "See you, Mary."

We left quickly enough that it didn't seem at all strange that she didn't answer.

Once again when we were outside and the door was closed, I felt myself breathe easier, underscoring with newfound clarity just how unhappy I'd been there, with Mary, with my father.

"So," Jack started, "anything on the agenda for today?"

"Nothing big. We're planning Italy for Rick tomorrow night, so tonight is just hanging out."

"Italy, huh? Wine and pasta?"

I chuckled. "Among other things."

"Bread?" he joked.

"Yes, bread. We're shooting for a picnic in the Italian countryside."

He nodded. "It's really kind of incredible, what you're doing for him."

"He's very well loved. I only wish there was more we could do."

"Do you think you'll be over there late tonight?"

"I'm not sure. There's no real agenda, why?" I asked stupidly, realizing my mistake too late.

"What do you think about joining me for a friendly-very-patient-with-no-kissing dinner?"

"Oh," I answered, the word a breath as anxiety over my impending refusal set in. "Jack—"

"Before you say no, I'd like to state my case."

"All right," was all I could say.

"As mentioned, I am patient, though maybe more persistent than

I let on. I like you, Elliot. I like you, and you're shouldering a lot. You could use a night away, a night out where you don't have to think about anything but yourself and what you want. You don't have to worry about Mary or the kids or Rick or broody guy. You could use a safe place, and I happen to be extraordinarily safe. Maybe when things settle down we can be more than friends, but for now, I'm perfectly content with that, if it's what you want. I just … I like you, and I'd like you to join me for dinner tonight. Will you do me the honor?"

He quieted down, giving me a moment to think about how to respond as we approached Rick's house. It wasn't untrue, me needing a safe place, but I had no intention of dating him, and it felt wrong to proceed without him knowing.

We slowed to a stop at the steps of the house, and when I looked up at him, I saw his hope fade as he took in my expression.

I touched his arm, and he took my hands. "Jack, I'm sorry. You've been … well, you've been a great friend to me in a time when I needed one. But …" I collected myself and told him the truth. "Time won't change the fact that I'm in love with someone else."

He nodded down at our hands. "Let me guess. Broody guy?"

I pursed my lips and released them. "Yes," I answered quietly.

"I should have known." His words were soft, blameless. "Judging by his reaction to seeing us the other day, I think he's in love with you too."

"It's been that way for a long time. It's just not so simple as us being together, that's all. I'm sorry. I … I didn't mean to mislead you."

He shrugged, still looking down. "It's okay — you didn't. You were pretty clear from the start. I'm just not great at taking the hint." He met my eyes and smiled. "We can still be friends, though, right? Real friends, if I promise no expectations of more from my end?"

I smiled back, relieved. "Of course. I really have enjoyed spending time with you. I hope we can still have that."

"I wouldn't have it any other way." And with that, he cupped my cheek and leaned in, pressing a kiss into my other cheek chastely as I stood there, frozen to the spot. "I'll see you around, Elliot."

"See you, Jack." My cheeks were on fire, my heart racing from the surprise of his gesture, and he smiled at me once more with his hand on my cheek before turning and walking away.

I took a deep breath and tried to put it all behind me. I'd cleared the air with Jack, spent the morning compositing my thoughts, and now I was ready to face Wade, to talk to him, to tell him how I felt.

Nerves flitted around my chest, and I smiled. I was in love with Wade, and there was a chance he was in love with me too. Seven years had disappeared into thin air at the thought.

I climbed the steps and knocked on the door, my hope sliding down into my shoes when it swung open to Wade, shoulders square and eyes sharp and flinty as steel.

"H-hi."

He said nothing, just turned and walked away, leaving the door gaping.

I stepped inside and closed it, my heart clanging, my uncertainty shaking me. He'd walked into the living room and to several stacks of books, which he sorted through, stacking them with noisy thumps. One slipped off the top and hit the ground, and a swear word hissed through his lips as he reached for it, slamming it on another stack.

I crept into the threshold of the room. "Are you okay?" I asked quietly.

He didn't turn or look up. "No, I'm not fucking okay." Another book stacked with an angry thud, but it was too much force, knocking the pile off center, and the stack fell over.

I moved toward him, hands outstretched for the books. "Let me help you."

He blocked me with his body, still not looking at me. "I don't want your help."

I pulled my hands back, wounded, somehow still surprised that he would once again shut me out. But clarity washed over me — of course today he would be different.

He was as unreliable and inconstant as the weather, and I stopped myself from reeling, recognizing the situation for what it was. Last night he'd just been caught up in the moment, emotional, sentimental. Wade was upset about his father; nothing about what happened had been about me.

I was through guessing which version of him I'd get when I walked through the door. I was through being pushed and pulled and toyed with.

But even still, I wanted to help him. Even still, I wanted to heal him.

"What's wrong, Wade?"

At that, he looked over his shoulder, his eyes full of hurt and anger. "What's wrong?" He stood, turning to face me like a brick wall. "*What's wrong?* Everything is wrong, Elliot. I've been sitting in this house for a week waiting, just waiting. Waiting for the seconds, the minutes to count down until the end. I've got my dad to think about. I've got my sisters to think about. I've got *everyone* to think about before myself. So no. I'm not okay. And no, I don't want your help."

I couldn't breathe, the shock hitting my lungs, freezing them as he blew out of the room, snatching his coat off the peg before opening the door, disappearing just before it slammed behind him. Ben glanced at me apologetically as he trotted toward the door, coat in hand, and the door opened and closed once again before I could finally take a breath.

Sophie hurried in, concern on her face, and she reached for me, pulling me into a hug. "My God, what happened? I'm so sorry."

I shook my head numbly. "I … I don't know. I just tried to talk to him and he just … just …"

"Ben will bring him back. He'll apologize, I know it — he didn't mean it."

I pursed my lips to stave off my tears, not believing that his frustration with Rick was all there was to it. The realization dawned on me that the room overlooked the street, that he could have seen outside. And Jack had kissed me.

I pushed the thought away, wondering if I would have a chance to talk to him. Wondering if he would listen to me if I did.

She pulled away, her eyes searching mine. "Elliot, I'm sorry."

"You don't have to be sorry. You didn't say it."

She shook her head. "No, I'm sorry because I haven't been here for you. You've been suffering too, and I've missed everything. Something's going on between you two, isn't it?"

"I ... I don't even know. But please," I pleaded. "Please don't do that. If I needed you, I'd tell you."

"No, you wouldn't. Not right now."

I marveled at the change a few words could make, how they could take me from the top of the world to the depths of emotion with a string of syllables and punctuation.

I pulled Sophie back in for a hug. "No, I wouldn't. You're right. But I'm all right. I'm here for you, not for me."

"But I'm not the only one in pain. Who will help bear yours?"

My chest ached from the weight. "Don't worry about me, Sophie. I'll be all right." I whispered the lie, wishing it were truth.

WADE

My jaw ached, clenched so tightly spots swam in my vision as I barreled down the sidewalk, ignoring Ben, who called my name from behind me.

I hadn't been watching for her out the living room window, not exactly, but I'd found myself at the front of the house more often than usual, my thoughts on her, my eyes searching for her beyond the windows to the city as I recited the admissions, the truth about how I felt about her, the apology for hurting her over and over.

And instead of making it better, I hurt her again. I was destined to hurt her forever.

What I'd hoped for was a homecoming. What I'd wished was to tell her everything in my heart. What I'd expected was the sweetness of forgiveness, for which I'd waited so long.

What I didn't expect was him. I didn't expect what I'd seen. I didn't expect to have my wishes, my hopes, exploded with napalm, detonated by a kiss that wasn't mine, laid on lips that were.

I couldn't see what all happened — she was blocked by his body — but I didn't need to. The image of her hands in his, of her flushed cheeks when he pulled away and I could see her again, it was all too much. Last night, I thought she'd made another promise to me. I thought she'd promised herself to me.

Wrong again.

"Wade," Ben called after me. I walked faster.

My intentions hadn't been as clear as I thought. Or they had, and they didn't mean to her what they meant to me. I should have told her the night before, when the truth was laid out in front of us. And because I didn't, I had no idea how she felt or what she thought. I hated myself for thinking we could be more, that we could go back or forward or anywhere.

I was too damaged, too broken, and I'd only keep hurting her.

"Stop," he said, grabbing me by the arm. I spun around, ripping my arm from his grip.

"*What?*"

His eyes narrowed, and he squared his shoulders. "What's the matter? What happened?"

My nostrils flared as I pulled in a breath. "Doesn't matter."

His jaw ticked as he flexed it. "You're not getting out of this. What happened?"

I swallowed, not wanting to admit anything, not wanting to say it out loud for fear it would make it more true. So I stood there silently for a moment, grappling with the words.

Ben shifted, folding his arms.

Another deep breath, and I said it. "Jack kissed her. I saw it."

"Jack?"

"*The guy.*"

His eyes widened with recognition. "You need to talk to Elliot." He said the words like I was overreacting, and my anger flared.

"Why? I don't need an explanation. I got all the explanation I need." I gestured back toward the house. "So, no. I'd like to be spared the rejection. I've had enough of that from her for a lifetime."

Ben scowled at me. "You don't even know what happened. Don't assume—"

My hackles rose, the hairs on the back of my neck standing at attention. "Don't you get it? I can't hear her justify *Jack* to me, not after everything. I don't care. *I don't care.*" I yelled the lie as if volume could make it true.

He didn't say anything, just watched me with a stern look on his face.

"You don't understand," I said as the wildfire burned in my chest. "We're too far gone, Ben. Sometimes things are too broken to put back together. I should just stay out of the way. At least he's here. He can be what she needs. Sometimes you've got to walk away, let it go."

His eyes softened, colored with sadness. "Because that's been so easy for you to do before? With an ocean between you and years gone by? How will you manage with her right there in front of you?"

I hung my hands on my hips, eyes on the ground like the cracks in the sidewalk held the answers. "I don't know, Ben. But I don't have a choice."

I wished that I did. I wished it could have been me. But I'd ruined my chances with her years ago, and I of all people knew that there was no way to go back.

Rick called my name from the library, and I turned away from the window overlooking the street. I'd been watching for him, waiting. Always waiting. But he'd never come. He probably never would, not the way I wished for.

"I'm here," I answered, trying to put Wade back in his box as I walked down the hallway and into his room. It's just that the lid wouldn't stay on.

Rick's hand was outstretched, beckoning me, and I hurried over to take it.

"You heard," I said.

His eyes were sad, but smiled the half-smile that was now so thoroughly his. "Hard not to."

I nodded, swallowing down my emotions.

"Sit with me." He nodded to Sophie behind me, and she nodded back, leaving the room and closing the door behind her.

I sat on the edge of his bed, and he squeezed my hand.

"Give him time."

The sun poured in through the window, a slant of light that served as a stage for dancing dust motes. "We've had seven years, and it hasn't gotten any easier or simpler."

"No, I suppose it hasn't. But it's different now, wouldn't you say?"

"It is different. It's harder. When he was gone, it was easier to miss the idea of him than to face the reality of him. He … he hates me. He hates what I did, what I'm doing, what I've done with my life."

Rick shook his head. "No, Elliot. He loves you, and that love hurts him because he regrets everything."

My breath shuddered as I inhaled, my eyes on our hands, his old and mine young.

"He punishes himself by pushing you away. It's easier to believe he can't have you, easier to think you're out of reach, because if he *can* have you, he'll have to deal with his regrets, his mistakes. He'll have to deal with his grief."

"It's too much," I whispered.

"Elliot, look at me."

I met his eyes, eyes that pleaded with mine. "He loves you. He always has, just as you've always loved him. Please, don't give up. He needs you now, and he'll need you even more when I'm gone."

Tears slipped down my cheeks as I wondered how, wondered if it were true, if patience were all I needed. Because I could give him time if he loved me. I could withstand the push and pull if he loved me.

I would give him anything if he loved me.

Rick reached for my face, brushing my cheek with his knuckles. "Don't do it for me. Do it for you. I know … I know you will find your way back to each other, back to yourselves after being lost for so long. And you're the only one who can bring him back, Elliot. I … I don't know how he'll survive this without you."

"Rick …" A sob swallowed my words, tears blurring my vision, and I blinked to push them out of the way so I could see him.

"Don't cry. Please. You will live long after me, and you will do great things. And I will live forever here," he cupped my head. "I know you'll miss me, but remember what I said — I want you to *live*. Honor me with that life and keep me alive. Don't be afraid. Because you are braver than you know."

I shook my head. "You've given me hope and purpose. You've shown me what it means to be loved and cared for, and I don't know what I'll do without you."

"You have Sophie and Wade. This house will stand here, waiting for you. This room will remain just as it is, as it has been for a hundred years, and you will come here and remember. You are loved and cared for, with or without me. So please, don't break or bend. Don't crumble and fall. Stand up tall and face the sun and remember me."

I was left without words, so I curled into his chest, the father I'd always wished for, the man I admired so much, and I cried with his arm around me until I was empty.

WANDERING
VOICES

So simple:
Breathe in, breathe out,
The motion never considered
Until it's gone.

—M. WHITE

WADE

The lawyer's hand gripped mine the next morning, firm and solid and despondent as we shook in parting after several hours of signing papers. The final adjustments to his will. The deed to the house, which as of that moment was mine. The guardianship papers for Sadie, who wouldn't be eighteen for another year. The power of attorney for Dad. The Do Not Resuscitate.

I was numb from the battering of emotions, past the point of being able to discern how I felt about anything, my soul burned to ash.

The door closed with a click, the house quiet, everyone gone. I hadn't seen Elliot since I'd blown out of the house the day before; she was gone by the time I could bring myself to come back. I was thankful for her absence, thankful and sorrowful and full of regret.

I would see her again tonight, and I had no idea how to handle it. The ground I'd gained, I'd lost just as quickly. And I was angry. Angry at her, at Jack, at myself, at life. At the universe for stripping me of the things I wanted most in the world.

No one was home but me and Dad — everyone had gone to run errands for our Italy date, knowing he and I would need some time with the lawyers, with each other.

As I walked back into the library, I saw him with fresh eyes — the slightness of his frame, the exhaustion written in the lines of his face, his eyes laden with the weight of the day, of the days before, of the sickness inside of him.

I pulled his blanket up when I made it to his side. "Want to sleep for a bit?" I asked gently.

"In a little while." He laid his hand over mine.

I sat on the edge of his bed so I could be close to him.

He cleared his throat and blinked slowly before turning his head to face me. "There are too many things to feel. I don't know how to sort through them all."

"Neither do I." My words were rough, burning my throat.

"Sadness and fear. Worry for you, for your sisters. Guilt for the burden I'll leave you with. Is it strange that I think more about you than I do myself? I think about what happens when I'm gone, and that hurts me more than the thought of not existing."

"Don't worry about us, Dad. We'll be fine," I lied, my mask firmly in place for him. I would do anything for him.

His smile told me he knew the truth. "I don't know how to make it all right. I don't know how to make it easier other than to tell you that I don't want you to hurt or suffer. Don't mourn me; celebrate me. Don't think of me with sadness, think of me with joy."

I swallowed once, then again, but nothing could stop the feeling that he was saying goodbye. "I promise."

"There's so much I want to tell you and not enough time. I don't know where to start." His eyes roamed my face. "Your sisters will look to you for everything, but don't let that weigh on you. Just let them breathe. Guide them. You all know what to do … my job was easy, raising you all." His gray eyes were just like mine, but his were filled with urgency and intention as he spoke. "I want you to know that I am proud of you, so proud. Your mother would have been too, and you've honored her memory with your life, with your heart, sacrificing yourself and what you want for the greater good. You are everything we hoped for, everything we imagined when we held you for the first time."

I squeezed his hand, unable to speak, so he continued, taking a deep breath.

"The day she died, when she called …"

"Dad …"

"No, it's okay. You need to know. I want you to know." He drew another breath. "It was chaos, people yelling and screaming, the sound of their footfalls as they ran down the stairs. But I could hear her smiling, smiling and crying when I answered, relieved to have reached me, I think. We both knew … we knew. And she told me goodbye. She told me … she asked me not to forget her, but told me not to hold on. She told me to let her go. I never understood why she said it, until now. I cursed her name for asking the impossible of me, to let her go, and I never did. But now where I sit where she sat, I wish I had. Not for me. For her."

My breath hitched, tears slipping silently down my cheeks.

"I need you to let me go, son."

"I …" *Can't. Never. Won't.*

"It sounds impossible, but this is what I'm asking of you. I can't leave this world without knowing you'll try."

I nodded, unable to deny him anything. "I'll try."

"Life is short, so short, so precious, every minute, every day. Don't let the people you love, the people who make you happy, the people who bring you joy — don't let them go. Hang on to them, even when it hurts. When it seems impossible. Hold on to the things that breathe life into you. Listen to your soul and honor what it tells you. Live. Fight for what you love. Because one day, you'll be where I am, and in that moment I want you to look back gladly, with no regrets."

"Elliot," I whispered.

He nodded. "You've been in the dark for so long, from the moment you lost her. But she's right here, right now, and she loves you. If you don't love her anymore, then let her go too, right along with me. But if you do, hold on to her. You don't know how long you'll have the chance."

He looked down at our hands. "All I want for you and your sisters is your happiness. I want your dreams and your hopes, and I'd do anything to give them to you. But I'm out of time, so I can only tell you my wishes so you can remember them, so you can hear them when I'm gone. Live and live well." He shook his head. "I'm sorry. I'm sorry to put this on you, but I can feel it." His voice dropped. "I feel it pressing on me, feel the time pass."

"Don't say that, Dad. There's still time."

"I know," he said with a sad smile, tinged with placation. "We'll have a little bit longer. Italy tonight?"

"Italy tonight."

"Promise me gelato."

I chuckled. "Promise."

"Will you read to me?" he asked after a pause.

"Of course. Any requests?"

"Emerson," he said sleepily, settling into his pillows. "'My Garden.'"

I reclined his bed just a bit and found the hardbound book of Emerson poems, flipping to the one he asked for and read as he closed his eyes to rest.

Wandering voices in the air
And murmurs in the wold
Speak what I cannot declare,
Yet cannot all withhold.

When the shadow fell on the lake,

The whirlwind in ripples wrote
Air-bells of fortune that shine and break,
And omens above thought.

But the meanings cleave to the lake,
Cannot be carried in book or urn;
Go thy ways now, come later back,
On waves and hedges still they burn.

These the fates of men forecast,
Of better men than live to-day;
If who can read them comes at last
He will spell in the sculpture, 'Stay.'

I kept reading, knowing he was asleep, not interested in silence, wishing the words would tether him to the world forever.

All he had to do was speak and his words hit my heart, hung over me, illuminating me. I had to let Elliot go or I had to hold on to her. When the choice stood before me that plainly, I knew there was only one answer. I'd tried to let her go for seven years, and last night was proof that I hadn't. I couldn't.

It was time I stopped trying. My only hope was we could finally sit down and have the conversation we should have had years ago when we were young and afraid. The conversation I couldn't give her when I was in the thick of war. The one I didn't think she ever wanted to hear.

Now I believed she did, and I hoped she would forgive me. I would honor my father and honor myself. I would put my fears aside, and I would do whatever it took to get her back.

An hour later, I was still reading, my voice rough. The nurse had let herself in and sat next to me, checking the machines and working on paperwork while he slept — neither of us wanted to wake him — and the only sounds in the room were my voice and the ticking of the clock, the ever present marker of seconds and breaths and heartbeats.

When his arm jerked in his sleep, I stopped reading, lowering the book. When his body stiffened and jolted off the bed, I leapt to his side, my heart stopping, my breath freezing, blood cold in my veins. And as he seized, body shaking, chin pointed at the ceiling, I held his face, cried his name. And my mask, my heart, the fabric of my soul shredded as I watched over him, weeping and lost forever as he breathed his last.

VANISHED

Like boiling water,
Scalding, churning,
Steam slipping silently
Up and up,
And when it vanishes
I watch, wondrous,
Disbelieving
That it had ever been real.

—M. WHITE

ELLIOT

"**H**e's gone."

Wade's voice was a thousand miles away, quiet and numb and small.

I slipped to the ground in my room, hands trembling and numb and whispered, "No."

"Please, come. We need you."

My cold hand cupped my mouth and I nodded, realizing after a moment that he couldn't see me. "Okay," was the only word to leave me.

The line disconnected.

I pulled myself up and gathered my things, stunned from shock, muttering blindly to my family that I had to go, unable to say where or why, unable to utter the words.

At first I walked, my mind tripping and skittering over the impossibility, over the inevitability, and then I ran, tears streaking my face. And then I was walking in the door of the house, the loss overwhelming me.

His absence was tangible, as if his spark lit the house, and now it was too still, too quiet. Sophie rushed me when I entered the library, and we fell to the ground in each other's arms. I couldn't breathe, couldn't speak, couldn't move, but my eyes found him where he lay in bed. He looked peaceful, as if he were sleeping as the nurse by his side solemnly disconnected him from the machines. Ben and Sadie sat on the couch, Sadie sobbing, Ben's face colored with the things I felt as he held her up. And Wade was nowhere, gone.

The light caught glimmering glass scattered all over the floor, and I saw the gears, the casing — a clock, smashed and broken, and we sat among the wreckage.

The day crept past us in a strange warp where hours were minutes and minutes, hours. We stood by his side and held his hands and cried. We said our goodbyes and kissed his skin as it cooled.

The funeral home came and took him away. A van from hospice came and collected the equipment. The nurse gave us condolences and left us there with an empty room and empty hearts.

Wade never came home.

Ben called with no answer, and we waited in vain as the daylight slipped away, crawling across the room imperceptibly until it was gone. And we sat in silence in the dark, no one possessing the energy to turn on a light, the twilight sifting through the glass from the clock on the ground, still chronicling the time without the need of its gears.

Sadie fell asleep first, and Ben carried her to her room in the dark. I took Sophie to hers, putting her into her bed, sharing a final burst of tears, trying to hold each other together for a moment longer before she fell asleep too.

Ben was downstairs, standing in the living room with his eyes trained on the sidewalk beyond the glass, and I stood next to him in silence. I couldn't stay, I told him — I needed out. And he promised he would be fine there without me, that he'd call if that changed. That he'd wait for Wade. It was my only solace as I pulled on my coat and stepped out into the bleak night.

The cold pressed down on me, the air charged as I walked home, and the snow began to fall in slow, lazy swirls, gathering quickly, a blanket of white against the dark of the night.

The house was quiet when I walked through the door, and I headed downstairs, numb from the cold and my loss. My room was warm and familiar, and I stripped down in the dark, unthinking, automatically, leaving my clothes where they fell. I shook as the cold seeped from my bones, kneeling naked by my fireplace to light it, not knowing why it was important, but it was. A fire had gone out and a new one was lit, a spot of warmth in the cold, a light in the dark. And then I slipped into my bed and lay beneath the blankets shaking, with my eyes on the flickering flames, a ward against the black of night.

Time moved, though I didn't, not as the shadows deepened or the temperature fell. Not until the window opened, and he slipped inside.

He was lit half in flames, half in shadow, his eyes sharp with pain and soft with sorrow. Snow dusted his dark hair and the shoulders of his jacket, and I sat slowly, holding the blanket to my breasts, dreaming with my eyes wide open.

Broken. Broken and sorry. He'd flung away the no, the why, stripped his soul bare, and what he was, what was left was the truth: he was broken, maybe irreparably. But I could be what healed him, mended him. It was why he came here, I knew, and selflessly, this was what I wanted, for him to be whole again. Selfishly, I wanted nothing but him, only him, broken or whole. Anything was better than nothing at all.

He begged me to understand without speaking, and I did. I understood when he moved to my side, the cold wafting off of him, touching my skin in tendrils. I knew when he touched my face, his hands warming the moment our skin touched. And when he breathed, I wished to be his air.

My eyes never closed for fear if they did, I'd open them to find him gone.

I felt his lips a second before they closed over mine, agony and hope, a fire burning in the empty space left by death. But around the edges was the solace in submission, after seven years of wanting, of waiting and loss, of loving without return. Our bodies came together, winding around one another with the memory of home and pain and love in our hearts.

His hands were around my back, my arms around his neck, our lips laced with relief and regret, with apology and forgiveness, deepening with every heartbeat until he tipped his head, pressing his forehead to mine, our breaths ragged and eyes closed.

"I need you," he whispered. "I love you," he breathed. "I'm sorry," he begged.

"I'm yours," I sighed, and he kissed me again, his heart broken and singing and flying into the sun.

He stood next to my bed, watching me as he pulled off his coat in the firelight, undressing as I sat with the sheets pooled around my waist, breath shallow, body on fire.

His body was strong, no longer that of a boy, but a man, hardened and chiseled by his work, scarred from the war with cuts and burns. I reached for him, tears falling as he sat next to me, my fingers tracing the ruts and tight skin. His fingers circled my wrist, and he brought my palm to his lips, eyes closed, reverent and solemn. And when his eyes found mine again, they were alive with regret, with intention.

He held my face in his big hands, eyes searching mine, and he tilted me gently, laying me down, kissing me with lips that knew me, knew my soul. Lips that had burned their imprint on me so many years before, a brand I'd never been able to wipe away, a brand that ignited again under his touch.

His fingers trailed down my body, pulling my hips into his like they'd never forgotten me, like they knew they owned me. It was his skin against mine, his lips and my own. Our legs scissored, bodies flush, hands roaming, touching, reveling in exploring every familiar curve.

His chest was warm and hard, his heart thumping wildly under my palm as it passed over, moving down, down to him, needing him, wrapping my fingers around his length. He gasped against my lips at the contact, his hand flexing on my hip, fingers digging into my skin before sliding down the back of my thigh to hitch it over his waist. And I stroked him gently, our lips and tongues moving in time as his hand kept moving until his fingers found my warm center. It was my turn to gasp, thighs flexing at the contact, relaxing as his lips moved down my neck.

When I found composure, I flexed my hand, and he did the same, slipping the tip of his finger into me, and I sighed, heart pounding with his face buried in the curve of my neck.

I could heal him, but he would ruin me. I would make that sacrifice without question, simply because he needed me, and I loved him.

He shifted at the sound of my sigh, a noise escaping him from deep in his throat that hit me deep in my belly. He broke away and hovered over me, his legs between mine shifting to open them more, his eyes on mine, noses only inches apart for a moment that stretched out. And then, he kissed me.

He kissed me with abandon, pressing me into the bed with his body as I felt the tip of him against the edge of me. With a gentle thrust, he slipped into me, the feeling taking over every sense, the moment too much, and I broke away, arms circling his neck, breath gone. He filled me, holding still when our bodies were connected, caging me in his arms, pinning me with his chest and hips, his face in the curve of my shoulder, my hands in his hair and cheek pressed against his head. We were as close as we could get, and we lay shuddering, breathing once, twice, three times before he moved.

His hips flexed as his head rose, his lips finding mine, our bodies moving together. Time seemed to speed up and slow down, my heart racing as my hips slowed and his moved faster, rocking against me, the rhythm of our bodies and hearts matching pace until they sped, until we were overcome. And our bodies broke free with a gasp and a whispered name.

The unspoken words were of no consequence for a long, singular moment.

But that moment was all we had.

As our bodies slowed, as he sagged against me, I felt the weight of his heart return, heavier than before. And he shook his head against me, the final fissure in the cracked surface that broke it once and for all.

"I'm sorry, Elliot," he whispered as he pulled away, slipping away from me like smoke.

"Why are you sorry?" I asked, though I knew the answer.

"I shouldn't have …" He swallowed hard and sat on the edge of the bed, the pain on his face mirroring the pain in my heart. "I can't do this to you, to me. Not now. I need time."

"Time?" I asked as I sat, my heart weak and broken. "I asked for time once, and you wouldn't give it. I've given so much." The words trembled and broke.

He stood, and I watched the expanse of his back and broad shoulders flex and release as he reached for his pants. "I'm sorry. Forgive me."

"No," I whispered, an answer and a plea. I'd known our fate, knew my sacrifice, but that knowledge was no consolation. My facade fell, my braveness gone — I couldn't take everyone's pain like I had so willingly. I couldn't give any more because I had nothing left.

He pulled on his pants hastily, stuffing his feet in his boots. And then he was at the window, dejected and desolate, ashamed and repentant. The rest of his clothes and his coat were in his hands as he opened the window, casting a tortured glance over his shoulder at me before disappearing into the falling snow, his footsteps vanishing within minutes as if he'd never been there at all.

BLANK

The page is blank
Like new fallen snow,
As is my heart,
As is my soul.

—M. WHITE

WADE

My hands lay on the surface of a mahogany table, palms pressed against the glossy surface, with my eyes on the reflection of the funeral director sitting across from me. Everything was in order, the details for tomorrow approved, and I'd just signed the rest of the paperwork, finalizing the funeral.

None of it fully reached me through the fog I'd been wandering through for the last two days.

Everything felt far away, distorted and fishbowled, like looking through the wrong end of a telescope. We were all grieving differently. Sadie was inconsolable. Sophie spent her time wavering between finding calm for Sadie's sake and crumbling, beside herself. And I was numb, grieving by not grieving, completely empty. There were too many things to do, too many people to talk to, and I was too busy to feel anything at all. Even in the dead of night, I lay in bed, not sleeping, not thinking, just watching the moonlight stream in through the window, warming to the blues and purples of dawn. And when the clock told me it was the right time, I would get up and dress to face another day.

"Mr. Winters?" he asked from across the table.

My eyes snapped to his. "I'm sorry, I didn't catch that."

He smiled genuinely. "It's all right. I just asked if you had any other questions for me?"

"No." I pushed back my chair and stood, and he did the same, mirroring me as I extended my hand.

"Then we'll see you tomorrow. Just call me if you need anything before then."

A curt nod was my only response, and I turned to leave the room. I was fifteen blocks from the house, but I didn't hail a cab — instead I buttoned my felt coat and flipped the collar up against the cold, burying my hands in my pockets. But the cold seeped through, slipping into my skin, muscles, bone, and I welcomed it, wishing it would turn me to stone.

There was only one moment since the day he died when I could still feel, and I felt everything, my grief compounding in layers.

As he lay in the hospital bed with the light shining in on him, still, gone, I stood disbelieving at his side, knowing what I had to do. First was Sophie. I'd heard the phone drop to the ground, then Ben's voice telling me they were on their way.

Then I called Elliot.

Her voice split me open. The second she gave me a response, I'd disconnected, unable to take anything more.

And when I looked at him again, I knew into the depths of my soul that he was gone.

I knew I was gone too.

I left the house, not knowing what I was doing or where I was going. And I walked. I walked until the sun disappeared and the snow began to fall, walked until my feet carried me to her. And as I stood in front of her window, I knew what I needed, what I wanted, the only thing I had left.

Her.

That was the moment I came alive. I crawled through that window and into her arms. I poured myself into her until I was empty again.

I'd been empty ever since.

I left simply because I couldn't stay. I'd made a mistake, crossed a line in going there, unable to see past myself. And when I left, I broke her again with my clumsy, numb hands.

The emptiness was complete. I couldn't feel her in my arms. I couldn't feel my heartache. I couldn't feel my soul or my feet against the pavement. All I had was the stinging cold to let me know I was alive.

The house was full of quiet movement as Ben, Lou, and Jeannie worked on setting it up for the wake. Something was baking in the kitchen, but I couldn't eat, hadn't eaten, knew I should. Instead, I hung my coat on a peg in the entryway and spoke to no one before walking up the stairs and into my room, closing the door behind me with a snick.

The light at my desk was still on, shining down on the blank paper like a spotlight, waiting for me to find something to say. How do you write a few words to sum up a man's life? How could I explain what he meant to me, to the world, on a sheet of paper? How could I describe the loss that had consumed me, leaving nothing? Because I had nothing. Nothing to give, no words to speak.

But I pulled out the chair and sat down, staring at the paper, blinking and breathing, heart beating, autonomous, lost to myself. The pen was heavy in my fingers, the words heavy in my mind, and when the ball-point touched the paper, words slipped out unbidden, unwanted as the tears fell from my eyes, unabashed, unashamed. And I realized then that I wasn't empty. I was broken; the sharp pieces of what was left of me were buried under shock that had collapsed, decimating me. But they resurfaced like the undead, cutting their way through the wreckage to open me up once again.

TO LIVE

To live
Is to feel
So you know
You are real.

—M. WHITE

ELLIOT

Dark eyes looked back at me in the mirror, dark hair framing my face, dark dress on my body. The world seemed to be bleak, quiet and empty, the sky shrouded in miles of fog that signaled snow. It made me feel small, a miniature in a world of miniatures.

I was not ready for today, and there was nothing that could stop it from happening. Today was here and waiting to be endured, survived.

I twisted my hair into a bun at my nape and turned my back on my reflection, the floorboards creaking to mark my movement as I stepped to the bed where my heels stood, slipping my feet in one at a time, smoothing the black skirt of my dress as if I could smooth the wrinkles of life away, make it straight and perfect. The poem sat on my desktop, the paper heavy between my fingers as I folded it into thirds and slipped it into my clutch. And with that, there was nothing else to keep me in my room where it was safe.

My family waited in the living room, dressed in black, half of them with a drink in their hands. They'd wanted to come, though I believed it nothing to do with Rick and everything to do with their own devices. Even Jack was there, standing somberly next to Charlie with his hands in the pockets of his slacks, his jacket bunched up at his wrists, looking impossibly handsome. But I wanted him less today than I ever had before. Today I didn't know if I'd ever want anything again other than to turn back the clock.

They chatted amongst themselves, moving around me as they donned jackets and gloves, and I felt as if I were the center of a storm, moving separately, more quietly than the rest. And when we were all ready, I followed them out of the house, into the cold. Jack hung back, laying his hand on my back, asking me softly if I was all right. I nodded my answer, because how could I tell him the truth? How could I tell him that my life, my heart would never be the same? How could I tell him my soul had been shredded and thrown to the wind?

We split up into several cabs, Jack and I ending up by ourselves. But he didn't press me, didn't speak, just let me exist, my eyes trained out the window as the first snowflakes began to fall.

Three days had passed, and I hadn't stepped foot in their home. There was nothing to be done there, not by me, and Sophie had come to me. She didn't want to be home, either. So we spent the days in my room when she wasn't with Sadie, who'd been staying with a friend too.

What I hadn't told her was that Wade had come to me that night. She spoke about him as if things were the same as they had been, as if he hadn't come to me for comfort and left when he'd gotten what he'd come for.

And still, I understood him. But the truth of my sacrifice was too much. He'd finally consumed all of me, fueling his fire with my soul's tinder.

He'd barely spoken, Sophie'd said, only gone from meeting to meeting, handling the funeral and the beginnings of the estate paperwork, all the details kept separate from her, which she was grateful for. She couldn't decide anything; not what she wanted to eat or wear, whether or not she wanted to sleep, how to occupy her time in the long hours of the day.

My heart cracked and crumbled with every word. He was in

pain (I knew, I could feel it as if I'd taken a part of him with me) and he didn't know how to manage that pain (I knew this too, without a shadow of a doubt). But I'd been used up and left alone.

He was dangerous. Letting myself have hope was dangerous. And now, I would pay penance for that. Because I loved him still, and I always would. I just didn't want to hurt anymore.

I didn't want to speak to him, and he didn't reach out to me, not that I'd expected him to. If there was one thing I'd learned from his return, it was that he wouldn't come to me, ever. I'd written him a dozen letters in those three days, the old habit as easy and comforting as it was painful. I'd written the words I wanted to say and never would, sometimes on tear-stained paper, sometimes on paper that met its end in the clutches of my fists. And I kept all those words secret, sacred. I couldn't trust him with them.

The cab pulled to a stop behind the others, and Jack got out first, extending his hand to help me out. But he didn't let it go, just tucked it into his elbow to steady me. I looked up at him gratefully, my legs and heart less steady with every step, and he patted my hand with sad eyes that expected nothing.

I wished again that I could let myself be with a man like him. But my heart wasn't mine to give. It never had been.

Ben greeted us at the door and showed us to the second pew, his eyes lingering for a brief moment on the point where my hand hooked in Jack's elbow. He pulled me aside, telling me softly that Sophie wanted me with her. But first, I had to see Rick.

I was last in line behind my family, and for that I was thankful. Because when I stood next to his casket, I wasn't rushed, didn't have to hurry. I couldn't have even if I'd wanted to.

He looked different, waxy and foreign but the same as always. Just ... gone. I wanted to touch him but stopped myself, wishing I could hold his hand again, wishing I could smooth his hair. But instead, I leaned into his coffin ever so slightly to whisper, "*For in that sleep of death what dreams may come / When we have shuffled off this mortal coil, / Must give us pause.* Goodbye, my friend, my father."

The words caught in my throat, and I backed away, turning for the side room as hot tears rolled down my cheeks. I brushed them away before I pushed open the door and stepped into the room, stopping just in the threshold as the door swung shut quietly behind me.

Sophie looked up, rushing into my arms, but my gaze was locked on Wade across the room.

He stood, tall, strong, his uniform crisp and neat, dark and somber. He looked bigger, larger than life, invading every corner of the room with his jaw sharp, lips flat, eyes that cut through me, leaving me shaken. Sadie's arms were wound around his waist, her face buried in his chest, which was covered in medals, but he looked at me for a long moment, our souls tethered.

Sophie pulled away, and the tether snapped. "You're here," she breathed.

"I'm here. I'm always here."

His eyes hadn't left me — I could feel them on me like a flood light, exposing me, illuminating my pain. Sadie broke away from Wade and moved to hug me. I closed my eyes and held her, and he watched me still. I couldn't meet his eyes again, couldn't feel the weight of them, didn't want it. Didn't want to know what he wanted, what he thought. Not right now. I was resigned to never know.

I pulled back and looked her over, smiling gently as I opened my clutch and found my handkerchiefs, touching up her makeup with one. I pressed it into her palm when I was finished and gave another to Sophie.

"We'll survive today," I said, cupping Sadie's cheek, trying to convince myself just as much as them. "Today, *this* will be hard, to share our grief with everyone. But we will survive, and we'll survive whatever comes next."

The funeral director ducked quietly into the room. "It's time."

I nodded and straightened Sadie a little more, adjusting her blazer, moving to Sophie to smooth her hair and press a kiss to her cheek, and then only Wade was left. His Adam's apple bobbed, betraying the hardness of his face, his eyes burning with things left unsaid.

I looked away and ushered the girls out.

They sat next to their aunt, and I kept walking, planning to sit with my family, but he grasped my hand, sending a shock up my arm and to my heart, pulling me to a stop. His eyes told me he needed me, told me he was sorry, begged me as he sat and tugged my hand, and still, against all that I wanted, I took the seat next to him, my heart hammering and soul aching. Because I loved him, and that love destroyed me.

The warmth of his body transferred to mine as a friend of the family stood in at the podium and sang "The Only Living Boy In New York," one of Rick's favorites. But I wasn't relieved to have Wade there next to me. I wasn't comforted. I was confused about everything and nothing, the injustice of it all stifling me through the stiff collar of my dress, which suddenly felt too small, too tight.

Rick was gone, and he'd never come back.

Wade was back, but he may as well have been gone.

He took liberties, doing what he liked, taking what he liked when he liked it, rejecting me over and over again in between, and I let him.

I was a slave to my hope.

But I couldn't hang on any longer. I watched as it slipped through my fingers, fading to a pinpoint of light.

The singer finished and sat, marking my turn. The poem was in my purse, then between my fingers, then resting on a podium stand as I stood before the people who loved Rick, their eyes on me for words of comfort. But the eyes I felt the most were Wade's, like a stone tied around my ankle, dragging me down, down into the dark.

I looked down at the poem, took a breath, and willed myself not to cry.

Life is a walk,
A very long walk
That begins with a crawl,
A toddle and tumble.
But we walk on,
Sometimes to trip or fall,
Sometimes to run and laugh
Throwing our faces up to the sky
And our voices to the wind.

Friends come and go
Through the very long walk,
Our paths meeting,
Sometimes parting,
Sometimes meeting again,
Sometimes not.
But we weather the days we have
Finding comfort and joy
In togetherness.

When we meet the one,
The one to walk with us,
The one to hold our hand,
The one whose arms we fill
When the nights are cold,
The one to comfort
When their tears fall,
Trail of diamonds
On a porcelain cheek.

This is when we feel
The value of our lives.

We walk through the spring,
Our eyes on the long blades of grass
Reaching for the sun
The smell of life and beginnings
Filling up our souls;

We walk through the summer,
Lazy in the heat
Warmed by that sun
Which coaxed the blossoms from buds
Opening their petals to offer themselves
Freely, gladly;

We walk through the fall,
And the green leaves breathe their last
In a riot of color as they languish
The tree yawns and stretches bare branches
To sleep, just for a while;

We walk through the winter,
And the cold is bitter
The days of spring and life gone
The quiet deafening, a fog with no edges
But still we hold hands: it vanquishes our fear.

And when our walk is done,
The miles behind us,
A trail of footprints

Converging, parting;
When we look behind us
At all that has passed,
The ones we love,
What we leave behind,
What we cherish,
Is what makes our lives
Worth living.

WADE

Elliot didn't meet my eyes again, only folded up her paper and walked off the stage with her head down, though I willed her to look up, waiting for her to sit next to me so I could hold her, take her pain and press it against mine until they were the same. But as my fingertips tingled, imagining themselves against her skin, she kept walking, passing me by to sit in the pew behind me.

My body went rigid, every muscle tense from my jaw to my thighs, leaving my lungs empty. A professor from Columbia made his way to the podium to read an Emerson poem, my eyes on my father's coffin, more alone than I'd ever been in my life.

She didn't want me, didn't even want to be near me. I'd broken her, just as I feared, and now … now …

Nothing made sense. Not the things I wanted. Not the things I'd lost. Not the moment I found myself in or the moments to come. Not my uniform, scratching at my neck like a noose, and not the hard pew under me where hundreds of people had sat, saying goodbye to someone they loved for the last time.

I could feel the letter in the inside pocket of my jacket, resting against the backs of the medals I didn't feel like I'd earned pinned to my chest. That paper reminded me that I had one job left to do before I could find peace for a moment. And I needed peace before I succumbed to the war inside of me.

"Catch the Wind" was sung as my sisters sobbed silently beside me, but nothing could reach me through the veil. And when the song was through, it was my turn. I stood, walking up to the podium, keeping my eyes down as I teetered on the precipice of my anguish.

I cleared my throat, pressing my palms against the surface on either side of the letter I'd written to my father.

"This piece of paper sat on my desk, blank and mocking me for days before I was able to write a single word. It was empty, and I'd been tasked to fill it with an explanation of what he meant to me, what he meant to everyone he knew. A description of his accomplishments and platitudes about how he lived.

"To say he lived would have been untrue. He didn't just live — he breathed life.

"I could have talked about his years at Columbia and the influence he had there. I could have told you about the books of poetry he wrote, or about his love of words or gifts as an orator. I could have told you how he liked his eggs or took his coffee, or which of his sweaters was his favorite, or how he always slept on one side of the bed, as if my mother were still sleeping next to him. But that wasn't who he *was*.

"How could I answer that question? How could I put into words who he was and what he meant? Because that story is different for every one of us. Each of you sitting before me knows in your own way what he meant to you, and that's why you're all here.

"Maybe it was because he supported you — it was one of his favorite things to do. He believed in all of us, an unflinching hope that we would all see our potential realized. Maybe he taught you things

235

that you'd have otherwise never known. I know that for me, that was true. He taught me how to tie my shoes and how to read. He taught me how to love unconditionally and how to forgive, though those lessons were lost on me later in life, when they mattered the most. But even in the end, he taught me grace and compassion, even tried to teach me how to grieve him. Of everyone, he knew how impossible that task was, but he believed in me even then.

"In grieving, he asked us to celebrate him. He asked us to remember him. He asked us to live because in living, we would honor him. I am not his only legacy. His legacy will live on forever in every heart and every mind in this room. So live, and live well. Take all of the things that he taught you and keep him alive too."

I finally looked up, and my eyes found her as they always did.

Emotion bent her brows, her lips hidden behind her handkerchief, her eyes pinched closed, the line of her long lashes against her cheek visible from even afar. But that wasn't what clamped my throat closed. It wasn't what set my pulse galloping or the heat climbing up my neck as tears from my words burned my eyes.

It was Jack's arm around her, her body curled into his side, his face, which didn't hold sorrow but something else, something sinister as he watched me watch them with defiance flickering behind his eyes.

She'd given herself to me, but it hadn't changed anything. We were here again, in purgatory for eternity.

I scooped up my letter after a split second of shock. But I couldn't sit down, couldn't stop moving. Jeannie held Sadie, nodding at me once as I passed — she'd take care of them, because I couldn't.

I rushed down the stairs and out the side door, not knowing what I was doing, not knowing where I would go. I only knew I couldn't stay there. It was too much. My father in a box made of oak and satin. My sisters crying, dressed in black. Elliot lost, lost to me as she ever was. Me, lost to myself.

The snow crunched under my feet, hand in my pocket around my hat, and I was halfway across the courtyard when I heard my name from her lips.

I turned, my chest rising and falling with shallow breaths — I couldn't get more than a sip at a time, like I was suffocating — the air puffing from my lips in foggy bursts.

"Wait," she called, her face touched with pink, nose and cheeks and chin. Her eyes were big and dark, shining and shimmering. "Where are you going?" The words were broken, lilting with emotion.

"I can't do this," I answered and turned to walk away, but she grabbed my arm.

"Wade, please. You can't leave, not right now."

I turned to face her, my words cold and hard, like my hands, like my heart. "There's no reason for me to stay."

I tried not to watch the snowflakes that fell on her cheeks and melted, the specks of white in her hair and on the shoulders of her black dress, on her rosy lips that parted, trembling with the words she was afraid to say. They were words I couldn't wait for, words I'd never hear. So I walked away, leaving her standing in the snow, the darkness of her marring the blanket of snow like the gash of my heart.

GROUND ZERO

The quiet point
Of impact,
The sooty blankness,
Tells tale of all
That was lost.

—M. WHITE

ELLIOT

I **stood in Rick's library, surrounded** by the chatter of dozens of people in black and the sound of Bach filling the spaces between, my eyes across the room on nothing, my ears straining to hear the front door in the hopes that it would mark his presence. But he never came.

Hours had passed since I'd seen him, hours that gave me no relief. And rather than speak to the guests who had come to pay their respects, I followed Sophie like a shadow, offering myself as support when she needed, even if it was just in the form of a warm hand or a word of encouragement as she handled the party by herself, without her brother by her side.

She kept a cellophane lid on herself, thin and transparent to me who knew her so well, but to everyone else, she seemed the picture of strength, accepting condolences and offering those of her own. She shepherded her sister, who was morose, attention turned inward, keeping her away from those who would pry, who would speak clumsily. Sadie's best friend had shown up just after the wake started, and the girls disappeared. I was grateful for that, because Sophie needed me. So there I was.

My family lurked around the bar, eating and drinking and gossiping until the kids finally had had enough. And with their exit, my burden was lighter. Jack hung back, asking me again if I was all right with his hand on my arm like I was his, and I let him because I didn't have the strength to fight.

Jeannie and Lou managed the gathering itself, their presence another blessing, Ben at Lou's elbow all day or answering the door, the honorary usher, everyone keeping things running while Sophie did her duty, even though I knew it took everything out of her, even though she wanted to be alone.

That's what no one ever tells you. Funerals are a selfless act, a long day of grief to share with others whether you want to or not. They're not about the ones closest to the impact of the loss — those closest must endure the arduous day with their grief put on display, a tamped down, quiet version of the screaming truth. The others feel the loss but don't have to hide it, don't have to pretend, don't have to *give* in a time where they have nothing to give.

But Sophie gave. She gave alone when Wade should have been there, shouldering it with her. But he was gone, not participating, grieving on his own. As much as I understood, I hated him for it. I hated him for running, for hiding, for grieving somewhere no prying eyes could see. I hated him for leaving Sophie here. I hated him for hurting her. For hurting me. For hurting.

And somehow, I loved him too, even though our love had been ground down to dust, blown away by the lightest breeze.

It was dark by the time the last guests had gone. I helped clean up the house and pack the food away, stopping only a few times to pour Sophie a very strong whiskey Coke. She sat drinking it silently in the library, her eyes on the fire, alone for the first time all day.

Sadie had gone to her friend's to spend the night, and Jeannie left a bit after as Lou and Ben waved goodbye in the hallway. His arm was around her, her body leaning against his, the two of them the picture of the exhaustion I felt. So I thanked them for all they'd done, which was more than they could ever be repaid for, and I sent them to bed, clicking off the lights behind them as I made my way back to Sophie.

Her eyes were glassy after the series of drinks I'd supplied, and she didn't look up as I sat down next to her in the dark room.

"He didn't come home," she said, her voice rough from disuse.

I drew a long breath, training my eyes on the fire. "No, he didn't."

"I can't believe I just did that alone."

"Me neither, but you did, and you did it well."

She chuffed.

"I mean it. You survived today, which was the sum of what you needed to do. Now it's behind you."

Her face fell, slipping into apathy. "Now I just have the whole rest of my life to live without Dad."

I swallowed hard, tears stinging my eyes again, just when I thought they'd run dry.

"Why would he leave like that, Elliot? Why would he just … just *abandon* us like that, right then? Today, of all days."

I didn't answer for a second, pausing to find my footing. "I … I think it's my fault."

Her face swung to mine, apathy gone, anger in its place. "If he left because of you, then he's more of a coward than I realized."

It was my turn to look away, wanting to tell her everything in my heart, but there would be time for that. Just not tonight. "I don't think it's only because of me, but … Sophie, I make everything harder for him, harder than it has to be, that's all I'm saying. It's another layer of pain atop something already impossible for him to deal with." I blinked slowly and took another breath. "I shouldn't have been here so much. I shouldn't have done this to him."

She grabbed my hand and squeezed, leaning toward me, begging me with her body to look at her, so I did.

"Elliot, *you* didn't run out of a funeral. *You* were there for me all day. *You* have been the strength we've needed to help us through it, even Wade. In fact, you were the only person who thought to chase him out and make sure he was all right, even though he's been cruel to you. I don't care what he said to you or why you feel like this is your fault, but it isn't. It was his choice to behave the way he has. He acts like this isn't hard for all of us."

"No, please don't say that. He knows, he just … I don't think he knows what to do with himself."

"So he runs away? It's so self-serving that I don't even know what to say. If only we could all run away when things get hard." She shook her head, leaning back on the couch, eyes on the fire and drink to her lips.

Flames licked the logs, flicking and jumping in yellows and oranges, whites and blues. "I think it's best if I don't come to the internment tomorrow."

Her brow bent, the hurt on her face in every plane and angle. "What?"

"Sophie, Wade needs to be there, and he needs to be there without me."

"But … Elliot, Dad loved you. He would want you there."

"I know, but Wade *needs* to be there. Don't you see? It's easier if I'm not there. He can have that final moment … it's his father. I've said goodbye, Sophie. I don't need to be there for this, not like the three of you do."

Her chin quivered, nostrils flaring as her breath hitched. "I hate this. I hate this so much."

"Me too," I said to the fire, wishing they could burn the words up, burn them down, make them disappear.

WADE

My frozen feet hit the pavement, one in front of the other, over and over, left, right, left until miles passed beneath them. The sun went down, dropping the temperature even more.

I'd found my way home for a moment, and I stood across the street in the falling snow, willing myself to walk up those stairs, through that door.

But I couldn't.

Nothing was right, nothing in the world. The air was too sharp. The city too loud. The sidewalk too hard, sending shocks up my legs with every step.

Thoughts had appeared and disappeared like ghosts, saying everything before dissolving into vapor. He was gone. I left my sisters, left his funeral. I failed him, and I hated myself for it. I left Elliot. She gave herself to me because that's who she is, because she gives everything, and then I pushed her away. I could have had her back, but instead I ruined her. I'd ruined everything.

I had all the excuses. I had no excuse.

I had all the feelings, all the thoughts. I could make no sense of them.

It was late, and I was so cold and so far away that I decided to hail a cab. I hadn't realized just how cold I was until I tried to give Dad's address — my address, the house was mine now — and my lips and tongue were sluggish, forming the words like Dad's after the stroke. And as the heat hit me, hit my hands, my legs, my feet, they started to tingle and burn, the frozen nerves firing painfully, coming back to life.

But I didn't want to feel, not anything. Not my icy hands, not my icy heart. I didn't want to face my sisters after leaving them, because I couldn't explain. I had no words for what I felt, no way to tell her that I couldn't pretend. I couldn't be calm for the sake of others. I couldn't listen to people like Elliot's father, who didn't know Dad at all, tell me how much he'd be missed. That they were sorry for my loss. I couldn't stand next to Elliot and pretend I was fine.

She was my curse, the wound that never healed, the truth-bringer. I couldn't hide my feelings around her, couldn't mask my pain for my father. And the truth was, I didn't know who I was anymore, didn't know what I wanted, didn't know how to live.

That was what Dad wanted. He wanted me to live, and I didn't know how.

I'd failed him there, too.

My hands and feet were on fire by the time we reached the house, and I took comfort in its darkness, hoping everyone was asleep as I climbed the steps and unlocked the door.

Everything was quiet, the house all shadows, but as I hung up my coat, I saw the fire flickering in the library and made my way down the hall.

Sophie sat on the couch, still in her clothes from the funeral, drink in her hand and eyes on the fire. She didn't look at me as she moved her drink from the arm of the couch to her chin, speaking before she drank.

"Welcome home."

I waited a beat, bracing myself for a fight. "I'm sorry," was all I could say.

"You should be."

"Sophie—"

She leveled me with her eyes. "How could you do that? How could you just leave?"

I didn't answer right away. "I'm sorry. I know it was wrong. I tried—"

"I don't give a fuck whether you tried or if you're sorry, Wade. This? This was one of the hardest days of my life, and you should have been here. You should have fucking been here." Her voice wavered, and she took a breath. "You let us down. I know you're hurting, but what you did … I don't even know if I can forgive you. I can't tell you it's all right because it's not, not by a long shot."

I folded my arms. There was nothing to say except, "You're right."

"And Elliot … Elliot seems to think this is in part because of her. Please. Please tell me she's wrong."

I watched her for a moment. "I can't. She's part of it. Not all of it, but she's part of it." The truth burned my throat as it left me.

She looked back at the fire, her lips flat as she shook her head. "Unbelievable," she muttered.

"You asked me a question, and I gave you an honest answer. Don't diminish my pain."

"I'm not. I'm saying that you're selfish, and that you should have endured your pain like I had to, like Sadie had to in front of all those people. I had to tell them all where you were, what you were doing, make excuses for you. Do you think it was easy for Elliot? Do you think she's just been *fine* with you here? But she showed up. She did what she had to do just like the rest of us, everyone but *you*. You ran away and left us all here to handle this without our biggest support, without the strongest of us. Or I thought you were. Guess I was wrong." She took another drink.

"You're drunk."

"Fuck you, Wade," she said, edging hysteria. "Fuck you. Leave me alone."

"Let me at least—"

She held up a hand. "You've done quite enough. So, please. Just go."

I felt it all inside of me, the explanation, the excuses, the words that meant nothing because my actions had failed me. I was too tired to fight, too bare to push back, so I gave her the only thing I had to offer her: her wish.

NO MORE

At the edge
Of no more
Is where we find
Our truth.

—M. WHITE

WADE

I *was awake long before dawn* broke, lying silently in the cold, in the dark.

My mistakes haunted me, my regrets too many to count, and yet every decision was justified in my mind.

I contain multitudes, Whitman wrote, and I understood the sentiment more deeply than I ever had before. I'd left the funeral because I'd needed to, because I couldn't contain the emotion, didn't know what I would do, what I would say. I left to save them from myself, even though I hurt them by leaving.

There was no answer, no choice I could have made to change the outcome. I would hurt them no matter what. It seemed to be the state in which I existed now, a dead end where I could only be wrong, where I could only damage everyone around me, even when I tried to remove myself from the equation. The fight followed me wherever I went; I couldn't escape.

I dressed when the room began to light in hues of gold. My uniform was stiff, formal, unnecessary today, but I had no suit and no interest in buying one, and when I looked in the mirror to knot my tie, I saw myself as if from the outside.

Cold eyes, hard jaw, brow that gave nothing. Broad shoulders, square and sharp, where the yoke of my pain sat. Strong hands, callused and rough, used for making a mess of my life.

I didn't know that man any more than I knew the boy who had stood in that spot seven years before, a lifetime, the span of a space that was too wide to bridge. I was a stranger to myself. And I'd lost everything I'd ever cared about.

The stairs creaked as I walked down them toward the sound of my sisters in the kitchen. They stopped speaking when I appeared in the entry, their grey eyes as cold as mine when they landed on me, accusing without breathing a word.

Sophie turned her back to me with a snap and click of her heels, coffee cup in hand as she moved to the sink. "So you actually showed up. Sadie, how long do you think until he bolts?" she asked flatly.

My eyes narrowed.

"Twenty minutes, tops," Sadie answered, equally flat.

My gaze fixed on her, but she wasn't looking at me, just picked up her coffee and took a sip as if I weren't there.

"I said I was sorry," I prompted through my teeth.

"And I said I didn't know if I could forgive you."

"You can't be serious."

Her eyes told me she was when she turned around. "What you've done is inexcusable. There's nothing you can say to me that will change that, no explanation that will make it all right. You left when we needed you the most. Why you left doesn't matter."

"You make it sound black and white," I growled, trying to keep my composure. "You didn't seem to mind that I've taken care of everything since I walked into that hospital. Hospice. The funeral. The will. The endless paperwork and lawyer meetings. You were perfectly happy to stay out of all of that, and I shouldered it alone. In fact, you *expected* me to handle it all without your help. You didn't even offer, Sophie, so don't be sanctimonious about me leaving yesterday when you haven't been present for *weeks.*"

"This isn't about me." Emotion edged her voice, shaken by my words. "You should have been able to hold it together long enough to be there. To be present. You can't ever get that back, that time, those moments. Life is hard. We have to stand up and live it anyway."

I took a sharp breath, chest heaving. "Don't tell me about life being hard. Don't tell me that with your privileged life that you have any idea what it means for life to be hard. This? This is nothing. We didn't lose Dad to an IED. We didn't see him shot or his body shredded from a mortar. I know life is hard. I've seen it. I've heard the song of the dying. I've been standing up and living it since I left home."

She took a deep breath, eyes shining, arms folded across her chest. "Then why couldn't you do this?"

"*I don't know!*" I yelled, hands fisted. "It's too much, too close. I'm sorry. I told you I'm sorry last night, and I'll keep saying it. I don't know what else you want from me. I don't know what else to do."

"Well, I told you last night that you've done enough." She blew past me to the peg where her coat hung. "We're going to be late," she said in lieu of a request or a demand.

I followed my sisters out in silence, the wall between us impenetrable.

There was nothing else I could say, and frustration mingled with my anger over the fact. We should have been hanging on to each other for this. I should have been there yesterday. I should have done a lot of things, but I didn't, and here we were, the three of us riding to the cemetery like silent islands, disconnected.

The funeral director met our cab and escorted us to the plot. Everything was covered in snow except the dark slash of his grave, dug just next to my mother's. Her name called to me from the marble slab, topped with flowers to match the ones on Dad's coffin. It rested on a platform with a lowering mechanism, surrounded by plastic turf, and as we approached, I heard music playing softly from somewhere,

Chopin's Nocturnes.

We were given single flowers and we filed to the coffin to lay them on the glossy surface. First Sadie, hand pressed to her lips and shoulders shaking gently. Then Sophie, her tears falling silently, streaking her cheeks. And finally me, my heart twisted and aching in my chest. I set my flower next to my sisters' before pressing my palm to the dark wood, imagining him on the other side, hearing him whisper to me to let him go. But I didn't know how, didn't know if I could.

I didn't want to step away. If the seconds had ticked past slowly before, when he was still alive, the moments we were in were the final, the last, and they stretched on endlessly. It was very nearly done; when I left his side, he would be gone forever. I wanted to scream, to cry, to fight for him. But there was nothing left to fight for, because he had left us with an empty vessel, lying on a satin pillow in a box we would place in the ground and cover with earth. It was insane, a ridiculous, ludicrous tradition, meaningless because it wouldn't help us, and he didn't care anymore what happened to him. We would never move on, we would never forget, and we would never forgive the universe or God or ourselves for the loss.

But there was nothing left to be done. So I said goodbye, sent my heart out of myself, into the air, and I stepped back, not taking my eyes off the coffin as I took my place next to my sisters.

Our eyes were all forward, and no words were spoken, the gentle piano music slipping over us as the coffin began to lower slowly, inching down silently, and my tears fell as he disappeared into the earth, taking my soul with him.

Sophie sobbed, a strangled sound, her body wavering just before her knees gave out. I caught her, held her as she clung to me, her eyes on the hole in the ground, her body wracking with sob after sob, but after a moment, she pushed me away, shaking her head. She didn't want my comfort, not even now, and I took my place by her side again, wounded and alone.

We stood at the edge looking down, and I felt the loss, felt the quiet absence of him acutely, as if my heart had been waiting for the moment to break entirely. I didn't know how long we waited here, but with the nod of the director, the workers came, rolling up the turf, disassembling the machine that had placed him where he'd rest forever. None of us seemed to be willing or able to move as Chopin played on and the small bulldozer pulled up. The director looked to me for approval, and I gave it to him with the smallest of nods.

We stepped back as the machine approached with a load of dirt, tipping its maw, the earth falling down to hit the lid of the coffin with a hollow thump. My sisters jumped from the shock of the noise, Sadie reaching for Sophie, Sophie clutching Sadie, and me, separate, solitary.

It was all I could take. But I endured it through the end, which was really no end, only the limit of what we could take. We turned our backs on the gravesite and walked away to the sounds of a roaring machine on the wings of Chopin, through the winding path of the cemetery to the street, where I hailed a cab.

The girls slipped inside, but I waited there on the curb, my body shaking with mounting hysteria. The mask was gone, the support that had barely been holding me up fallen, leaving me exposed.

"You're leaving us again," Sophie said, the plea rough, thorny and coarse.

"I'll be home later." I didn't wait for an answer before closing the door.

She trained her eyes forward, her jaw set and lips flat as the cab pulled away. But nothing I could say would absolve me. I needed to think, needed to get away, needed to understand. I had nothing left to give to her or to anyone.

I was in full uniform, and the eyes of passersby followed me, marking me, judging my behavior, but I couldn't stop moving. I was lost, aimless, frantically digging through my thoughts for the bottom, but there was no bottom, no end.

I had lost everything.

And I needed to know why.

E L L I O T

The doorbell rang in the quiet house — everyone was gone, busy at work or shopping, and the kids in school, leaving me alone, which was where I wanted to be.

The day had been spent transferring my grief onto paper, trying not to think about Rick or Sophie or Wade, trying not to think about the cemetery and smell of wet earth. And when the doorbell rang, when the sound marred the silence, I should have known who it would be.

And yet, beyond all reason, I was surprised.

Wade stood on the stoop in his uniform again, his face alive and eyes on fire, and I stood in the doorway, frozen to the spot with no idea which version of him I would get.

"Is everything all right?" I asked quietly, not knowing what else to say.

"I need to know why," he said, something on the edge of his voice that made me feel like I was wrong, as if he were accusing me of something.

I had no idea what he meant. "Why what?"

"Why didn't you choose me?"

I blinked, pulling away from him in shock. "Wade, I would have always chosen you—"

"But you didn't. You didn't choose me, and I want to know why."

"You know why," I offered gently. He was wild, distraught; there would be no reasoning with him.

He shook his head. "Why didn't you come with me? Why didn't

you leave your family? If you had only come with me, everything would have been okay."

"Please, come inside—" I said, but he spoke over me, his eyes wild.

"I need to know why you're still here. Why did you have to be here through this? I can't … I don't …." His chest heaved, and I said nothing as my heart broke again for the thousandth time, the porcelain pieces so small that I didn't know how I could keep putting it back together. "Why don't you want me?" he asked in agony, voice sharp. "For seven years I've perfected this mask, pretended to forget, pretended to survive, and now everything's ruined. I'm ruined. All I ever wanted was you, but after I came to you, you showed up to the funeral with *him.* Every time I wanted to speak, *he* was there. So tell me, why did you choose *Jack*?"

Anger filled me like creeping smoke, filling me up, my face and my heart on fire. "No."

He blinked at me. "What do you mean, *no*?" he spat. "You can't even answer—"

"Stop it, right now." The words were low, the warning clear. "You don't get to do this."

"You owe me an answer—"

"I owe you *nothing*," I shot at him, my back straight and breath shallow. "*You* did this to us, Wade. *You* put us here, but you're asking *me* why? When I've given you everything I have, you ask *me* why? Three days, and I heard nothing from you, and now you come here and accuse *me* of being the ruiner? I have questions of my own. Why don't you tell me? Why didn't you answer my letters? Why didn't you give me more time? Why have you treated me the way you have since you've been back, through everything with your dad?"

He said nothing, the shock written on his face at my anger, and I realized he didn't think I'd fight back. He'd expected me to bear his pain, shooting me down with his words. *No more.*

My heart hardened at the thought, forged by my pain at remembering what he'd done, how he'd hurt me. "Why did you come here that night, Wade? Why did you take without giving? And why do you presume to know what I feel, what I think? No one cares to ever ask me anything, you all assume and push and take until there's nothing left." I shook my head at him, finished being a rubber band for him to stretch. I'd finally snapped, and clarity found me with the sting. "I can't keep doing this with you. It's killing me, Wade. You're killing me."

He shook his head. "You don't understand. You never understood."

"I understand just fine, and I'm not participating in it anymore. I'll love you forever, but that won't stop me from telling you that I'm through. It won't stop me from telling you that I don't know the man who would do what you've done. I refuse to be hurt by you again." I stepped back into the doorway with my heart a jackhammer, and he panicked, eyes flying wide, stopping the door with his palm.

"Just tell me why," he begged.

"You first."

But he said nothing, his eyes searching mine as if he'd find courage there. In the end, there was none, only the war behind those eyes I loved so much.

I swallowed hard and nodded. "That's what I thought. Goodbye, Wade," I said gently and moved back, leaving him, closing the door to the vision of him standing there in the cold in his uniform, strong and weak, broken and begging me once again to acquiesce without saying a single word.

But I'd already bent as far as I could go.

DISPLACEMENT

Displaced by the weight,
The excess of what we believed
Spilling over curling edges,
Kissing the floor sweetly
As it crawls away,
Lost to the cracks,
And gone.

—M. WHITE

WADE

stood there on her step, staring at the door in the freezing cold, the madness that had consumed me ebbing as the wall I'd built so carefully crumbled, falling to the ground.

Her questions had hit me in a burst of explosions, each one ripping me apart a little bit more. She was right — I couldn't answer her. I couldn't give her any answers because I was broken. I couldn't be honest because the truth hurt too much to speak. I'd piled up that truth like sandbags and had been hiding behind them for protection.

I'd given her nothing, but expected her to give me everything. But she didn't owe me a thing, and I owed her everything.

I turned slowly and walked down the stairs, my jagged thoughts needling me from the inside.

The whys tormented me, all the whys I'd pointed at everyone else like weapons, holding them in front of me for protection when I should have turned the barbs back on myself.

Why had I done this to her? Why did I keep hurting her when all I wanted was to love her?

Why was I so broken? Why couldn't I do the right thing?

Why couldn't I be who she deserves?

The whys had been on me the whole time.

The truth of the circumstance was a relief and a regret. I'd pushed her to this, forced her to fight, backed her into a corner. All she'd ever done to deserve it was give me everything without condition, without expectation.

I chased the fleeting thought of confessing to Dad, realizing too late that he was gone.

The pain in my chest was unbearable, the loss so complete.

There was nowhere to go but home.

The blocks passed under my feet in a haze until I was standing on the stoop with my hands shaking as I tried to unlock the door. When I walked in the door, I found Ben waiting for me in the living room. His jaw was set and his eyes narrowed.

I kept walking, passing the entrance to the room, not ready to talk. I didn't know that I'd ever be ready.

"Wade," he called after me, his voice firm.

"Not now," I answered as I reached the stairs.

"Stop."

The command gave me pause, and I turned to face him, exhausted and drained. "What do you want from me?"

"Just to talk for a minute."

I eyed him, and he put his hands up in surrender.

"I'm not going to yell at you."

I relaxed only by a degree.

"But I might say some stuff you don't want to hear." He didn't wait for me to respond, just gestured for me to follow as he headed for the kitchen. "Come on. You need a drink."

I watched his back for a second before following him, still wary.

"Sit," he ordered, and I did, at the island bar. He poured us each a neat whiskey and handed mine over, which I took gratefully, sagging into the counter, propped up by my elbows.

I took a sip, and so did he, setting his drink on the surface. Neither of us spoke for a long moment.

He was the only safe place I had left. So I told him the truth.

"I was wrong."

Ben only watched me, letting me breathe.

My eyes were on the amber whiskey. "All this time, it's been me. I've hurt everyone I love with my own words, with my own hands."

"Elliot?"

I nodded. "I went there today. I needed someone to blame, and I chose her. I wanted to blame her for everything: Dad, my life, us." I ran a hand over my mouth, ashamed. "What is wrong with me? Why do I destroy the things I love?"

"Because you don't know how to give or receive love anymore. You've been this way as long as I've known you."

I took a drink, the heat burning a trail down my chest.

"War never healed anyone, especially not you."

I shook my head, still unable to meet his eyes. "I don't know who I am anymore, Ben. Do you?"

He took a long, heavy breath and let it out. "Sometimes I do and sometimes I don't, though the longer we've been away from the war, the more often I feel like myself. But we can't just shake off what we've seen, what we've done, what we've survived. It's a part of who we are now."

I swallowed, my voice low and shaky. "I don't want to feel like this anymore."

"Then you've got to change."

"I don't know how."

"I do."

I picked up my drink to take a sip. "Please, enlighten me."

"You've got to own up. You've got to be honest with yourself and with the people you love. You've got to apologize and make amends." He shook his head. "You're so busted up inside, and still you keep smashing the bits with a bat as penance. To make yourself pay over and over again when all you need is forgiveness. Forgiveness that they'll give you, if you'll only ask for it."

"I don't deserve their forgiveness."

"Your sisters will forgive you. They love you, and they need you, especially right now."

"And Elliot?"

His eyes were sad. "There's only one way to find out. And if you don't feel like you deserve her forgiveness, then maybe you should think about how you can earn it."

I considered that as I stared at the whiskey, looking for answers. "For so long, I've just compartmentalized everything. It was the only way I could survive her, survive deployments. You know how it is. You just pack everything away and focus on the task at hand. And since I've been here, I haven't been able to. I can't pack it away because the task at hand is the thing itself. There's nowhere to hide from it. Not from Dad. Not from Elliot. And all of my feelings were displaced. Today I put it all on her, and part of me, a big part of me, expected her to take it. To look at me with those eyes of hers like it *was* her fault."

"But she didn't?"

"She didn't."

"Good. You earned this, Wade. There's no one to blame for what's happened, and you can apply that across the board. But you're responsible for your actions, and your actions have hurt just about everyone around you since you came home."

I nodded, drained and tired. "And now, I make amends."

"You make amends. Starting with your sisters. When they come home, at least."

"They're not here?"

"They came home, changed, and left again. We talked before they left — Sadie's at her friend's, and Sophie's staying with Elliot."

I stretched my neck, tipping my chin to look up at the ceiling. "They don't even want to come home," I muttered.

"They're hurt and grieving. It's not just because of you. This house is a reminder of your father, and I don't think they want any more reminders. Not today."

"Can't blame them." I took another drink, considering drowning myself in the bottle on the counter.

He watched me again. "Want to talk about your dad?"

I shook my head. "It's too deep — I can't see the bottom."

"Anything I can do?"

I pushed away from the counter and stood, shaking my head again. "Thanks. I … I'm just going to go upstairs for a while."

"I'll be here if you need me," he said, his eyes earnest and sad. "For what it's worth, I'm sorry."

"Me too," I answered softly as I made my way to the stairs, climbing them to the top.

I paused in front of his room, still just as he'd left it the night before the stroke, less a few things we'd taken to the library. His side of the bed had a dip in it where he'd lain every night. His shaving kit was still in the bathroom, having let his beard grow in his last days. His things, all of his things, the reminders of him we could never erase, didn't want to erase.

Tears stung my eyes as I turned and headed for my room, another space frozen in time. I found myself at my closet, duffle bag at my feet. Then my hands were inside, fingers closing around the wooden box I took everywhere with me. And I sat on my bed and opened it as I did so often, looking for answers in the past.

Could I earn her trust again? Could I earn her forgiveness?

I wanted to more than anything.

And with newfound resolve and clarity, I began to devise a way to make it right.

THE
TRUTH
LIES

The truth lies
Still and quiet,
Waiting for the moment
It finds its voice.

—M. WHITE

ELLIOT

"'ll get it," I called** as I trotted up the stairs to answer the door late that afternoon, finding Sophie on my doorstep looking defeated. "Oh, Soph," I said softly and pulled her into my arms. She leaned against me for a long moment before pulling away.

"Thank you for letting me stay with you tonight," she said as we walked in and I closed the door.

"Of course. Come on, let's go downstairs before they catch us." I nodded toward the living room.

"Let's. I can't handle conversation about the weather. Not today."

We headed downstairs and into my room where the fire was going, the two of us climbing into my bed and under the covers. Sophie lay on her back, staring up at the ceiling, blankets up to her neck. She sighed.

"Maybe I'll stay here forever."

I chuckled. "I think that almost every day." I watched her profile for a second before speaking. "Tell me about today."

The color rose in her cheeks and nose, her eyes tightening as they filled with tears. "It was harder than anything before. Harder than finding out. Harder than when he died. Harder than the funeral. This time, I knew what it meant. I knew I'd never look at his face again, never hold his hand, never hear his laugh. It was so very final." A tear slipped down her temple and into her ear.

There was nothing I could say, so I offered nothing but my attention and heart, waiting patiently until she spoke again.

"Wade and I fought last night, then this morning before we left. He's just completely checked out, giving us nothing. He left us at the cemetery as soon as it was done. I just …" Another tear fell, her voice hitching. "I feel so alone. Isolated. Like no one understands or cares or can reach me. You're the only one who's been there for me through all of this, really there, whenever I needed."

"And I'll always be here."

"I thought when Wade came home, we would bear it together. But I was wrong."

My chest ached at the thought of him, pain blooming at the sound of his name. "I think he's grieving the only way he knows how."

"I know. And I know I shouldn't be angry with him for that, but I am. I'm angry with him for so many reasons. You know, I confronted him about you."

I took a shallow breath. "You did?"

"He said you were part of the reason he left the funeral. I just … I don't understand any of it, Elliot. It was so long ago. I know … I know things are hard for you both, but I just can't believe he'd let that get in the way of Dad."

"It's not just about the past, Sophie," I started, not sure how to explain the details of everything and nothing that had happened between Wade and me.

Her brows pinched together, and she turned her head to meet my eyes. "What do you mean?"

"He … he came here the night Rick died."

She blinked. "To talk?"

"No, not to talk."

Her mouth made a circle as she gasped. "Oh."

"He left just as quickly as he appeared. After the funeral I think … he thinks I'm with Jack. He's confused and scared. Angry. When he was here this afternoon—"

"He came here?" The words were an accusation.

I nodded. "He wanted answers, but I don't have any. I've given him everything I can." I let out a heavy breath. "Jack was right. I make excuses for everyone who hurts me, bend and bend under everyone else's weight."

"I can't believe Wade would do this," she spat. "I can't believe he'd come here, sleep with you, leave you, treat you the way he has. It's not fair, Elliot."

"Don't. Don't do that, Sophie. I can take care of myself. And you know what else? It's my fault I've been treated this way by him — I let him do it. But no more. I just … I can't keep doing this with him, and I told him as much."

"Elliot, I'm so sorry. I hate him right now, for what he's done and not done. But I miss him and need him too. I don't know which emotion is stronger."

"Don't hate him for what he can't control."

"He can't control himself?"

"Right now, I don't think he can." She didn't speak, and neither did I for a moment. "I miss him and need him too."

"Do you think he'll come around?" she asked quietly, and I rolled over onto my back, staring up at the ceiling alongside her.

I sighed, chest aching as I gave the only answer I had. "I don't know."

Sophie left early the next morning after we set a date for the next day to start packing up Rick's things. She didn't want to wait, she said, felt like she needed to do it before she went crazy thinking about it. I only hoped she was ready.

So I'd spent the day alone writing; the kids were still in full-time daycare, and my family happily carried on without me. I'd heard almost everyone leave early in the day — Charlie gone to work, Dad and Beth gone out for who knew what. But Mary was home after working the night shift, though she'd been asleep for most of the day.

It was early afternoon before I ventured out for lunch, setting my leather-bound journal next to my bed with my stomach rumbling. Once on the main floor, I realized the house wasn't as empty as I'd thought.

Voices wafted in from the kitchen, low and angry; an argument. I heard Mary's voice, the sniping, hissing tone sharp and quiet, like she was trying to keep it down. And I heard a man, but not Charlie. I stopped just before I reached the threshold when I realized who it was.

"Keep your voice down," she whispered.

"I told you what would happen, Mary," Jack bit, something in his tone dark, with an edge that sent goosebumps sprinting up my arms.

"But *Elliot*? For fuck's sake. It's the most ridiculous thing I've ever heard of. You and her. As if she could ever have a real chance with you."

I couldn't breathe from the second I heard my name, hanging in the air like an omen. And I stood paralyzed in the hallway, unable to do anything but listen.

"It's not ridiculous. She looks a lot like you, you know. But smaller, softer. Those big, brown eyes that just want to give you everything you ask for." He sounded like a snake when he spoke. I slowly realized that's what he was after all, and I was just a mouse he thought he'd caught.

"Don't do that," she said, her voice hard and biting. "Don't you do that, make it sound like you were interested in her. You only did this because of me, to get me back. To piss me off."

"It worked, didn't it?"

She made an infuriated noise. "I fucking hate you."

"No, you don't. You love me, and I'm through waiting." He paused, and when he spoke again, his voice was softer, cajoling her, persuading her. "Just leave Charlie. That's all you have to do. Come with me and all of this will be over. You won't have to deal with Elliot or the kids or anything you don't want to. I'll take care of you, you know that. Please, Mary. I love you." He kissed her; I could hear the soft sounds as I told myself to move.

She sighed. "I love you too. I just … I wish it were easier."

"It's never gonna get easier, babe. And we've waited long enough to be together. No more sneaking around. No more secrets. No more lies. Just us."

Move. I took a breath and stepped into the doorway to find them in each other's arms, his hand cupping her cheek, her eyes hot and locked on his. Until she saw me.

They burst apart like shrapnel.

"God, Elliot! What the hell are you doing?" she yelled as the flush rose in her cheeks.

"I could ask you the same thing," I said with more calm than I felt. My eyes met Jack's, and he at least had the decency to look ashamed of himself.

Mary's gaze bounced between me and Jack as panic set in, visible on her face, in her voice. "How much of that did you hear?"

"Enough."

Jack straightened up, his face tight. "Elliot, it's not what you think."

I ignored him. My eyes were on my sister, the liar. "I can't believe you would do this to Charlie."

"Oh, please." She tightened up her face and deflected, shooting insults at me to justify her wrongdoings. "Don't pretend you know what it's like. You've been alone your whole life — you don't understand what it means to be married or have kids. You don't understand what it's like to have a demanding career or real responsibility. You sit around all day and write in your stupid notebooks and hang out with Sophie and take care of someone else's kids because you have no life. It's pathetic."

My eyes narrowed, and I drew myself up, feeling taller, bigger, wider than I had before, fueled by my anger, by the betrayal. "You're right. I don't know what it's like. I don't know what it's like to be selfish and self-absorbed because I work every day not to be like you. I don't know what it's like to hurt everyone around me so I'll feel better about myself because I try to put other people's needs above my own, even yours. I don't know what it's like to cheat on the man I promised to spend my life with—"

"Because you have no one," she scoffed. "You are so pious, Elliot."

I glared at her, emboldened. "And you are such a bitch, Mary."

Jack's face bent in anger at Mary. "Leave her alone, Mary."

"What?" she shrieked, gaping at him, betrayed.

I ignored her, instead leveling him with a look I felt burning from deep in my belly, undeterred by his standing up for me. "And you. How could you do this to Charlie, to your best friend? To Mary, even, who you say you love? How could you? You used me to hurt her, but I'm not a weapon or a tool to be used by you or anyone."

"I'm sorry," he said, looking not at all sorry, "but I only did what I had to do to get her back."

I shook my head. "I should be hurt that you didn't really care about me, but I'm not — I never wanted you. I'm only sad that you used me to hurt the people I love." *Wade. Charlie.* I looked them both over. "You have until tonight to tell him or I will."

Mary's face turned a furious shade of red, her eyes flashing. "You can't do that."

"I can, and I will." The words were flat, direct. "I will not lie for you. I will not hurt the one person in this house who's been there for me. I will not betray your children by lying for the sake of you, who cares about no one but herself."

Jack turned to Mary, taking her arm. "It's fine. Let's tell him tonight. Together."

She ripped her arm away and turned on him, fuming. "No. I won't be blackmailed by *her*."

"You're going to tell him anyway. Why not make it tonight?"

"She won't do it," she said, looking at me, but talking about me like I wasn't there. "She doesn't have the guts. Sweet little Elliot, the doormat."

"Try me."

Something in her eyes faltered, like she was seeing me for the first time, but she slammed the door closed on the thought when Jack reached for her arm again.

"Mary, we'll tell him tonight."

"I don't *want* to," she yelled petulantly.

His face hardened. "Because of her or because of me?"

"Don't do that, Jack. Don't make this about you and me."

Something in him changed, something fundamental, and it was like an iron curtain slamming between them. "You've had me waiting for years. *Years*. And I was stupid enough to think you'd actually go through with it." He stepped away, and her face sprang open with regret.

"Jack, wait! I want to tell him … I'll tell him, just not—"

He brushed past me. "No, you don't. You won't. I should have known," he said to himself as she chased him down the hallway toward the door. "It's really too bad you couldn't be more like Elliot. She would give anything for the people she loves. You can't even give yourself to me, not in the way that matters."

"Wait! Please, talk to me." She grabbed his arm, and he spun around.

"I'm through talking." And with that, he blew through the door, slamming it hard enough to make the windows rattle.

She stood there in front of the door with her back to me, shoulders heaving for a long moment. And when she whipped around, her face was twisted, contorted with rage.

"You," she whispered. "Get out."

I swallowed. "Whatever you want," I said as I walked to my coat, slipping my feet in the boots that I'd left in the entry after the snow.

"Get out. Get out! *Get out!*" she shrieked, and I slipped on my coat, grabbing my bag.

Heat radiated off of her as I walked past and opened the door. "I'm telling him tonight." My words were firm, quiet, and when I closed the door behind me, she screamed, the sound punctuated by the thump of something hitting the door.

REVELATIONS

Revelations
Begin and end
With the truth.

—M. WHITE

WADE

The front door opened and slammed shut, and Ben and I shared a wary look, neither of us expecting Sophie to blow into the living room, fuming.

"I need to talk to you." Her eyes were razorblades.

Ben nodded. "I'll, ah, give you guys a minute," he said as he left, abandoning me.

Her lips pinched, her whole body coiled up like a spring. "You slept with Elliot."

A jolt shot up my spine. I nodded.

"How could you do that to her, Wade? How?" she said, the words like daggers. "You know she still loves you, and you still love her, but I don't even know if you deserve her. Not after what you've put her through."

"Sophie—"

"I used to, you know," she said as she began to pace like a caged animal. "All this time I've tried to be understanding, tried to see your side, had your back and supported your decision even though I disagreed. I never asked you about her, not once, even though I knew you were both hurting. Especially her. Because, unlike you, she actually talks to me."

"Sophie, if you would just listen—"

"And you come back here, treat her like a pariah, and then go over there and take advantage of her?" She shook her head. "I don't even know who you are anymore."

"Stop!" I shouted, her words cutting through me. "Just hang on and let me speak."

"Why? Are you going to deny it?"

"No, but—"

"So you've just got a bunch of excuses. Imagine that," she scoffed.

I stood, frustration coursing through me, making it impossible to sit still. "It's not like that."

She crossed her arms and glared at me. "Well, then, explain it to me."

"Are you going to interrupt me?"

"I'll give you two minutes."

I ran my hand down my face, pressing my eyes with my fingers, sorting back through the days, trying to decide where to start. So I started at the beginning.

"I've always loved her, since the first moment I saw her, and that has never changed. Didn't matter how badly I wanted it to."

Her face softened by the smallest degree.

"If things had been different, if I'd come here for any other reason but for Dad, maybe I would have known what to do about her. But I didn't. I didn't handle anything the way I should and now … now I've ruined everything, hurt everyone. Even you and Sadie. I went there that night because I knew she was the only person in the world who would understand, the only one who could remind me that there was a reason to live. She was the only one I could turn to. And then … I was scared. I've been scared since I walked into that hospital, all the way up until we put him in the ground. But right now I'm not scared. Now I'm only ashamed, empty, wounded. This whole time, I've needed her, but I couldn't have her, couldn't see past myself to tell her. And now that I understand what I've done, it's too late."

Her anger melted away, and she covered her lips with her fingers, shaking her head as she sank onto the couch. "Wade …"

"I'm sorry, Sophie," I pleaded. "I'm sorry I haven't been here for you, but I didn't know how. I'm sorry I hurt you, but I was too hurt to give of myself. I'm sorry I left you over and over again, but I was afraid of what I'd do if I stayed. Please, forgive me."

"I forgive you," she said quietly after a moment. "Why didn't you talk to me? Why didn't you tell me?"

I took the seat next to her and leaned forward, resting my forearms on my thighs. "I didn't know what to say, how to act. I couldn't deal, Soph. Not with any of it. And to have Elliot here on top of everything was just too much."

"You've got to talk to her."

I clasped my hands between my knees and squeezed. "I want to. I do, but I … I've made so many mistakes. So many. Too many."

She laid her hands around mine, and I looked up to meet her eyes. "Wade, she loves you. You just have to find a way to tell her you love her too. Make it up to her. Get her back, beg her forgiveness. She'll say yes — I know it. Maybe not at first, but she's been waiting here for you to forgive her for seven years. Give that to her and tell her you were wrong and I don't think there's a chance she'll say no."

After what I'd said to her, after what I'd done, it seemed like forgiveness was a pipe dream, a carrot on a string I'd almost had in my hands over and over again. I needed to think, needed time.

Time. Time. Time.

It was the one thing I'd never been afforded, no matter how I begged and pleaded. And now … now I knew I needed to make the most of it.

Sophie gripped my hands. "Just think about it."

I nodded, and when she shifted to embrace me I found myself overcome.

The doorbell rang, and she pulled away. "I'll get it," she said, touching my shoulder before she walked away.

Elliot's voice carried into the room from the entry, and I straightened up, my heart ticking faster with surprise and anticipation. With fear. But I pulled myself up and ventured out to face her.

"She told me to leave. I found her in the kitchen with—" She stopped when she saw me, and her face shut down, closed off. "With Jack. Mary and Jack are having an affair."

Sophie gasped, and a war of emotions washed over me. Relief that they weren't together. Rage that he could hurt her. Sadness that I couldn't have protected her. My chest ached at the realization that I couldn't even protect her from myself.

"I can't believe it," Sophie breathed. "For how long?"

"Years. I was apparently a pawn in his attempt to persuade her to leave Charlie."

"Oh, my God. Are you all right?"

Elliot nodded. "I never wanted him like that. He was only a friend." She didn't look at me once, but I knew the words were meant for me.

"Poor Charlie. And the kids." Sophie shook her head, mouth gaping in shock. "What … what are you going to do?"

"I told her she has until tonight to tell Charlie the truth before I did."

Sophie blinked. "You're kidding."

Elliot shook her head. "I'm going back over there tonight, but … I might need a place to stay for a little bit. I'm so sorry to even ask, but—"

"Don't be ridiculous," Sophie said, taking her hand. "You can always stay here, as long as you need."

"Thank you." Relief was heavy in her voice. "I'm going to have to figure something out. I don't know if I'll ever be welcome there again."

"You're always welcome here," I said, wanting some interaction with her, anything. But she stiffened, her lips and voice flat and formal.

"Thank you."

Sophie asked, "Want to sleep in my room?"

Elliot softened again when she looked back at Sophie. "That would be nice."

"Then it's settled." Sophie's phone rang, and she swore when she checked it. "It's Jeannie. I've been avoiding her calls since yesterday. Give me one second, okay?"

Elliot smiled and began unwinding her scarf. "Okay."

Sophie answered and walked toward the back of the house, and Elliot and I stood in the entry in silence. She went about the business of taking her coat and hat off, hanging them on the pegs on the wall as I fumbled with what to say, how to start.

"Elliot, I—"

She turned at the sound of her name, her eyes deep and sad. "Please, don't," she said softly. "It was hard enough to come here without us doing this again. I just had nowhere else to go."

I nodded my response. She didn't want to talk to me, as I suspected, and I knew better than to force her. Because I could, and she might submit. But I didn't want her to submit. I wanted to earn her love.

I would give her that precious time she needed, but I wouldn't give up. I wouldn't run away. Not this time.

$$\boxed{\text{E L L I O T}}$$

My heart hammered in my chest at the confrontation, but he didn't press me, only nodded and turned for the stairs, making his way into his room. The second his door closed, I could breathe freely again.

I was standing in the last place I wanted to be and the only place

I could think of to go. I needed Sophie, but Wade was where she was, and the unsuspected consequence of pushing him back was that it felt like I'd made everything worse, more complicated.

But I wasn't sorry. And I didn't want to hear what he had to say.

I'd exhausted all hope that he'd tell me he wanted me, that he would say that he loved me, that he was sorry, that he wished he could erase the last seven years all the way up to yesterday and start over. The likely answer was that he wanted to argue more, blame me for everything, and that just wasn't something I could take. Not today. Not ever.

Sophie appeared again. "God, I'm sorry. She needed to know we were all still breathing over here, but I just couldn't deal with it yesterday."

"I'm sure she understood."

"She did, thankfully." She slipped her phone into her back pocket. "So, I think I know what we should do while you wait to detonate your sister's marriage." I flinched, and Sophie took my hand, smiling. "I'm kidding. She handled all that C-4 well enough on her own."

A chuckle puffed out of me.

"I think we should bake cookies."

"That does sound like it would make life a little better."

She hooked her arm in mine. "It's science."

We spent the next few hours making and eating cookies until we felt sick. The house was relatively quiet — Wade never came back down, Ben was out with Lou, and Sadie was staying with her friend still. No one faulted her for that, and I don't think Sophie or Wade knew if it was right or wrong. They'd be her parents now, an overwhelming task that neither of them knew how to perform.

But that afternoon, nothing else mattered. There were no

problems other than how much sugar we had left and if there were enough chocolate chips in the batter. There was just me and Sophie and the task at hand, our conversation finding its way to us, easily, happily, devoid of anything important. But in that simplicity, we found comfort, levity in an otherwise weighted day, week, life.

Things always change, I said to myself, finding comfort in the platitude. Life is fluid — sometimes with cresting, white-capped waves, other times with an eerie stillness, a quiet surface. But it was never the same, day to day. And as sure as one day was up, the next may be down. Letting yourself ride the surface instead of kicking and fighting or sinking to the bottom like a stone was the only way to survive intact.

The sun had gone down and the temperature dropped, and too soon, I had to go back. The thought of walking through the door of my sister's house gripped my stomach, but there was no choice left to make. No more would I let her have her way. No more would I suffer, nor would I let Charlie suffer for the sake of what she wanted.

They'd never cared for me, my family, and I'd sacrificed so much for them. My self, my future. Wade.

My sister's betrayal and my loyalty to Charlie and myself fueled me, and I put on my coat and hat and scarf like I was going into war, not knowing who I'd be when I returned.

It was cold outside but warmer than it had been, as if my fire had warmed up the whole world. I felt strange, changed, alive and brave, even though I was scared. But what I'd realized was that the brave aren't immune to fear. It's only that their fear doesn't stop them.

I stood on the stoop for a long moment, staring at the knocker, gathering myself up. And then, I knocked.

Mary opened the door with a whoosh that sucked the cold air past me and over her, making her shiver just once as she glared at me, teeth bared.

"Get out of here, Elliot."

"Did you tell him?" I asked simply.

"*Leave.*"

"Who is it?" Charlie asked, approaching the door. "Elliot? Why did you knock?" he asked with confusion on his face. "You have a key."

Mary warned me with her eyes, furious eyes edged with fear, shouting warning at me. I ignored her.

"Mary told me to leave, so I didn't think it was appropriate to just walk in, given the circumstance."

His face bent even more. "Asked you to leave?"

"May I come in?" I asked.

"No," Mary shot just as Charlie said yes. He made a face at her and pulled the door open wider, touching her arm to move her from where she stood blocking my entry.

"What's going on?" he asked her as I passed.

"Nothing. She was just leaving, weren't you?" she asked pointedly, and I turned to face her, accusing.

"I have nothing left to lose, which leaves you nothing to bargain with."

Charlie watched us, trying to find his footing. "Let me take your coat."

"No, that's all right. I won't be staying long." I looked into his eyes, apologizing with all my heart, hoping he'd understand. "Mary didn't tell you, did she?"

"Tell me what? Will somebody please tell me what in God's name is going on?" he asked with wide eyes and fear riding his voice.

I looked at my sister. "It's your last chance."

Her face wrenched up, red and angry as tears flooded her eyes, catching in a line at her lashes. "Don't. This is none of your business, Elliot. Just shut up. Shut the fuck up right now."

I took a deep breath and released it, hoping he knew how sorry I was. "She's having an affair with Jack."

Charlie stood dumbfounded next to me, brow bent as if he didn't understand what I'd said. "That … that can't …"

I said nothing.

"She's lying," Mary cried, reaching for Charlie, fisting his shirt in her hands. "Please, believe me."

He searched her face before looking back to me, then back at her. "Why would Elliot lie?" he asked.

"Because she hates me." Mary was frantic and feverish, her eyes searching his for purchase. "She's jealous because I have everything she wants. She just wants to hurt me, hurt *us*. She's probably in love with you and wants me out of the way. You know she's obsessed with mothering the kids. *Our* kids."

But her words couldn't touch me — I kept my eyes on him and my heart on task as my father and sister appeared next to the staircase, staring silently. "They were here in the kitchen this afternoon. I heard everything. Jack only pretended to be interested in me as leverage, to convince her to leave you. They said they've loved each other for years … and when I walked in, they were kissing."

"No," he whispered.

Emotion welled in my chest at the impossibility of it all. The right thing felt wrong, so wrong, the betrayal and disbelief on his face breaking me.

"You liar," she growled through her teeth. "You fucking *liar*," she shrieked and flew at me. We tumbled to the ground as she slapped and scratched at me for a split second before Charlie pulled her away.

He grabbed her by the arms and bent to level his eyes with hers, holding her still. Her eyes were still locked on me.

"Mary," he commanded, and she finally looked at him, her anger melting away, turning to pitiful sorrow. "Is it true?"

Her mouth opened to speak, but nothing came out, her eyes bouncing between his, her brows pinched.

He shook her once. "Mary! Tell me. Tell me the truth." A fat tear slipped down her cheek.

"It wasn't supposed to be like this," she whispered.

His chest heaved, jaw locked, nostrils flaring as he took it in. "With Jack?" he asked after a moment.

"We never meant to hurt you," she said feebly, her words shaking, and he let her go, backing away from her slowly. She lunged for him, grabbing his shirtfront. "Don't, please don't go. Please, let me explain," she begged, desperation thick in her voice.

He ripped her hands away, holding her back by her wrists. "Nothing you can say will change what you've done." He let her go and turned his back on her, his hands shaking as he helped me up. "Are you all right?" he asked gently.

"Who cares about her? This is *her* fault," she screamed as I nodded. Charlie whipped his head around to glare at her.

"No, this is *your* fault. You did this to me. To our children." His voice broke. "You did this, and it can't be undone." He turned for the stairs. "Get out, Mary. Take your things and leave. And don't come back."

"*Charlie!*" she cried, scrambling up the stairs after him. "Please. Please don't say that. Don't do this. If you'd just talk to me—"

"You can talk to my lawyer." He stormed up the rest of the stairs and slammed the bedroom door.

Mary stood halfway up the stairs, her eyes on the space where he'd stood only a few seconds before. And in that moment, she seemed small, stripped of her pride, of her marriage, her dignity. I reminded myself that she'd made this choice. That it wasn't my fault.

It didn't stop me from feeling responsible all the same.

She finally turned, her rage contorting her face. "You couldn't keep your fucking mouth shut, and now look at what you've done. I've done *everything* for you, you ingrate, and this is how you repay me?"

"You treat me as if I've done nothing for you. Like I haven't endured you for all these years. You ask me to lie when you've never given me anything, not even something so simple as your love. But if you cared about anyone other than yourself, you wouldn't have asked that of me. You wouldn't have cheated in the first place."

"Get out, Elliot!" she screamed. "*Get out.*"

Charlie appeared at the top of the stairs again, his face flat and angry and cold. "Leave her alone, Mary. You've bullied her long enough."

"Fuck you, Charlie! Don't tell me what to do in *my* house."

He rushed down and grabbed her by the arm, wrenching it at an awkward angle as he kept going, taking her down the stairs with him, then past us.

"Ow, you're hurting me. Where are we going?" she yelled, trying to wriggle away from him.

"To the office until Elliot is gone for the night. I don't know that she's safe here with you."

"What the hell is that supposed to mean?" She broke free and stood there, staring at him.

He towered over her. "It means if you hit her again, I'll call the police, and I don't think you want to get arrested, not if you want custody of your children. So get down the stairs and into my office or so help me God, *I'll pick you up and carry you.*"

He grabbed her arm again, and she went more compliantly, shooting daggers over her shoulder at me. When the door closed, I realized I was shaking all over.

My father fumed. "What the hell is the matter with you?" he spat. "None of this was your business, and now you've meddled and *all* of us will suffer for it! What are we supposed to do now?"

"I don't know, Dad," I offered, exhausted. "Go home?"

His face was red as he blustered, "We can't go home! We *have* no home!"

My brow dropped in confusion. "What do you mean?"

"I mean we were evicted, you idiot. We have no money, no means. Why else would we be here? Do you really think I wanted to come back *here*? And now you've ruined everything."

I watched them in utter disbelief and absolute understanding. "Of course. It all makes perfect sense." I tried to walk past them to my room to pack a few things, but he grabbed me by the arm.

"Where do you think you're going? You need to fix this, Elliot Marie."

I pulled my arm away, meeting his angry gaze with one of my own. "Fix it yourself. It's you who made the mess in the first place."

"You're just like your mother," he spat like it was an insult.

"Thank you. Because in this world, one thing I will always be grateful for is that I am not like you." My eyes cut to Beth, who held Rodrigo, scowling at me. "Your hate has only strengthened my desire to be kind. Your anger has only made me more compassionate. I'm only sorry that I wasted it on you for all these years."

And with that, I walked away from my family once and for all.

THE LENGTH OF LOVE

Love is a line
Spanning the distance
Between two hearts.

—M. WHITE

WADE

tried to keep myself busy in the kitchen the next afternoon, but knowing Elliot was upstairs had me on edge.

The words I wanted to say swam around and around in the fishbowl of my mind. She'd come back late the night before — I'd still been awake, talking with Ben in the living room. She was upset, and when she glanced at us, her eyes begged us not to ask any questions. So, we didn't, though I wanted to. I wanted to know that she was all right, wanted to comfort her. I couldn't imagine that her breaking up her sister and her husband would have been easy or simple. In fact, I knew she was hurting and afraid.

I only wished I could be there for her.

She'd spent the rest of the night upstairs with Sophie, and that morning she was subdued, making eye contact with me only once, the force of her sadness nearly bringing me to my knees.

Sophie never left her alone with me, not even for a second.

There was so much to say, but I had to bide my time, give her space, let her breathe. If I pushed too soon, I'd lose her forever. She might have already been lost to me.

I could hear the murmur of their conversation up in Dad's room as they packed away his things, and I recounted every moment I'd spent with her since I'd come home, all the years I'd spent so many miles away with her on my mind, wondering what if. I thought about that night, the night he died. I thought about the need my soul had for her, and she gave herself willingly, as she always did. Because she was unfailingly kind, even at great personal cost, simply because she loved with all of her.

I only wanted to be whole enough to give myself to her. For so long, I'd been in pieces, and in my darkest hour, she'd been my only light. But I'd laid waste to the gift she'd given me before I'd told her what it meant to me.

The kitchen — and the rest of the house — was spotless before long, and Ben was at Lou's again as he spent all the time with her that he could before he left. I'd walked the equivalent of the length of Manhattan in the time since I'd stepped off the airplane, and now that I'd found my bearings, I didn't want to run anymore. But being downstairs in the house, all alone, in the quiet … Dad's absence was loud, deafening.

I decided to read and made my way up the stairs, not able to sit in the library. That room was almost more his than his room. But when I heard the sound of my name as I approached his room, I paused.

Elliot and Sophie sat by the window, the light streaming in around them, illuminating them, leaving them with halos of sunshine. Boxes surrounded them as they worked through a pile of his clothes.

"Wade and I got this for Dad for Christmas a few years ago," Sophie said, running her hand over the front of a sweater that lay in her lap. She sighed. "It's so hard to choose what to keep and what to donate. Almost everything here has sentimental value."

Elliot didn't respond right away, but finally said, "It's okay if it's too soon. We can put all of this away and go for ice cream instead. Or whiskey."

That elicited a chuckle from Sophie. "Both sound nice. But I've got to do this. I haven't been able to stop thinking about his things in here, just waiting to be sorted through."

"All right." She looked around. "Well, let's say you can keep ten things. Fifteen, if you really need to push it, so if it's not important enough to make the top ten, it goes in the donate pile."

"Thank God you're here, Elliot." Sophie shook her head. "It's silly to love a sweater in place of a person."

Elliot reached for another sweater and held it up. "Oh, I don't think it's silly at all. Especially this. You can put it on when it's cold, and it'll keep you warm. He would have appreciated that."

Another sigh from Sophie, heavy and sad. "Can I ask you something?"

"Anything."

"Do you think that there's an end to love?"

Elliot considered for a second.

"What I mean is," Sophie continued, "the longer someone's gone, do you think the love … diminishes? Is there a limit to its length?"

Elliot laid the sweater in a heap in her lap, her hands buried somewhere inside of it. "I think that every day the answer to that question is different. Some days the loss is as fresh as the day the love left. Some days, you can breathe, not think of it for a stretch, sometimes just for an hour or a few minutes, sometimes for days. Sometimes you'll go a day or a week without breathing once because the loss is suffocating. It takes different faces: anger, hurt, longing. Sometimes it's bittersweet joy, because for a moment, you had it all. I want to tell you the pain gets easier, but it doesn't. You only learn to bear it. But there's comfort in knowing you loved and were loved in return, even though it's no consolation. Only a truth you carry around with you forever."

Sophie sniffled, and Elliot leaned in to hold her.

"There is no length to love; it's infinite. It lives in you always. Hold on to it."

"But it hurts," she sobbed.

"That's how you know it was real."

I leaned against the wall without the strength to stand on my own for a long moment, and I pressed my forehead to the cool surface, eyes closed. Those words — her words — were meant for me, not my father. They were about me, an echo of what I felt, what I'd felt every day since the day I left.

And now, now that I knew what I stood to lose forever, what was in my grasp, I felt the truth of it, of her, of my heart. I heard my father telling me to live. And for the first time in seven years, I knew exactly what to do.

TO SURVIVE

Inch by inch,
Second by second,
Pulling yourself from the
wreckage,
Leaving it behind you
To survive.

—M. WHITE

ELLIOT

he afternoon was up and down as we worked slowly through Rick's things. Sophie and I vacillated between reminiscing and laughing to bearing the pain of our loss and the tears that always seemed to follow. Wade had stayed away, thankfully. I was too bruised, too worn to take any more. He'd tapped me dry.

Charlie had texted me that morning to ask if I'd come by the house at some point, promising me that my family was nowhere near. So after we'd finished for the day, I left for home, not sure what I'd find.

The only sound in the house were the sounds of the kids playing and the rumble of Charlie's voice. I smiled when I heard him laugh, thankful for even a small show of happiness after everything he'd been through.

And of everything that had happened with Mary, Charlie was the one I felt most guilty about — putting him through all of that was the end cap on the horrible damage I'd done.

"Hello?" I called from the entry as I closed the door, wondering if I should have knocked instead.

"Elliot?" Charlie called. "Up here."

I hung up my things and made my way upstairs, my heart lighting when the kids jumped up and ran for me.

"Hi, guys," I said, smiling and crying, just a little, their joy bringing me joy. I pulled away, holding them at arm's length, feeling like I hadn't seen them, really seen them, in ages. "I've missed you."

Sammy bounced. "Where've you been? Mommy's gone. Grandpa too, bye, bye, bye," he crowed, flapping his arms merrily.

Charlie looked older than he had a few days before, the lines in his face speaking of a sleepless night and his sadness. "I don't think they even miss her," he said, defeat heavy in his voice. "I don't know how this happened, Elliot."

"Oh, Charlie," I said, pulling Maven into my lap as Sammy found a dump truck and pushed it around the room making truck noises. "This isn't your fault."

He sighed deeply. "And Jack …"

I shook my head. "This *isn't* your fault. They made a choice."

"But I didn't see it. It was going on right under my nose, and I didn't see it."

"They're good liars."

He chuffed.

"What happened last night?"

He scrubbed a hand over his face. "Well, I kept Mary in the room with me until you left, and she pulled out all the stops. Begged. Screamed. Threatened me. Promised me. But in the end, I made her leave like I told her to."

"Do you know where she went?"

"Not to Jack's. I went there this morning, early."

"How early?"

"Still-dark early. She wasn't there, and he said he was done with her, that he'd waited too long. He even said he was sorry, but I didn't buy it, and it didn't stop me from decking him."

I gasped. "Oh, my God. Did you really?"

He held up his right hand, bloody knuckles out, looking quite pleased with himself. "Sure did."

"How did it feel?"

"Like vengeance."

I chuckled. "I'm not usually the vengeful type, but in this case … well, he deserved that."

"You can say that again." He shook his head. "I just can't believe this. I didn't sleep at all, just lay in bed in the dark, thinking about everything, wondering if they had sex in our bed, considering every time she wasn't with me, wondering if she was with him. My best friend and my wife. I … I just can't even comprehend it."

My chest ached. "Charlie, I'm so sorry. I'm sorry I was the one who told you … I really wanted it to be her."

"She's too much of a coward for that. Her life was a very delicate web, complete with pitfalls she put in place herself. I'm not sure she knows what it's like to be happy — she sabotages every good thing in her life. She'd labeled all of us a burden. Me. The kids. Even you, who's always been there, whenever we need. I just don't understand."

I helped Maven with the puzzle toy she fiddled with in my lap. "She's always been this way, even when we were children. She wanted it all, and Dad gave it to her, feeding her selfish nature, and when she was older, she did the same to him. They're fire and air, the two of them. Where did Dad and Beth go?"

He sighed. "By the time Mary and I came up last night, they were in their room, and when I came back from Jack's, they were packing their things, spewing bullshit at me the whole way out the door about the sanctity of marriage. As if I were the one who had defied that vow."

Sammy marched around the room like a soldier saying *bullshit, bullshit, bullshit.* Charlie grabbed him and roared, tickling him until he'd forgotten the dirty word all together.

As I watched him with his kids, anguish filled me again at the realization of what I'd done. "I hate this, Charlie."

His eyes were sad when they met mine. "Me too. But you know what? I've always known it wouldn't work out between us. Is that wrong to say? That I married a woman I didn't truly love and who didn't love me?"

"No. It's not wrong, especially if it's the truth."

He looked away, shaking his head. "I thought she would … I don't know. Grow up. Change once she had Sammy. But I was naive, and now … well, now I'm not entirely sure what I think."

"Do you know what you're going to do?" The question was vague; I didn't know how to ask him anything more specific than that.

"I've already put in a call to a buddy of mine from college to handle the divorce, and I called a nanny agency today looking for someone to help. My parents are coming to stay for a few months from Chicago, to help out and for moral support. Because it's not going to be pretty, this divorce. She's going to fight me for everything, whether she wants it or not, like the kids. Elliot, she can't get them. She … she can't. She won't care for them like I can, like I will. They'll just be something for her to use to manipulate me, to hurt me."

"I know," I said quietly.

"This is early to ask, but …" He watched me for a second before speaking. "If I need a witness, will you speak on my behalf?"

I swallowed the lump in my throat, swallowed the regret that Mary had done so much damage, hurt so many people. There was no question as to what I'd do. "Of course I will."

"Thank you," he said, sighing his relief. "I wanted to talk to you about something else."

"Anything."

"I wanted to thank you for the truth. I know how hard that must have been for you, and I wanted you to know that I appreciate you — I always have. You can stay here as long as you want, and I mean that, even if it's forever. But I don't want you to feel obligated to be here. What I mean to say is that … I don't want you to wait or to hold back. You've sacrificed years of your life for us, for *them*," he said, nodding to the kids. "So, what do *you* want? Because I think it's time you did that. You're free — we won't hold you back anymore."

I tipped my chin, pressing a kiss to Maven's crown to hide my face. "Thank you, Charlie."

"No, thank you. For everything." He looked around to Sammy. "Now, who's ready for ice cream?"

Sammy laughed. "But Daddy, it's cold out!"

Charlie grabbed his son and hugged him tight. "Good, then it won't melt."

And I smiled at them, comforted by the knowledge that they'd be all right, no matter what, because they had a father who loved them.

THE CONSTANT

In life
(Unlike death)
There are few constants:
The sun will rise;
Your lungs will breathe;
Your heart will love.

—M. WHITE

ELLIOT

T *he ice cream was cold,* but our hearts were warm as we walked back to the house in the dusk. I reflected over the last few weeks, on the vast changes all of our lives had taken, at the sheer breadth of space between who we were then and who we were now.

I felt like I'd climbed a mountain and was nearing the peak; the light glimmered against the edge, promising an end. Or a beginning. Either way, the shift was tangible, and I marveled over the power of my losses and gains, that they contained the means for me to change. And change I had, elementally.

For so long, I had been still and quiet, waiting. Waiting for what exactly, I didn't know, not even as I looked back. Perhaps inspiration to guide me to a profession I'd love. Or maybe I was waiting for the courage to submit my work, realize my dream to write. I was waiting for something definitive to break the chains of my family, something to convince me that they held me back. I'd still been waiting for Wade, even after all those years, after all that we'd been through since he'd come back.

But there would be no more waiting. Not to seek out my career. Not to walk away from my family. Not even for Wade.

It didn't matter how much I loved him; my love couldn't change him. So I'd go on loving him silently through the rest of my days, as I didn't know that I could ever move on.

As we walked up the street, I saw the shade of a figure sitting on the step, shrouded in the failing light. But the moment he stood, his name filled my mind, my soul recognizing the lines of his body.

My feet slowed as my heart sped, betraying my promise not to wait for him. He waited there at the foot of the stairs, shoulders straight, the collar of his peacoat flipped against the cold. As we came closer, I saw that his face was set in determination, his eyes filled with sorrow and apologies. A wooden box rested in his hands, elegantly carved, and my thoughts raced with possibilities.

I reminded myself that he'd rejected me, blamed me, hurt me over and over again. This would only be another version of that cycle we'd found ourselves caught in. But hope sprang despite it all, like a shoot of grass in the snow.

I stopped, though Charlie and the kids kept going, making their way inside. When I looked up at Wade, the nearness of him was stifling.

"What are you doing here?" I asked, girding my heart for the answer.

He looked down at the box in his hands. "You said you didn't owe me anything, and you were right, Elliot. But I owe you everything."

My breath was thin as I stood still, waiting, wishing, hoping, dreading.

"I have been unfair and unjust. I've been resentful and angry. I've been so many things I'm ashamed of, but the one constant is that I've always been in love with you." He met my eyes, pinning me down as he so easily could. I was his, irrefutably. "You asked me why I came to you that night — it's because you have possessed my soul from the start. You were the only one … the only one who would understand, who could show me that there was love still in the world, in my heart."

He took a deep breath, shifting, eyes dropping once again to his hands. "You asked me why I never wrote you back. But I did, Elliot. Every day, to every letter."

He opened the box, and I watched him as my tears chased each other down my cheeks. Inside were my letters, dozens and dozens of them, each in my hand, and in the center was a leather bound journal, fat and bursting with papers.

"When I left, I was angry, so angry. But through boot camp, I didn't have time to think about anything. I got every letter, but I couldn't throw them away. I couldn't open them either. So I tossed them in my foot locker and ignored them. I took them with me when it was over, because I still couldn't get rid of them. And when I got stationed in Texas for training before deployment, the letters kept coming, and every one added to the pile was another log on the fire."

He swallowed, meeting my eyes and dropping them again as the wind ruffled his dark hair. "It wasn't until I was in Iraq, when my mail finally caught up, that I opened one. There were twenty of them, all with your handwriting on the envelope, and where I was, so far away, I … I found I wasn't mad. I only missed you. So I opened one. Then another. Then I couldn't stop, not until I'd read them all."

Tears stung my eyes, and I blinked them back, steeling myself.

"And then, I wrote. Letter after letter poured out of me, the things I'd wished I'd said. Some were angry. Some were happy, some sad. But they were all wrong. I didn't know how to tell you I was wrong, that it wasn't your fault but mine. And I was, Elliot. I was wrong. I was selfish and scared, and I've regretted that for a long, long time." He took a breath. "I thought when I came home, maybe you could forgive me. We could talk, make it all right. Go back to the old plan. I couldn't answer you while I was there because … well, because of no good reason, I see that now. But at the time, I was stuck there. The only concession I gave myself, the only allowance to feel anything, was when I sat down to write you a thousand letters I never sent. Friends died, I saw things that made me feel like I wouldn't make it out. I had nothing to offer you, nothing to give, no promises to make, not until I was home. And when I finally did get back, when I opened your first letters, I realized just how wrong I was."

He met my eyes, and I saw his were sparkling with tears.

"You changed your mind."

My breath hitched, and I nodded.

"I didn't know," he breathed. "I would have come back before leaving for deployment. I would have married you then, if I'd known you'd been begging me to come back that whole time. The answer I wanted was given to me over and over again, piled up in a locker in the dark. And when … when I read them, I knew there would be no going back. I believed at the time that I'd lost you forever without even asking you because how could you ever forgive me? I pushed you and blamed you, and you believed I didn't want you because I didn't come home. I could have married you then, but I had too much pride. I was young, young and stupid. And by the time I realized how wrong I'd been not to reach out to you, it had been years. Your letters had stopped. You were through. But I kept writing you back, every day, even after you stopped. I never stopped loving you, even though I thought you had stopped loving me."

He set the box on the concrete rail and picked up the journal, unwinding the strap, opening it to one of his letters before he offered it to me.

The leather was soft, the book heavy in my palm as I read his words, the words I'd imagined for so long.

Elliot —

Every day that passes takes me farther away from you, from us, from what we had. I sit in the mountains, surrounded by men who are each alone entirely, and I think of you. I can remember you so vividly that sometimes I feel like you're here, and I imagine what you would say, what I would say. Sometimes I imagine that we talk about nothing, that I make you laugh, that you kiss me and tell me you'll always be waiting. Other times, I imagine us saying all the things we'll never have a chance to say.

I wish I were brave enough to send these letters to you. As much as I love you, as much as I always will, when I sit under the stars on the other side of the globe, I know that you and I can't fit into each other's worlds. But there will ever only be you, for all my life.

I ran my trembling fingers over his words, then across a letter I'd written him that rested in the crease, folded like a paper boat. I flipped back through the pages, letter after letter, his words breaking me, his sorrow, his longing. His heart had been through what mine had.

"It's always been you, Elliot. Every night when I lay my head on the pillow, every morning when I rise, it's only you. Tell me I'm not too late. Tell me there's still a chance for us, and I will spend every breath I have earning your forgiveness. Tell me that you still love me, and I will give myself to you completely."

I was overcome, unable to speak as I closed the journal and clutched it to my aching heart. And because words could not find me, I stepped closer until our bodies met, laid my hand on the hard line of his jaw, tilted my chin, and kissed him with everything I possessed.

His lips against mine transferred truth, singing softly as they parted and closed against mine in a song of deliverance and salvation.

He wrapped his arms around me, breathing me in deeper with every second as the kiss went on and on forever just as it ended too soon. He searched my face, only a few inches from his, his breath warming my skin.

"Is it true? Is it real?" he asked in a whisper. "After everything I've done, could you still love me?"

"I have loved only you," I whispered back, and his face lit with joy, bent with grace as he kissed me again. And with a few simple words, he was mine and I was his, as it had always been, even when it was unspoken.

He dipped his chin, breaking the kiss as he pressed his forehead to mine.

I was home.

WAIT

Waves lap my feet
Eyes on the horizon
Love in my heart
As I wait
For you.

—M. WHITE

W A D E

closed my eyes, certain I'd open them to find her gone, but there she was with love and forgiveness in her eyes. And my new mission was to earn that forgiveness with everything I did.

I kissed her again, pulling her into me, drinking her in with every breath, every touch. When she broke away, she smiled up at me.

"What do we do now?" she asked with swollen lips.

Within a split second, I had my answer. I smiled back and took her hand. "Come with me."

"I'll follow you anywhere. Where you go, I go."

I couldn't resist another kiss, slipping my hand into her hair before I pressed my lips to hers, transferring all the gratitude and triumph I felt. And then, I hastily packed away my notebook and closed up the box, tucking it under my arm as I took her hand again.

Anticipation crackled between us, popping with wonder. Her hand was in mine, and she was smiling. She was happy, but not as happy as I was — she'd given me everything I wanted, everything I'd been hiding from, the things I thought I'd never had. But all I'd had to do was ask.

"Where are we going?" she asked as we hurried down the sidewalk.

"To my house, is that all right?"

"Perfect," she answered.

We didn't speak along the way, both of us too busy with our thoughts, with our awe and reverence, and before long, I was towing her up the steps of the house and through the door, up the stairs and into my room, closing the door behind me.

She stood in the middle of my bedroom catching her breath, looking around with wide eyes that scanned the walls and furniture.

"It's just like I remembered it," she said half to herself as she unwound her scarf absently, walking to my desk to hang it and her coat on the back of my chair. The cork board still held our photos, my boutonniere from senior prom pinned next to our picture, a poem she'd written me there alongside it. She trailed her fingers across the words. "It feels like a lifetime ago."

I took off my coat too, tossing it on my bed, stepping behind her to hold her around the waist. My chin rested on top of her head, and she covered my arms with hers.

"Feels like yesterday," I said. "Time is a funny thing, isn't it?"

"It is," she answered quietly before turning around in my arms. "I've missed you. Every second of every day."

I brushed her cheek with the backs of my fingers. "I thought I could forget you. I even convinced myself I had, for a time. But it was impossible. You left a mark on my soul I couldn't erase."

The feeling of her body against mine, the weight of her hands on my chest reminded me she was real. And then I kissed her, compiling the sensations blissfully.

"I want to know everything," I said, pressing my lips to her temple. "Everything I missed, everything that's happened."

She chuckled. "So much. Seven years' worth."

"I've got all the time in the world to listen."

She sighed, the sound full of perfect happiness. "Where should I start?"

"From the minute I left."

"That," she said sadly, "was not a very tale-worthy time."

"But I want to know all the same."

She took my hand and led me to my bed, climbing in to lie against the wall, and I lay next to her. Her body curled and molded to mine, our legs wrapping around each other, her arm over my chest and mine under her shoulders, her dark hair fanned out and my hand unable to leave it alone. I slipped silky strands of it between my fingers, lost in the moment with her.

We lay like that for a little while before she spoke.

"You read my letters, so you know a bit."

I nodded and kissed her forehead.

"For almost two years, I floated through life, not knowing if I'd ever recover. I just kept writing letters, an exercise likened to stamping your feet in the cold to keep the blood flowing. It was the only way I could survive, to get the words out and away from me. Except the words were wind. They meant nothing to anyone but me. Or, I thought. I wasn't sure if you'd even gotten them or if you did, if you'd read them."

"I did. I read every one, just not when I should have."

She was quiet for a moment. "I think I'd rather hear what happened to you through all that time. I've missed it all."

"I ... Elliot, I don't know how to tell you what it was like."

"Words, strung together, one at a time."

I took a deep breath, her arm riding the rise and fall of my chest. "When I left, I left my soul here, with you." I paused, not sure how to put it but trying to, regardless. "I was empty at first, focused only on basic training. Every day was scheduled, every minute from the time I woke to the second the lights went out, and it seemed the next thing I knew, I was shipped off to Iraq."

Her hand shifted, resting in the hollow of my chest, just above my heart.

"It was … extreme, intense is the only way I know to explain it. You know, during the war, we had ways to call home, ways to keep in touch, but none of us did. I mean that — not the guys with kids or families, no one. It was too hard, knowing that back home, everyone went about not knowing, not seeing the world for what it is, not knowing what we knew. I barely spoke to Dad or the girls, but they wrote, and you wrote. But I couldn't answer. I tried. I was going to. But there was a moment …" I paused. I'd never spoken about it.

"You don't have to talk about it," she said softly, as if she knew.

I squeezed, holding her to me as I pressed a kiss to the top of her head.

"It's okay. It was a long time ago. Our truck hit an IED and flipped. My friend died, and I knew I couldn't answer you because I was sure, certain in that moment that I would die before I could get home to you. I dug a hole, a deep hole in myself, and I hid there, burying that most precious part of me so it would survive what I went through, all I saw. The only problem was that before long, I'd forgotten where it was buried. I don't think I uncovered it again until I found you again here, now."

Her fingers closed, clutching my shirt.

"But I wrote to you every day. I'd write them over and over again. Admission after admission. Some days, I'd just tell you what I did that day. Some days I'd beg for your forgiveness. And some days, more days than I'd care to admit, my words were angry, hurt, unforgiving. But no matter what I wrote, I couldn't send one back. I needed to be cut off from the rest of the world. From you. It was the only way I could survive everything I'd seen and the only way I could protect you from losing me. You'd already lost me. Better that than to give you hope. And part of me thought that if I didn't respond that you'd stop, that you'd be quiet and leave it alone, all while hoping you'd never stop, riding to every mail pickup with my heart in agony and hope.

"I was in Afghanistan when you finally gave up on me. I'd brought the box with me to every station, the only personal effect I kept with me always. I bought it on my first tour to Afghanistan in a village nearby from a man who'd learned to carve from his father, who learned it from his father and back generations. A few months after I bought it, that village was laid to waste. I always wondered if he'd survived to teach his sons. But I never saw him again."

She took a shuddering breath, and I pulled her closer.

"It wasn't long before the letters didn't fit, and I'd gone through a journal. Then another. So when I came back to the States, I kept only the ones that meant the most. Every time I came home, I switched them out, and every time the ones I kept changed, with the exception of just a few. I have thousands of them in Germany, all worn, the creases soft from folding and unfolding them so many times over the years.

"I volunteered for tour after tour, never wanting to be back here. It's … easier over there. When we come home, we can't forget, can't walk away from war, especially knowing we'll probably be sent back, so I just kept going. At least over there, everyone understood. We were all in the same place, hurting in the same way, pretending we were fine because it was the only way we'd survive.

"By the time the war was over, I'd changed so much, withdrawn into myself. I didn't know how to be the old me, and I wasn't sure who the new me was. I was still angry, so angry. And even at that, I thought about trying to find you. But there was no way to reach out. Not after a thousand letters I'd never answered. Not after ignoring you when you changed your mind and begged me to come home. After your last letter, I … I was sure it was over. I told myself I could move on, that it was time. But it was empty, and so was I."

"*This will be my last; my heart can't take any more,*" she recited from the letter, her voice distant, just as I'd imagined when I'd read it over and over again.

"*I hear you. Your silence is deafening, the answer clear. Since I'm sorry will never be enough, I'll only say goodbye.*"

We lay in silence for a few long minutes, hanging on to each other, the years folding up like a paper fan until the length had been shortened, bringing us back together again.

"I don't deserve your forgiveness," I whispered, and she propped herself up, looking down at me with her face framed by curtains of dark hair.

"I wouldn't have forgiven you if you hadn't changed."

I reached for her face, thumbing her cheek. "How can you be sure I have?"

Her eyes, her bottomless eyes told me only of her faith. "I can see it here." She ran her fingers across my temple. "And here." She touched my lips. "I can feel it here." She laid her hand on my heart. "I know you, even when you don't know yourself. Even when you pushed and pulled me, deep down, I knew how you felt. But I couldn't fix you, couldn't help you because you didn't want help. You wanted to be broken, and you wanted to hurt all of us, to warn us away. It almost worked."

"You believe in those of us who didn't love you the way you've deserved. Why?"

"Because," she said as her lips smiled small, "I knew all that you could be, and I wished for it with all of me."

"I'll spend every breath that I have proving you right." I pulled her down to me, my hands in the curve of her neck, her lips against mine, her breath my own.

So many years I'd missed. So many kisses, so many words from her sweet lips. How happy we could have been all that time — my chest burned at the thought. But I was through looking back to the past when my future was right in front of me, right there in my arms.

There was no urgency, only the long kiss, the kiss that never ended, only flowed from one moment to the next, softly, gently. I broke away after what felt like an eternity or a moment and climbed out of bed, walking around to turn off the lights. Snow fell beyond the window; the ground had been covered in the time since we'd been inside, and the full moon reflected off the crisp white canvas, lighting the room in shades of indigo. I reached over my shoulder, grabbing a fistful of sweater to tug it off. Then my shirt. Then my jeans, leaving me just in my underwear.

She'd pushed herself up to sit, taking off her sweater and jeans before climbing under the covers in a tank and her underwear. I slipped in next to her, the heat of her body radiating, mingling with mine as we lay chest to chest, our legs entwined, her arms folded and curled against my chest, my arms around her back, hands in her hair.

It was a moment I'd dreamed of, a moment I'd rejected. It was a moment we'd shared so many times, so many years before. It was *the* moment, the now, the present. The beginning and the end. The end of our pain. The beginning of our future.

"What happens now?" she asked, her breath skating against the skin of my collarbone.

"Now, we start over. I've got weeks left before I have to go back, and there are still so many things I need to do here. Like spend every second I can with you."

"And then what? What happens when you leave again?" The fear in her voice was slight, controlled — her heartbeat betrayed her.

"That's up to you." I leaned back so I could see her face. "If you're happy, if you still want me, then you can tell me what you want. If you want to come with me, you can. If you want to stay, I'll wait for you. I'll wait forever, if you want. I'll give you anything, if you ask."

She closed her eyes for a moment, opening them again to show me her shining irises. "I've waited for a second chance to answer this question. I've dreamed of what it would be like to give the answer I wish I had so long ago. And now I can tell you that I will follow you. I will follow you to the ends of the earth, if you'll give me your heart in exchange for mine."

"My heart has been yours as long as it's been beating. It'll be yours until it beats its last."

A sparkling tear rolled down her cheek, and she cupped my jaw, leaning in to kiss me, sealing the promise.

As my fingers wound through her hair, the kiss deepened, the urgency we'd lacked before now present in her hips pressing against mine, in her hands holding my face. The time apart had erased nothing — I knew her body if it were my own. The last time I'd been with her, I'd been driven by fear, by pain. Now, I was only driven by my love for her.

My hand trailed down her ribs, down the valley of her waist, to the curve of her hip. I savored every touch: the warmth of her skin under my palm, the weight of her body against mine, the softness of her lips as they moved gently against my own. The moments of waiting, of pain and longing, they had washed over me, passed through me, leaving me clean and new.

Her hips rolled against mine as we kissed, her body asking to be touched. Her fingertips roamed from the seam of our lips to my jaw and neck, across the place where my heart thumped in my ribs and down the ridges of my stomach. And as she touched me, I touched her, hands slipping under her tank, pulling it up with my wrist, fingers hooking in the edge of her bra to bare her. My palm cupped the swell of her breast, my thumb grazing her peaked nipple, the sweet softness of her body memorized by my skin.

She gasped against my lips, her body arching, and she tilted her head, tipping her chin up. But my lips couldn't stop, and they made their way down her long neck, to her collarbone, to her breast as she clutched me to her, hands twisted in my hair. I was surrounded by her, my thigh between her legs, her arms all around me, her skin everywhere, and I wanted every inch.

Lower I went, my busy lips seeking work, making a trail down her body as my hands rolled her onto her back, then moved down her stomach, to her panties. My fingers hooked them, pulling them down her thighs, her calves, away, my chest aching at the sight of her stretched out before me, all porcelain skin and dark eyes. Her breath was heavy as she crossed her arms to reach for the hem of her shirt and pull it off, the two of us undressing quickly.

The last time I held her, I was broken, unseeing what I had, unknowing what she could be. But now, with Elliot in my arms, I took nothing for granted. I knew what I had, and I'd hold on to her until the last beat of my heart.

She reached for me, and I filled her arms; I'd give her anything she wanted, forever.

I hovered over her, and she held my face, telling me with her eyes alone all the things I knew to be true. That she loved me. That she was sorry. That I was forgiven. That it was forever. And then I kissed her, giving myself to her in all the ways I could.

For a long moment, our bodies were still as we kissed, our only focus that place where our lips touched, where our tongues danced, but with every breath, heat spread across our skin. She moved, shifting until her thighs rested against my ribs, opening her up to me, her hips angling as her body reached for me. I was pressed against the heat of her, and with a shift of my hips and a flex, I filled her, connected to her, body and soul.

Neither of us breathed, our eyes locked, my heart thudding desperately in my chest as her lids fluttered closed. She took a breath that sounded like a sigh. I took a breath that shuddered with emotion.

Every movement was long and slow, deliberate. Her head turned to the side, lips parted, body rocking against mine. My arms, my back, my legs trembled as I moved slowly, deliberately, my pulse racing faster with every flex, and a soft sound passed her lips. I pressed harder, and she gasped. Harder still and my name, a whisper, slipped into the air. And then, just before I lost my composure, her back arched, her breath gone, lost from between her parted lips, the squeeze and pulse of her body around me taking me with her. And I let go too, the past, my pain, my heart and soul. I let it go and gave it to her.

Our bodies slowed to a gentle wave, my heart thundering as I buried my face in the curve of her neck, her heartbeat fluttering under her skin against my lips as her arms wrapped around me, cradling me.

I thought I'd never find freedom again. I thought I'd never know home, never know love. But in that moment, in her arms, against all odds, I found it all.

ONLY

For time cannot stop,
But moments,
Seconds,
A fleeting smile,
A kiss in the sunlight,
Can live forever.

—M. WHITE

E L L I O T

The sun shone crisp in a cloudless sky, warming us in the cool in-between that spring so often brought. Wade stepped forward onto the mounded grass and placed a bouquet of flowers on Rick's grave, then another on his mother's. When he came back to me, he reached for my hand, and we stood silently, his final goodbye, for a while at least.

Almost two months had passed, bittersweet with grief over our losses and joy that Wade and I had found our way back to each other. Grueling and time consuming was the process of finalizing the details of the estate, paying off lingering debts and medical bills, setting up Sophie and Sadie to be able to manage the house with him so far away. But I'd been there through it all, and over the weeks, the hard shell of a man who'd come back after so long had cracked and fallen away, and I found Wade, my Wade, underneath it all.

I'd also submitted my work to a string of agents, a nerve-wracking and slow process. But I felt good and right, as if I were stretching my dusty wings for the first time in years and years. I found my light, my spark, and Wade had found his. We'd held each other's all that time.

I'd moved into the house with Wade and Sophie once Charlie's parents came to town and the new nanny was hired and settled in, though I still went by every day to see them, they seemed to be fine without me after all. Mary's absence was the likely culprit of ir adaptability — she would have only made it harder on everyone, ldren included, strictly for the sake of doing it.

I hadn't seen or spoken to her since that night. I didn't know that ver would again.

She'd disappeared, abandoning Charlie and the kids, and my ther and Beth had disappeared right along with her. It should have ade me sad, made me regret my part in the falling out, but I didn't. hat they blamed me for their circumstances only made it easier to walk away.

I'd been freed from chains I hadn't known I'd been wearing.

The grass was still damp under our feet from the morning dew — Wade's flight would be leaving soon. My heart skipped a painful beat at the thought of being separated from him, but I reminded myself it was only temporary. I'd follow him in a few weeks, and then forever after. Warmth blossomed in my chest at the thought.

When he left all those years ago, I'd been afraid to leave home, leave everything I knew. But what I'd learned since was that he was everything that home meant to me. Without him, I'd been lost, wandering through my life without moving an inch, searching for something to make me whole.

Now that I had him, I could do anything. I was unstoppable.

He squeezed my hand and began to walk away, and I followed, neither of us speaking until we'd left the cemetery.

"I don't want to leave you," he said once we were in the cab headed for the airport and I was tucked into his side, my head on his shoulder. "I don't want you to go, but I'll be right behind you."

He sighed. "Two weeks is too long."

I chuckled. "Seven years is too long. Two weeks is a heartbeat."

"I've spent every day for the last two months trying to memorize your face, trying to get my fill, but I can't. No amount of time will be enough with you to satisfy my heart."

I lifted my hand, touching his face as I kissed him. "Well, do think forever would be long enough?"

He smiled down at me. "Guess we'll see."

My heart fluttered, and I rested my head on his shoulder aga

"Do you think Lou is getting settled in?"

"Ben says everything's great. I just can't believe they ran off li that and got married without telling anyone."

"Oh, I dunno. It doesn't sound so crazy to me. And anyway, I'll b glad to have someone familiar in Germany."

"So I'm already not enough for you? I see how it is," he joked.

"You're a given. You're more familiar to me than my own reflection." He kissed the top of my head. "I love you, you know."

"Almost as much as I love you."

He sighed again. "Two weeks is *too long*."

I laughed and wrapped my arms around his chest as we rode the final minutes in the cab in silence, the ticking of the infernal clock never stopping. And too soon, we were standing at the passenger drop at LaGuardia, his duffle bag at his combat boots, cap on his head, shielding his eyes from me.

"For so long I didn't want to come back, and now I don't want to leave."

"*Yet let me not be too hasty,*
Long indeed have we lived, slept, filter'd, become really blended into one;
Then if we die we die together, (yes, we'll remain one,)
If we go anywhere we'll go together to meet what happens."

He smiled, a crooked thing, surprised and teasing and full of love. "Quoting a Whitman poem about death is supposed to make me feel better?"

"It's easier than saying goodbye, isn't it?"

He pulled me close, still smiling. "It's only two weeks."

"Two weeks is too long," I echoed, and he kissed me sweetly ore whispering in my ear.

"Two weeks, and then forever."

And at that, I cupped his cheeks, kissing him once more as the light danced across his grandmother's engagement ring resting on y finger, the same finger that was closest to my heart.

E P I L O G U E

He laid his hands gently on my jaw, my heart singing h[...]
name and tears stinging my eyes, and he kissed me, sealin[...]
the vow of our forever.

The people who loved us cheered and clapped from behind us, but
I barely heard a thing. There was nothing outside of his hands, his lips, in
that moment when our lives began. And when he pulled away, his hands
still warm on my face and the ghost of his kiss still on my lips, he smiled
at me with more joy than I knew one man could possess.

He took my hand, and we walked up the aisle, past Sadie and
Sophie, crying and smiling from the front row, past Ben and Lou with
her hand on her round belly, Charlie and the kids, as confetti rained
down, spinning to the ground like dervishes. Hanging candles in jars
and paper flowers spun above us in the light breeze, whirling the tiny
scraps of paper around us.

The Black Forest was magical, a fairy tale forest of trees stretching
up to the heavens, lush and green and older than time. The big trees
were so tall, so dense we could barely see the sky, the leaves and moss
so green they almost glowed. When Wade and I had come here to

…e venue, we'd both known it was the perfect place to start our

…le.

… year of planning after years of loneliness had brought us to that

…ent. We'd flown back for Sadie's graduation and brought her and

…ie back with us, and every day since then had been busy with the

…l of preparations, time mostly spent constructing decorations for

…y, this day.

All the paper cuts were worth it.

I'd typed up all of our letters on an old typewriter, and though

…wasn't the first time I'd read them all, every one hurt in its own

…y, sated only by the peace of forgiveness. But I remembered writing

…ery line, and I felt every line of his.

We'd photocopied the originals and used them to make a myriad

…f decorations, mostly paper flowers, some big, some small, some in

…ouquets, some to make garlands of, which hung all over. Some were

…nade into strips and used as streamers. A thousand more copies were

…shredded into confetti, confetti that floated around us like snow.

A thousand letters that brought us to that moment.

My heart skipped in my ribs as we walked together to the back

of the venue with my hand in the crook of his elbow, the long chiffon

spilling down from the empire waist of my dress, floating around me

like mist. And as we reached a curtain made of tulle strips strung with

flowers, he pulled me through it and stopped.

He was so beautiful, his uniform crisp and medals shining as he

smiled down at me.

"Mrs. Winters," he started as he brushed a scrap of confetti from

my nose.

"Yes, Mr. Winters?" I asked with a smile.

"I have dreamed of this day for eight years." His fingers trailed

across the lace capping my shoulder in a triangle.

"And was it all you imagined?"

At that, he smiled and tipped my chin with a single finger.
And now there is nothing left in the world I could possibly war
His kiss spoke the truth of his words, stealing my breath, sto
my heart, starting my life.

Because now, we would live.

With every end
Comes a beginning,
A new path forged
Through the pain
Of an end
Giving life,
Giving breath
That once caught cannot be lost.

—M. WHITE,

OTHERWISE KNOWN AS
ELLIOT MARIE WINTERS

THANK YOU

There are always so many people to thank, and I always for someone. Such is the curse of being a mad scientist type.

As always, the first person to thank is my husband, Jeff. Th time, more than any, you have stepped up and knocked it o of the park during what was the most taxing book I've read i years, during a time in our lives that was tumultuous on its own So thank you, forever and ever, thank you.

The second person to thank is almost as high up on the list as my husband, and that's Kandi Steiner. If I had the proper equipment, and if I wasn't already married, I would totally put a ring on that. There are days (too many, too often) when your support is the only thing to keep me moving. How can I ever repay you for that? <— Rhetorical: there is no way. But I'll do my damnedest to try, for as long as I live.

Third comes Karla Sorensen, who showed up in an unbelievably supportive way for this book. Not only did you talk my characters and plot through with me ad nauseam, but you slapped me around when I needed it, petted my hair when I needed it, and generally helped hold me up so I could make it to the end of this thing. You're an excellent fascist cheerleader, and I couldn't ask for a better friend than I have in you.

Next is Brittainy Cherry, the woman who knows my soul

even I don't. How can I ever express what you mean to
When I was in the depths, when I was so deep in this story
could barely function for the toll on my soul, you were
. You understood. You knew. And you told me I could do
e comfort, the love you've given me fills my heart up over
over again. Thank you will never be enough.

To my many, many Alpha, Beta, and Charlie readers: Thank
dness for you. Every one of you made an impact on this
ry. Every one of you helped to shape this story. Every one
you have a little piece of your heart in this story. Thank you,
ank you, thank you.

I'd like to also thank Kris Duplantier and her husband SSG
obert Duplantier for their insight, for the answering of all the
uestions, even when they were hard, even when they dug a
ttle too deep.

To Lauren Perry — you're a genius.

To Becky and Ellie — spit-shine polish, that's what you do.
Don't ever leave me.

And to my readers, thank you. Thank you for your time, for
letting me into your hearts and minds; thank you for existing.

ABOUT STAC

Staci has been a lot of things up to this po
her life: a graphic designer, an entreprene
seamstress, a clothing and handbag desig
a waitress. Can't forget that. She's also b
a mom to three little girls who are sure
grow up to break a number of hearts. Sh
been a wife, even though she's certainly n
the cleanest, or the best cook. She's also super, duper fun at a part
especially if she's been drinking whiskey, and her favorite word start
with f, ends with k.

From roots in Houston, to a seven year stint in Southern
California, Staci and her family ended up settling somewhere in
between and equally north, in Denver. They are new enough that
snow is still magical. When she's not writing, she's gaming, cleaning,
or designing graphics.

FOLLOW STACI HART:

Website: Stacihartnovels.com
Facebook: Facebook.com/stacihartnovels
Twitter: Twitter.com/imaquirkybird
Pinterest: pinterest.com/imaquirkybird

Made in the USA
Monee, IL
06 March 2020

22819954R10201